To Catch A Thief

Books by David Dodge

Novels

Death and Taxes
Shear the Black Sheep
Bullets for the Bridegroom
It Ain't Hay
The Long Escape
Plunder of the Sun
The Red Tassel
To Catch a Thief
The Lights of Skaro
Angel's Ransom
Loo Loo's Legacy
Carambola
Hooligan
Troubleshooter
The Last Match

Travel Books

How Green Was My Father
How Lost Was My Weekend
The Crazy Glasspecker
20,000 Leagues Behind the 8-Ball
The Poor Man's Guide to Europe
Time Out for Turkey
The Rich Man's Guide to the Riviera
The Poor Man's Guide to the Orient
Fly Down, Drive Mexico

TO CATCH A THIEF

DAVID DODGE

Introduction by Randal S. Brandt

Afterword by Jean Buchanan

Bruin Books
The Emerald Empire
Eugene, Oregon

Published by
Bruin Books, LLC
October, 2010
Second Edition

© David Dodge 1952
© renewed 1980
Introduction © Randal S. Brandt 2010
Afterword © Jean Buchanan 2010

This book was designed and edited by Jonathan Eeds
Graphics design by Michelle Policicchio

Special thanks to:
Kendal Lukrich, Randal Brandt and Jean Buchanan

Printed in the United States of America
ISBN 978-0-9826339-3-9
Bruin Books, LLC
Eugene, Oregon, USA

Visit the scene of the crime at www.bruinbookstore.com

For more information on David Dodge visit
*www.**david-dodge**.com*

Introduction

David Dodge

Set a Thief

Set a thief to catch a thief.
—Old English proverb

In the spring of 1950, American writer David Dodge (1910-1974), his wife Elva, and nine-year-old daughter Kendal landed on the Côte d'Azur. They had left the States after Dodge mustered out of the U.S. Naval Reserve where he had held down a desk job in San Francisco during World War II. By that time, while working as a tax accountant, he had written four moderately successful mystery novels featuring San Francisco tax-accountant-turned-reluctant-detective Whit Whitney. With the help of a modest inheritance that Elva had received, the Dodge family packed their car in 1946 and hit the Pan American Highway in search of new plot devices and cheaper living south of the border.

Latin America provided Dodge with settings for his next three-book crime series featuring an American expatriate private investigator, Al Colby, and launched his second writing career as the author of humorous, anecdote-filled—and best-selling—"travel diaries" that documented the family's (mis)adventures on the road.

He also began a long, profitable relationship with *Holiday* magazine as a freelance travel writer. After extended stays in Guatemala and Arequipa, Peru, then taking a steamer down the Amazon River from Peru to Brazil, the Dodges decided it was time to give Europe a try. Initial brief stops included the Canary Islands, Lisbon, and Barcelona. When they laid eyes on the French Riviera, the Dodges were so taken with the place that they immediately started unpacking their bags: "Five minutes on the Côte d'Azur and I burned to have one of the little villas on the hillside for my own. I knew home when I saw it."[1] They rented a house on a hill above Golfe-Juan, near Cannes, and soon afterwards the characters and plot for Dodge's next thriller virtually fell into his lap.

By agreeing to also act as gardener, Dodge was able to install his family in a furnished villa with a view of the Mediterranean and employ an elderly, partially deaf peasant woman named Germaine to cook and keep house. The Dodges' villa shared a garden wall with a villa owned by a millionaire industrialist that was the scene of frequent, glittering parties. Shortly after their arrival, David and Elva enrolled Kendal in a girls' boarding school at Cannes and left for Italy, where David had another assignment for *Holiday*. The night they left, the villa next door was struck by an acrobatic cat burglar who made off with a quarter of a million dollars' worth of jewelry from the bedrooms while the guests were dining on the terrace.

Of course, the mysterious American who vanished simultaneously with the jewels became the prime suspect in the robbery. Germaine, with a peasant's natural dislike of the *flics*, did not help matters when she refused to cooperate and answer questions. But, by the time David and Elva returned, all the excitement had died down because the actual crook, an Italian named Dario Sambucco, aka Dante Spada, was securely behind bars. Sambucco had subsequently pulled off several other gymnastic heists, but was caught after getting into an argument with a fence in Lyon. David Dodge, upon learning of the formidable dossier compiled against him by the local cops—and after the laughter at the thought of a self-described "middle-aged pear-shaped husband and father," being mistaken for an agile, daring "porch-climber" died down—"saw in the combination a fiction which was, for once, so much stranger than truth that it cried out to be immortalized between hard covers."[2]

The story that Dodge created centers around an acrobatic American cat burglar named John Robie (nicknamed Le Chat by the French press), now retired and living peacefully in the south of France, tending the garden of his hillside villa, with a faithful, partially deaf *bonne à tout faire* named Germaine. Robie is forced out of retirement when a copycat thief begins working in the neighborhood and the local police are convinced that Le Chat is up to his old tricks. In his efforts to catch the copycat and clear his name, he meets the cool, beautiful Francie Stevens and her rich and bejeweled mother—a prime target for the new thief—at the Hotel Midi (Dodge's fictional stand-in for the Carlton Hotel) in Cannes. Dodge gave his new novel the title *To Catch a Thief* and sent it off to the publisher.

A decade later, Dodge revisited the south of France in a non-fiction book he called *The Rich Man's Guide to the Riviera*, published in 1962. The title is a word-play on the title he had used for his most successful travel book, *The Poor Man's Guide to Europe*, which was an immediate best-seller when it was published in 1953 and was re-issued in revised editions annually through 1959. The *Poor Man's Guide*, written from the perspective of a tax-man, was described as a "tipsheet for nickel-nursers and skin-flints" and included practical information for seeing Europe on a tight budget mixed in with the humor. The *Rich Man's Guide*, on the other hand, is completely anecdotal and focuses on events surrounding the writing, publication, and aftermath of *To Catch a Thief*. The first chapter provides background for the novel that made Dodge, for the first time in his life, a "rich man," a multi-millionaire in fact, even though it was in devalued post-war French francs.

> *The* mise en scène *was shot with glamour as it stood, straight from the newspapers. Mrs. Industrialist's guest list at the time of the theft included, besides Madame Schiaparelli, lovely well-rounded names like Elsa Maxwell, M. le Comte Alain de Lechet, Lord and*

Lady Tavistock, Sir Duncan Orr-Lewis, the Marquise de Ricci, the Duke and Duchess of Leinster and a double handful of other fat walk-ons. The theft had taken place during a formal dinner served by candlelight on a gardened terrace overlooking the sweep of Mediterranean shore and sea that stretches from Cap d'Antibes to the Îles de Lérins, with a theme of soft gypsy music played by a string quartet offstage right. The whole picture came vividly to life in my mind's eye: the winking candles, a moon hanging full and high over the sea, banks of blooming flowers perfuming the night air, beautiful women—some of them, anyway—in beautiful gowns attended by distinguished Continental types in evening dress and ribboned decorations. Against this background I saw the agile figure of a thief appear in the shadows, the daring climb, danger, suspense, accomplishment, flight, pursuit ... oh, it was all just too gorgeous to be, the easiest eighty thousand words ever put together. The book practically wrote itself.[3]

The reception *To Catch a Thief* received far exceeded Dodge's modest expectations. In December 1951 the novel appeared in condensed form in *Cosmopolitan* magazine. When the hardcover appeared, in January 1952, the critics loved it, giving it nearly universal praise. It was also included in the *Reader's Digest Condensed Books* volume of Winter 1952 selections. All of which merely set the stage for what must have been a novelist's dream in the 1950s, an Alfred Hitchcock movie adaptation.

To Catch a Thief had been submitted in galley form to Paramount Pictures in July 1951, where it caught Hitchcock's eye. He purchased the movie rights himself for $15,000 in December of that year (rumors of which, appearing in some of the reviews, no doubt spurred sales of the hardcover).[4] Even though the film, which premiered in 1955 with Cary Grant and Grace Kelly in the leading roles, bears only partial resemblance to its source material, Dodge was enormously pleased with the result. Not only did it put real money in his pocket for the first time, but there was also "a credit line in the billing that you could read without any trouble at all by putting your face up real close to it in a good light."[5]

The film was a success. It was a hit at the box office and was nominated for three Academy Awards (winning for Best Color Cinematography). It also brought additional notoriety to Dodge's book. Dario Sambucco, by this time serving a ten to fifteen stretch in a Genoa prison, tried to sue Dodge and Paramount for the unauthorized use of his life story. "He dropped the complaint when his lawyer explained that a thief can't copyright his methods of thievery."[6] Other writers who had previously used the same title also tried to get a cut. But, since you also cannot copyright a title, they too were unsuccessful. The book then went through a new round of "condensation, boiling, digesting, redigesting, reprinting, book-clubbing and synopsizing in the foreign-language market."[7]

David Dodge continued to write well-received suspense novels throughout his career, most of them starring American protagonists in foreign locales, but he never regained the success he had with *To Catch a Thief*. The influence of that novel, however, can be seen in much of his later work. He capitalized on the novel's fame with a number of travel articles for *Holiday* on various aspects and attractions of the French Riviera. He also returned regularly to the south of France for literary settings, most notably in *Angel's Ransom* in 1956, also given a film treatment (this time, however, Dodge's novel was boiled down into a one-hour, utterly forgettable—except for a menacing performance by Hume Cronyn as the villain-made-for-television melodrama produced as part of the "Kaiser Aluminum Hour" on NBC), and in his final, posthumous novel, *The Last Match*, written in the 1970s and published in 2006.

Although *The Last Match* is filled with Dodge's hallmarks of compelling characters, exotic settings, expert plotting, and witty dialogue, when put into the context of his life and works, it is clearly an attempt to recapture the seemingly effortless magic of *To Catch a Thief*. The "hero" is an American con man and small-time crook known only as Curly. He is pursued by a beautiful British heiress, Regina "Reggie" Forbes-Jones, who is determined to reform him. Curly and Reggie are obvious reincarnations of John Robie and Francie Stevens; their first meeting even takes place at the Carlton Hotel in Cannes.

The Côte d'Azur bestowed upon David Dodge the raw material for his most successful novel. It not only presented him with a glamorous locale and romantic personalities, but also with the basis of *To Catch a Thief's* compelling plot. Enriched by this bounty, Dodge would certainly admit he owed the French Riviera a debt of gratitude. Always a stickler for balanced accounting, he was, in fact, able to reciprocate in a variety of ways for the rest of his life. The French government, recognizing his longstanding enthusiasm for *la belle France*, made him a *Chevalier de l'Ordre du Mérite touristique*—an honor normally reserved for French nationals—for his role in promoting the sparkle and allure of a country where anyone from an ex-accountant to an ex-jewel thief could live happily in a villa overlooking the Mediterranean.

Randal S. Brandt
Berkeley, California
August 18, 2010
www.david-dodge.com

¹ David Dodge, *20,000 Leagues Behind the 8-Ball*. New York: Random House, 1951: 235.

² David Dodge, *The Rich Man's Guide to the Riviera*. Boston: Little, Brown and Company, 1962: 8.

³ David Dodge, *The Rich Man's Guide to the Riviera*. Boston: Little, Brown and Company, 1962: 8-9.

⁴ DeRosa, Steven, *Writing with Hitchcock: The Collaboration of Alfred Hitchcock and John Michael Hayes*. New York: Faber and Faber, 2001: 87-88.

⁵ David Dodge, *The Rich Man's Guide to the Riviera*. Boston: Little, Brown and Company, 1962: 10.

⁶ David Dodge, "A Capsule History of Jewel Thievery." *Holiday*, 39, no. 4 (Apr. 1966): 61.

⁷ David Dodge, *The Rich Man's Guide to the Riviera*. Boston: Little, Brown and Company, 1962: 13.

This is for
KATHRYN, FRANCES
and MARIAN

1

THE *agents de police* came for John Robie sooner than he expected them.

It was a hot, still summer evening in August. Crickets sawed at their fiddles in the grass, and a bullfrog who lived in a pool at the bottom of the garden boomed an occasional bass note. John was burning letters in the fireplace when first the crickets, then the bullfrog, stopped their music. His setter, sleeping on the rug, woke suddenly and cocked her ears, but he did not need the dog's help. The crickets were better watchmen.

He had already changed his clothes and was ready to leave the house. He kicked the ashes in the fireplace, crumbling them, before he went into the kitchen. The setter growled, deep in her throat.

Germaine, his cook, was making a ragout, peering nearsightedly into the big iron pot on the stove and muttering to herself. She was too old and deaf to hear the dog until it began to bark. She heard John come in, but the ragout was more important at the moment than he was. She did not look up.

He said, "Germaine."

"M'sieu?" She still peered into the pot.

"I'm going away. Dinner won't be necessary."

She looked up at that, surprised and indignant. He had no time to tell her more. He said, "*Au revoir*," and ran up the back stairs. The dog growled again, more loudly.

He found his passport and billfold in the dark bedroom, buttoned them into the inside pocket of his jacket, and looked out at the rear garden from behind a window curtain.

It was early evening, not yet full night. A shadow was out of place against the wall at the back of the garden, just inside the gate. He could not be mistaken. He knew every shrub in the garden. Except for the olive trees that were there when he started, he had planted everything himself, down to the endive and the leeks and the *fines herbes* in the vegetable patch. He had not planted a shadow by the gate.

The dog began to bark. There was still no sound at the front door. He turned to a side window, saw another misplaced shadow, and went quickly to another window at the far end of the house. They had it watched from all sides.

The dog was barking steadily by the time the doorbell rang.

He had one path of escape open to him. It was not the easiest, but it would do. It will leave no doubt in their minds, if there is any doubt, he thought. When he heard Germaine's loose slippers slap across the floor as she went to answer the doorbell, still grumbling over the wasted dinner, he stepped out on the little *terrasse* where he slept on hot nights, climbed the low railing, balanced himself for a moment, and jumped.

The man in the garden below heard feet scrape on the railing of the *terrasse*. John, in mid-air, saw the white blur of an upturned face, and the dark blotch in it that was the *agent's* open mouth. The *agent* was too startled to shout, at first.

John had never made the jump before, even in daylight. But he had looked at it many times, subconsciously measuring the distance, estimating the knee-spring that would be necessary and the swing to follow after he caught the branch of the olive tree. He had it all timed and pre-calculated in his arm and leg muscles. He could not see the branch against the dark background of the tree foliage, but it was there when he reached for it, flat out on his face in the air and stretching. As his feet went down he bent at the hips, kicked hard on the upswing, let go of the branch while he was still rising, arched his back, and went over the top of the high garden wall with inches to spare.

It was a fine jump, one that the *agent* talked about for a long time afterward, when he was permitted at last to talk. John came down on his toes in the middle of the lane beyond the wall, and was running up the hill through a vineyard toward the shelter of the orchard at the top of the hill before the *agent* let out his first shout. By the time they came through the garden gate and began to hunt for him, their flashlights bobbing around like little bright balloons in the dusk, he was safe in the orchard.

There were only four men in all, not enough to search the whole countryside. They gave up soon and went back to the house.

He was not afraid of what Germaine might tell them. She knew nothing about *M'sieu* except that he liked her cooking and would not ordinarily abandon a good ragout. She was an old peasant, half blind, nearly deaf, a fine cook. He hoped she would stay on at the villa and keep the garden in shape. She liked green things growing around her. With the olives, the garden patch, a few chickens, and her way of making a little go a long way, she could live there comfortably forever, if nobody told her to leave. He meant to write her a letter after he was safe from pursuit, tell her that the Villa des Bijoux was hers. *M'sieu* would not need it any more.

But it was hard to think he would never see the villa again. There were too many things in it he hated to leave behind, too many ties to a good life—the books, the fine guns and fishing rods, the dog he had trained, the garden he had planted, the good wine he had laid down in the cellar, the comfortable chair by the fireplace. It was all finished and done with. He did not have even a photograph of the house.

It's just as well, he thought. From the orchard on the top of the hill he turned his back on the Villa of the Jewels and set off for the coast.

It was full dark by then, but he knew the country well. He knew all of the South of France well, even to the odors. Most of the farmers who were his neighbors cultivated patches of flowers to sell to the perfume factories at Vence or Grasse. All Provence was a flower garden during the summer months, and even at night the perfume was strong. It was not safe for him to go through Vence, where he was well known by sight, so he walked around the town by way of the heady, sweet-smelling flower patches, returned to the road on the other side, and kept on in the direction of Cros de Cagnes and the Route Nationale, where he could catch a bus.

It was a ten-kilometer walk. To be safe, he stepped off the road into the shadows whenever he heard a car coming, and at the bus station he bought a copy of *Nice-Matin* to hide his face. There was nothing about him in *Nice-Matin*. It would be still another twenty-four hours before the French papers picked up the Paris *Herald Tribune's* lead and spread it across the front page with headlines and photographs. He thought he would be safely out of the public eye before that happened; or on his way to a French prison. One or the other.

There was only a single passenger on the bus when he boarded it. He did not have to hide his face from her. She sat in one of the extreme rear corners, so that he could not take a seat out of her line of sight, but after one quick, incurious glance she paid no attention to him. He would not have given her a second thought except that caution made him observant, and she was clearly out of place on a rattletrap Route Nationale bus. She was dressed for the evening; a long gown, fragile, spike-heeled slippers, a fur wrap. He knew enough about furs to guess that the price of her wrap alone would buy an expensive car and pay the salary of a man to drive her wherever she wanted to go. She was one of a type he knew well, had made it his business to know. Girls of her class did not ride buses.

Force of habit made him look at her fingers and ear lobes. Afterward he watched her until a movement of her shoulders opened the wrap far enough to let him see her throat. She wore neither rings, necklace, earrings nor, as far as he could see, jewelry of any kind, not even a wrist watch. It was not in keeping with the wrap, any more than the wrap was in keeping with her presence on the bus. The class he knew always wore some ornament, frequently a great deal.

He wondered if the explanation could be that she had lost her jewelry to a thief. It was incongruous that he might be fleeing from the police on the same bus with one of the women whose losses had set the police on his trail. They would make some kind of a point of it, if they caught him now.

The bus filled gradually. When it reached the end of its run opposite the big pink stucco casino in Cannes, several other passengers were between him and the girl when she got off. He lost sight of her and did not think of her again.

He joined the strollers along the promenade of La Croisette, the boulevard skirting the beach. It was a lovely night for strolling; warm, with a quarter moon hanging low over the Mediterranean and a faint breeze blowing in from the water to rustle the leaves of the palms and plane trees along the promenade and make shadows dance on the sidewalk. He kept to the beach side of the promenade, where the lights were dim, and crossed the boulevard only when he was opposite the shabby front of the Hotel Napoleon.

The Napoleon was a poor, distant cousin to the newer, more fashionable hotels which faced La Croisette farther up the beach near the casino and the yacht harbor. It was not a popular place even with the people who stayed there. No one was in the musty hotel lobby but the concierge and a porter who doubled as elevator operator.

The faded red carpet had a new patch since his last visit. Bellini's sign near the elevator still advertised the same services in the same three languages. The English part of the sign read:

HENRI BELLINI
Insurance — Sales and Rentals — Tourist Agent
Imports and Exports — Domestic Help
Interpreter — Stenographer
Investments

MEZZANINE FLOOR

An arrow pointed up the stairway to the mezzanine.

He nodded to the porter as he walked by the elevator cage. His nerves were strung tight, but he did not hesitate climbing the stairs. He had complete confidence in Bellini.

~§~

Bellini was reading the Paris edition of the New York *Herald Tribune* in the cluttered cubbyhole that served him as an office. He had the paper spread open on his desk under the fan of light from an old-fashioned lamp with a green shade. He did not move when he heard the doorknob turn. The door had a spring lock and could be opened from the outside only with a key, but he always left the key in the outside lock, except when he had confidential business to transact in the room, so that his callers could let themselves in. He did not like to walk to the door unnecessarily.

John brought the key with him when he entered. He put it on the corner of Bellini's desk.

Bellini took off his spectacles and peered at him under the lamp shade, smiling his oily smile of welcome.

"I was wondering when I would hear from you," he said, chuckling. "Have you seen this very interesting article in the newspaper?"

He tapped his stubby finger on the paper. He read, wrote, and spoke seven languages. John spoke French and English almost equally well, but he and Bellini used English with each other because it was John's native language. One tongue was the same as another to Bellini.

John said, "I've read it."

Bellini chuckled again.

He had not changed in the months since John had seen him. He always looked the same; small, round, oily, and happy. A German soldier had broken his shoulder with a rifle butt during the Occupation. The bones had not been set properly, so the shoulder stayed hunched up around his ear in a permanent half-shrug, and one arm was shorter than the other. He wore heavy, horn-rimmed glasses that made him look like an owl. In the summertime he dressed in cotton trousers, a loose shirt, and slippers, and oozed perspiration. In the wintertime he wore all the clothes he could put on, toasted his feet on an electric heater wedged under his desk, and oozed perspiration just the same. He never stopped smiling, and no one could say anything remotely humorous in his presence without earning an apprecia-tive titter or gurgle or bubble of laughter. His manners were excellent, even too good; he had the smooth gra-ciousness of a professional confidence man. He had never been known to break his word. In addition to his legitimate business activities, he was an importer of smuggled goods, a black-market operator and a dealer in stolen property. He was careful to carry on these activities through intermediaries, and since he com-manded the absolute loyalty of everyone who worked for him, he had never been arrested nor had his reputation as an honest businessman challenged publicly. He was John Robie's best friend.

"You will ignore the implications, no doubt?" he said, peering at John under the lamp shade. He was still speaking of the newspaper article.

"The implications are too difficult to ignore," John said. "I'm leaving the country."

"The police?"

"They came for me tonight."

"And you?"

"Off the *terrasse* and over the wall."

"Like old times." Bellini giggled. "I would like to have seen the *flics'* faces. They never took you but once, did they?"

"No. I don't think they will take me again, if you can fix this for me."

He took the passport from his pocket. Bellini looked briefly at the passport, then up at him again, still beaming.

"What do you want done to it?"

"Change the number and name, set my birthday back ten years, and alter the date on the entry stamp so it won't be more than three months old when I leave. I'll dye my hair, pad myself around the middle, and have a new photograph taken. The only pictures they have of me are newspaper prints, and those date back to before the war. They won't have any reason to look twice at a middle-aged tourist. Once I'm out of the country, I'm safe."

"You are not afraid of extradition?"

"I don't think they will bother. I'm not that important. When they learn that I've left the country, and the thief keeps operating, they'll see their mistake."

"Will the thief keep operating after you leave, John?"

"There'll be no reason for him to stop."

Bellini chuckled again. He blinked behind the spectacles, looking wise and owlish.

John said, "Did you think that Le Chat had come back?"

Bellini lifted his good shoulder to the level of his crippled shoulder, then let it drop again.

"It's been a long time since I saw you last. A man might change his mind."

"It isn't Le Chat."

Bellini nodded, satisfied. "I was waiting to hear you say it yourself. Now, what can you do about this story in the newspaper?"

"What I told you. Run. It doesn't leave me any other choice."

~§~

He knew how soon the other papers would take up the cry. He had caught their attention before, although not as John Robie. French reporters, who coin a nickname for every public figure, named him Le Chat after his first thefts in 1936, at Nice and Menton. In the months that followed and until his imprisonment in 1939, only the gathering war clouds over Europe received more space in the French press than he did.

He was a thief who made good newspaper copy. He was never known to employ violence or carry a weapon more dangerous than a glass cutter, never stole anything but cash and jewelry, always operated alone, and was never identified, except by his nickname, until a receiver of stolen property in Paris turned him in to the Sûreté Nationale after an argument over the price to be

paid for a necklace of pigeon-blood rubies. The Sûreté
arrested the receiver when they arrested John, so the
betrayal helped nobody but the insurance companies.
Their losses from the activities of Le Chat in the South
of France for three years amounted to the equivalent of
three-quarters of a million dollars, in various currencies.
The several receivers who bought stolen stones from
him never paid more than 40 per cent of insurable
value, sometimes less, but he had nearly eight million
francs, then worth two hundred and fifty thousand
dollars, in several banks under several names when he
was arrested.

The police never learned about the money, and he
wasted none of it on expensive lawyers. He had no
defense worth presenting. The Sûreté agents who broke
into his Paris hotel room had taken him while he was
unsetting the stones from the necklace which the receiver had wanted cheaply and which belonged to the
wife of a Member of the Chamber of Deputies. Because
the theft had taken place on the Côte d'Azur, they
brought him back to Nice and tried him there before the
cour d'assises.

The prosecution offered for evidence a notebook
which had been found among the prisoner's effects. It
contained odds and ends of useful information about
such items as *Les Feuilles de Lotus* ("good jumbo
emerald surrounded by diamond-encrusted leaves,
thirteen pear-shaped emerald pendants, earrings to
match, all fine stones, easy to break up") made by Van
Cleef & Arpels of Paris for the Maharani of Baroda, or

the Pearl of Asia which sold for $50,000 at a Paris auction ("ugly; 76 millimeters long, 19 millimeters wide, 605 carats, silver twig setting, probably too well known to bring a price"), but they could not prove another theft against him. Except for the rubies, the stolen jewelry had long since been broken down to unidentifiable individual stones and sold. His careful maps of certain summer villas and their surrounding gardens, and his sketches of the floor plans of the more popular hotels on the Côte d'Azur were not admitted as evidence, even after the prosecution offered to show that a successful robbery had taken place at several of the localities mapped, and that the technique of robbery in each case was identical with the technique of the thief who had robbed the wife of the Member of the Chamber. The ruby necklace was enough. He received a fair trial and a maximum sentence under the law, twenty years.

The newspapers gave the trial front-page coverage. He was good copy to the end. He admitted nothing, denied everything, and offered no information about himself, who he was, where he had come from, or what he had stolen. He had no identity papers. No friends came forward to speak for him at the trial. The reporters knew that he was a young man, suspected from his accent that he was an American, and were reasonably certain, as much from the muscular development of his body as from his technique as a thief, that he was a trained gymnast, possibly a professional acrobat. The evidence that was not admitted in court got into the newspapers easily, along with some imaginings not far

from the truth; the story of Le Chat's climb up the bare
façade of a hotel in Villefranche to enter a third-story
window and depart the way he came with a string of
rose pearls around his neck; another story, exaggerated
but sworn to by the servant girl who had seen it and
raised the alarm, of his jump from the roof of a villa in
Eze to the ground forty feet below, and his bounding
leap from there over an eight-foot wall; another story,
solemnly reported in the French way, of a woman who
had lost diamonds worth twenty thousand dollars and
wakened in time to see Le Chat, in dead black clothing,
spread his arms and fly out the window with the stones,
like a bat. He read the stories in his cell and said nothing.

They sent him to serve his sentence at La Maison
Centrale de Fontevrault-l'Abbaye, near Saumur. He
arrived there a few months before the outbreak of
World War II. He had been in prison less than a year
when the German army arrived to take over the
management of that part of the country.

La Maison Centrale was full of cutthroats—a few
thieves like himself, but more murderers, gangsters,
and *apaches,* one step removed from the criminals who
were sent to Devil's Island. The Germans considered
them good material to pass over into the care of what
remained of the Third Republic. One night the entire
population of La Maison Centrale was herded into
trucks, driven into the Unoccupied Zone, and turned
loose.

It was one of several German errors. All the murderers, Frenchmen first and cutthroats only inciden-

tally, went into the *maquis* and began practicing their trade on German soldiers. John, with no place else to go, joined the others.

~§~

He met Bellini in the *maquis*. Bellini's shoulder had just been fractured, and it pained him so badly that he could hardly keep the happy smile on his face, or giggle at the way his arm grew shorter and more useless day by day. When he learned the identity of Le Chat from John's jailmates, he said, "It is a great pleasure to meet you, sir. A great pleasure indeed. I tried to make your acquaintance for several years."

"Why?"

"I would have enjoyed betraying you to the Sûreté," Bellini tittered. "Or having you strangled."

"Was I in your territory?"

"You were. You were a great inconvenience to me. Every time you made a theft, my organization felt the heavy hand of the law." Bellini chuckled at the memory. "You were clever not to try to dispose of the jewelry on the Mediterranean coast. I would have had you, as well as the stones."

"It wasn't cleverness. The prices were better in Paris."

"You were lucky, then. Do you have plans to return to the Côte after this business is finished? Because if you do, I must, warn you—"

"Not as a thief."

"You have reformed, then? A wonderful thing to hear.

I have always contended that the French prison system had its points."

John shook his head and smiled. Bellini amused him.

"Retired is a better word," he said. "I have all the money I need. Now that they know my face, I'm no longer safe. I've seen all of the French prison system that I want to see."

"Good. Good. I am glad to hear it. I should not like to be your business rival."

They both laughed. John said, "We would make better partners, I think."

They made good partners in the *maquis*. Bellini, in spite of his Italian name, was French, a Niçois. He was not a jailbird like the others, only a businessman with useful connections in *le milieu,* the French underworld. The Germans wanted him to use his connections on their side. When he refused, they broke his shoulder instead of shooting him, another error.

He organized his own band of *maquisards,* all *boche* killers. John, the only one among them without a Frenchman's inborn hatred for German invaders, caught it in time from the others. They murdered according to individual talent. Guns, except those taken from the Germans themselves, were hard to come by in the early days, before the British and Americans began to parachute supplies into the *maquis.* Because of the strength in his arms and shoulders, John was most often called on to strangle sentries or to climb quickly and quietly when climbing was necessary. A thin, anemic boy named Jean-Pierre ran up a good score of stray soldiers using a sharpened rat-tail file for a weapon. Le Borgne was a one-eyed man whose specialty was sharpshooting through lighted windows at night. Coco was an expert with a *casse-tête,* a skull-cracker. La Mule, a hairy mountain of a man, used anything that came to hand. He was a peasant farmer whose farmhouse the band used as a headquarters from time to time. His wife had been killed or abducted by the Germans, he never knew which, and he was left with two children to care for, a boy and a girl nine or ten years old, who smuggled food and carried messages. When the Germans finally raided the farmhouse, La Mule stayed behind and died in his own doorway under a mound of dead soldiers while the rest of the band got away. The boy and the girl had disappeared when Bellini sent men back afterward to look for them, and their bodies were never found.

But recruits always came to take the place of those who died. Bellini had nearly a hundred men in his gang, by then well armed and well supplied, when American troops landed near Saint Tropez in August of 1944 and the *maquisards* joined up with them in the drive north.

John was wounded twice, neither time seriously. After the fighting had ended, he left France for the United States. The disrupted French border controls had not yet been re-established, and he had no difficulty getting out of the country. To enter the United States without papers, he had to show that he was an American citizen, which he did by proving that he had been born in New York State. His birth certificate was enough. After establishing his nationality, he applied for a passport and returned to France on the first boat.

It was not recklessness. Bellini wrote that the Sûreté had made no attempt to round up the convicts of La Maison Centrale. The prison records had been destroyed by the Germans, and it was common knowledge in *le milieu* that no man who had killed Germans during the Occupation need worry about an unfinished prison term as long as he remained respectable. John intended to remain respectable. To do so, he needed the money that still stood to his credit in the French banks.

The franc had deteriorated badly and was still tumbling. He found that he was worth less than fifty thousand dollars instead of a quarter of a million, and that rigid currency controls made it impossible for him to take the money out of the country. Still, eight million francs was a comfortable fortune in France, and he liked France. He stayed.

He had used his own name on the passport. No one questioned him. He bought the villa on a hill above Vence, still using his own name, and called it the Villa of the Jewels because a name was needed on the mailbox, and the joke was a harmless one. He registered under his right name at the prefecture in Nice, where he had been convicted, and applied for a *permis de séjour* as a resident. The card came through, and still nobody asked if John Robie of the Villa des Bijoux was the thief of the same name who had been sentenced to twenty years at La Maison Centrale de Fontevrault-l'Abbaye for jewel robbery. Finally, after he had been at the villa for several months, the Vence *commissaire de police* came to call on him, riding a bicycle and puffing because of the steepness of the hill.

The *commissaire* was a short, broad man with sharp eyes and a soft voice. His name was Oriol. John gave him a glass of wine. He took one sip, to be polite, and did not touch it again.

"Your *permis de séjour,*" he said. "It came through in order?"

"Yes." He had made the first application through the Vence *commissariat*.

"I am glad to hear it. You plan to live here indefinitely?"

"Off and on. I like to travel."

"I see." Oriol's eyes wandered around the room. "You are very comfortable here, at the Villa des Bijoux."

From the way he said it, John realized that he knew. He went on slowly. "I hope you continue to be comfortable here, Monsieur Robie. I know of your record— with the *maquis,* I mean. I was in the *maquis* myself, for a time. Before that, I was a police clerk. At the *cour d'assises,* in Nice."

John waited. Oriol thought for a while, working out his sentences, before he said, "I recommended that the *permis de séjour* be given to you, Monsieur Robie. My recommendation was enough. There will be no further investigation of your background at present."

"I'm very grateful. What do you mean by 'at present'?"

Oriol turned over his hands, palms up. They had calluses on them. He worked in his garden and among his vines whenever he had time, like the good French peasant he was.

"I mean that there is nothing I know of now which would require investigation. What you may do tomorrow or the next day is, of course, another thing. If you were to attract official attention to yourself in any way, then I, as *commissaire* for this district, would ask more questions than I have asked."

"I do not intend to do anything to attract attention to myself. I hunt a little in season, fish, swim when the weather is good, and dig in my garden. That's all."

"You have adequate means to live on?"

"All I need."

"You do not think you will find it necessary, then, to adopt some form of gainful employment while you are in France?"

"No. I've retired."

"Then you should be very content here."

He stood up. They shook hands. Oriol motioned at the glass of wine and excused himself for not finishing it.

"It is very good, but I do not drink while I am on official business," he said. "I press a little wine from my own grapes. Not like yours, of course, but drinkable. Perhaps you would do me the honor some day soon—we will talk about the *maquis*—I live not far from here, myself."

John said he would be glad to do him the honor.

They shook hands again.

After Oriol had pedaled away down the hill, he drank the wine himself. He felt really secure for the first time since his return.

~§~

He saw Bellini rarely, and his other friends of the *maquis* only by accident. But he did Oriol the honor of drinking his wine a few weeks after Oriol's call, when the *commissaire* made the invitation specific, and through him met others of his neighbors, peasants and villagers and minor government functionaries like Oriol. He began playing *boule* with them in the village on Sundays. When the Grasse *boule* team challenged them to a match, he went up to Grasse to help defend the village honor, and was paired off against a big broad-shouldered man who introduced himself simply as Paul. He was the most popular man on the Grasse team, and their best player; likable, quiet, friendly. John thought he might be the village blacksmith. He was surprised to hear that Paul was le Comte du Pré de la Tour.

They were friends from the beginning. Paul, several years younger than John, went by the name of Du Pré, rarely using his title, but the title was old and honored, and John learned from Oriol that Paul had been decorated by both the French and British governments for his war record with the Free French Army. He had a steel plate in place of one kneecap, besides the decorations. His home was in Lyons, but he owned a little *domaine* in the hills above Grasse which he pretended to farm for profit, although he was independently wealthy. Actually the *domaine* was a summer rest home for his wife, Lisa, who was dying of tuberculosis. They were hopelessly in love, they both knew she was dying, and they never spoke of it to each other. Paul spent as much of his time by her bedside as she would permit, until she sent him away, made him go out and play *boule*, or trim his vines. After she had met John, and became aware of his friendship for her husband, she begged him to take Paul with him whenever he went on a hunting or fishing trip, which he did frequently.

"Get him away from me, John." There were tears in her eyes. "Keep him occupied. Don't let him think about me. I'm afraid of what will happen to him when I die."

"You're not going to die, Lisa. Don't talk that way."

"Yes. Soon." She squeezed her eyelids together against the tears. "I'm not afraid for myself. I'm afraid for Paul. Help him to find something, somebody, to take my place, John. Be his friend for me."

"I am his friend."

"I know." She pressed his hand in her thin fingers. "Don't forget."

For her sake, and because he genuinely liked Paul, he cultivated Paul's company. They hunted together, went on fishing trips, and, during a trying period when Lisa was confined in a Swiss sanitarium and Paul was unable to visit her, attempted the stony peak of the Jungfrau. Paul and the guide who took them were experienced mountain climbers, but John, who had never been on a rock face before, surprised them both. His strength, climbing skill, and immunity to the vertigo that bothers beginners made Paul question him later. He evaded an explanation. Paul, seeing his reluctance to talk about himself, did not ask again.

After the first experience, mountain climbing became the exercise he enjoyed most. Sometimes he went with Paul, sometimes alone. Between times he dug in his garden, read, played *boule* at the village, and enjoyed living. He was content. He did not look ahead to the day when he might no longer be content.

It was three years before Lisa died in the Swiss sanitarium where Paul had taken her again for treatment. He did not learn about it until Paul came back to the *domaine* alone. Paul was quieter than before, and smiled less often, but otherwise seemed the same. He continued to spend several months of the summer at the *domaine*. John did not know if it was because he himself was near by, or because Paul's best memories of Lisa were there. But he remembered his promise to Lisa. Although he never spoke of his own background to Paul, they talked about everything else, a bottle of wine between them to wet their mouths and sharpen their wits and the whole universe to discuss—life, and death, and why, and what made Provence more beautiful than any other place in the world. And war.

When the Russians first moved in Asia, Paul saw the ultimate end of Europe and everything it stood for. He was blackly pessimistic about the future of the world. After he had gone to Lyons to volunteer for the French contribution to the United Nations troops, and was rejected because of the plate in his knee, he wrote John that he was leaving France, that he would not come back to the *domaine* for an indefinite period. He did not feel that he was good company for anyone.

It was a curt, unhappy note. But John had no time to worry about Paul. Oriol paid him a second official visit on the same day that Paul's letter arrived.

He had been on a solitary fishing trip. It was a good day. He was covered with fish scales and sunburn, and had brought back enough of a catch for Germaine to make a bouillabaisse. He had not seen the newspapers.

He gave Oriol a glass of wine, according to custom. Oriol had been at the villa several times by invitation, and always enjoyed drinking what John gave him. This time he barely touched the glass to his lips, as he had done on his first visit. He looked solemn.

With no preliminaries, he said, "Did you ever, during your time with the *maquis,* hear of a man named Le Chat, John?"

John felt the sweat start along his ribs and on his back. After all that time it was a shock.

He said, "I know the name."

Oriol took a folded newspaper out of his pocket and held it out, his sharp eyes watching John's face.

"He was a famous jewel thief. We think he may be operating here, on the Côte. He began here, before the war. I wonder if he has returned."

John looked at the paper.

A Mme. Lisieux, staying at one of the resort hotels in Menton, had lost jewels valued at three million francs to a thief who got in through the window of her top-floor suite during the night by swinging himself down from the cornice of the roof. Nobody had seen him, but from all the signs he had gone out the same way, pulling himself back up over the cornice from a window ledge four stories above the street. The police suspected inside help and were questioning Mme. Lisieux's maid, because the jewels ordinarily remained in the hotel strongbox and were accessible to the thief that night only because Mme. Lisieux had worn them to a *gala*. Most of the article was about the thief's boldness and physical agility. The man who wrote it clearly had never heard of Le Chat, because the comparison was a natural one to make. Le Chat's name was not mentioned.

He returned the paper to Oriol. Oriol looked at him woodenly as he folded it.

John said, "I remember reading about Le Chat, years ago. This man's technique seems much the same. But it isn't the same thief."

"Can one ever be positive?"

"I can. Le Chat was killed during the Resistance. I was there when he died."

Oriol said nothing. John wanted to take him by the arm and say, "I swear it. I like being an honest man. I wouldn't steal again if I starved. All I want is to live my life, drink my wine, dig in my garden, and be let alone." But he could not say anything so bald. The amnesty that let him live peacefully at the Villa des Bijoux was not an official one. Legally, he was still an escaped convict, and Oriol a *commissaire de police*.

They talked about other things. Oriol still did not touch his wine glass. Before he left, John said, "I give you my word that Le Chat is dead, Oriol. He will never come back."

"I hope you are right."

Oriol went away on his bicycle, still looking solemn. A day later Mme. Lisieux's maid was released by the police. They had nothing to prove against her. They made no arrest.

Oriol was a conscientious man. As a *maquis* fighter himself, and a fellow *boule* player, he wanted to give John the benefit of every doubt. But he was not over-trusting, and because he, and he alone, knew John's identity and had taken upon himself the responsibility of extending the universally recognized but legally non-existent amnesty, he watched the Villa des Bijoux for several nights. John rarely went out in the evenings. When he did it was openly, and he came back openly. There were no further thefts. Oriol abandoned the night watch.

John read the newspapers every day. The Korean war pushed local crimes off the front page for several weeks, until the climbing thief moved back into the news.

Three villas were robbed in five days. They were all in the same neighborhood, in or near St. Jean on Cap Ferrat, and the total value stolen amounted to twenty-two million francs, about sixty thousand dollars. One of the villas had just been purchased by a wealthy British couple who planned to make it their permanent home. The house was crammed with wealth—the wife's jewels, the husband's diamond studs and cuff links, fur coats, valuable first editions, antique furniture, silverware, *objets d'art.* The thief took only the jewels and loose cash, as Le Chat had always done. The *inspecteur* in charge of the investigation questioned and requestioned the two servants, because there was a dog in the house and he had not been heard to growl all night. There was a high wall all around the yard, with glass shards embedded in cement on top. Again inside help was suspected, until a police *agent* with a curious mind climbed trees in the yard until he found rope burns. From that point, the *inspecteur* reconstructed the theft as it must have happened.

The thief had tossed a rope over a tree limb from outside the wall and pulled himself into the tree. From there he had moved to another tree, rerigged his rope, and swung over to the house without touching the ground, climbing in through a slit window ten inches across and thirty inches high, afterward making his escape by the same route, carrying the whole thing off so quietly that not one of four people or the dog sleeping in the house was disturbed.

The other two thefts bore the trademarks of the same daring, agile thief. The newspapers and the police agreed that the same man must have made all three thefts. Still no one thought to bring up the name of Le Chat. There were no arrests.

Oriol took up his night watch again, but abandoned it when John continued to go out infrequently and openly in the evenings. Oriol no longer played *boule* at the village, and John knew that the *commissaire* was avoiding him, and why. There was nothing he could do but follow the newspaper reports and hope for the thief's arrest.

Two weeks later there were new headlines. A villa in Monaco and a hotel room in Monte Carlo across the bay were entered and robbed between a Tuesday night and the following Friday morning. The season was then in full swing on the Côte, the summer villas occupied and the hotels full of wealthy foreign visitors making what many thought would be their last visit to the bright beaches and casinos of the Riviera before another war ended the world. Jewels and cash amounting to forty million francs were stolen in the two thefts. No one saw even the thief's shadow, and there were no arrests.

The local newspapers, neutral until then, began to take sides against the police. One editorial pointed out, in a hard-headed French way, that if the Côte d'Azur were to survive at all as an international playground for the rich, the thief was a greater immediate menace even than a war. Riviera businessmen would inevitably lose their wealthy customers unless the police did something drastic. An arrest, any arrest, was demanded. Still no one brought up the name of Le Chat.

By then it had been twelve years since his arrest. He knew that twelve years was a long time to be out of the public eye, but the thief's technique was so nearly identical with what had been his own that he did not see how the connection could be missed.

The hotel theft at Monte Carlo was spectacular. The thief left footprints on the marquee over the main hotel entrance, and marks on the front of the building to show where he had climbed one of the chains supporting the marquee from a hook at the level of the third-floor windows. The window he wanted to enter had been closed and locked, but he had cut the pane away with a glass cutter, worked the lock open, then gone in to steal Madame's pearls and rings while she was enjoying a run of luck at the casino. He had left behind only a crescent of glass cut from the window-pane, with a small piece of adhesive tape attached, and no fingerprints.

John knew that it would be only a matter of time after that. The thief had duplicated, almost action for action, one of Le Chat's boldest thefts, even to the use of the glass cutter and a piece of tape to keep the cut piece of glass from falling. It was as if he were inviting a comparison.

The Paris edition of the New York *Herald Tribune* finally made the connection between new thief and old. If it had been *Nice-Matin* or one of the other local papers, he would not have escaped when he did.

The *Herald Tribune* reached Riviera newsstands about noon or later, and he had an arrangement with the mailman to deliver a copy with the afternoon mail. Germaine brought in the paper at the same time she brought another letter from Paul, with a Madrid postmark. He never opened the letter, which he later burned with his other letters before he realized that he had not yet read it.

The newspaper headline was: *Has Le Chat Returned?* Underneath there was a blurry picture of himself, taken in the courtroom of the *cour d'assises* in 1939. The article which went with the picture put a series of questions, only suggesting some of the answers. It was an American paper and had no right to insult the French Sûreté Nationale. The French papers did that later, when they reprinted the article.

The *Herald Tribune* asked if it were true that the late spectacular series of jewel robberies on the Côte d'Azur bore trademarks similar to those of the thief known as Le Chat, who had committed several burglaries in the same locality during the years 1936-1939 and had been sent to La Maison Centrale de Fontevrault-l'Abbaye for twenty years in connection with a theft from the wife of a Member of the Chamber of Deputies. Was it also true, as rumored, that Le Chat and other notorious criminals had been released from prison by the Germans before serving their full terms, but that because of their good record with the Liberation forces during the war, the Sûreté had extended an amnesty against their further imprisonment? Was this what accounted for the failure of the police to make a single arrest in connection with the latest thefts? Had Le Chat truly returned, and was he immune from arrest?

There was more, including a review of the 1936-1939 thefts and his trial. He knew that Oriol, who spoke no English, would not ordinarily look at an English-language newspaper, but it could not be long before he heard of the story. John's arrest and return to prison would follow automatically, whether or not the real thief continued his activity.

He changed his clothes, burned his letters, took the money he kept in the house for an emergency, and left

the Villa des Bijoux by way of the *terrasse* and the tree
when the *agents de police* came for him. Now, with
Bellini's help, he meant to leave France. He had no
further plans.

~§~

Bellini, peering at him wisely under the green shade
of his reading-lamp, his round, happy face shining with
sweat, said, "If you leave, you can never come back. You
realize that, don't you? Once the Sûreté brings the old
charge out in the open—"

"It's out in the open now. That's why I'm leaving."

"Never to see *la belle France* again?"

Only a Frenchman could imply so much with a single
question. John, understanding the implication, said,
"It's not as bad as that. They'll forget me in a few years."

"And if France does not survive more than a few
years?"

"You sound gloomy."

Bellini chuckled.

"I am never gloomy. I am practical. Another war will
kill France forever, if it comes."

"I'm practical, too. I don't intend to spend the next
twenty years in prison. I'm going home."

"You went home once before, I remember. How long
did you stay? Three months?"

"That was different."

"Why different?"

"There's no point in talking about it. How soon can

you have the passport ready?"

Bellini lifted his good shoulder. "Two days, except for the photograph."

"I'll take care of the photograph. Somebody else will have to find me luggage and clothes. Where can I stay, without papers?"

"Where else but with your friends? Let me think."

Bellini thought, smiling at nothing.

"It would not be wise to remain here with me," he said at last. "There is Jean-Pierre, in Marseilles. He is probably safest, although not entirely safe. The *flics* have called on him three times in the past six weeks."

"What do they have against Jean-Pierre?"

"Nothing tangible. But he is a receiver now, in a small way, no longer a hero of the Resistance, and they do not believe him when he says he has heard nothing of the stolen jewelry. They have reminded him of an unfinished prison sentence he might yet be called upon to serve if The Cat is not caught."

Bellini thought again. "Le Borgne? No, Le Borgne is less safe than Jean-Pierre."

"Is he receiving, too?"

"Oh, no. He is practically honest now. But he was a burglar himself, before his joints grew too stiff. Never a clever fellow like you, only ordinary, and at his best he could never climb a tree. But the police are being pressed to make an arrest of some kind, and Le Borgne would serve if they can find no one else. He came out of La Maison Centrale when you did, you remember."

John said nothing.

Bellini went on. "Coco? No. They are watching him, too. Bernard? No, poor Bernard is in jail. So are Boum and Ali—" He broke off, giggling. "Imagine it, John. They are even arresting my Moroccans, for nothing more serious than a little cigarette smuggling. This thief is giving us all a great deal of trouble, I tell you. More, even, than you gave us, in your time. The police are making it difficult for everyone. I, myself, have had to suspend several of my more important activities."

"You and Le Borgne and Jean-Pierre and Coco and the others had better get together and do something about it."

"We have tried. Cautiously, of course, because at first we thought it might be you again, and one does not give an old comrade to the police, however inconsiderate he may be of his friends." Bellini chuckled. "We will have to try harder now. With this new thing"—he tapped the newspaper lying in front of him—"and the criticism of the police which will follow"—he gave his lopsided one-shoulder shrug—"it is going to be very dangerous for all of us until the thief is caught."

"The Sûreté will take him in time. They're slow, but they never give up."

"Certainly they will take him. In time." Bellini leaned forward under the lamp shade. "But what does that mean? It was three years before they took you, and he is as clever as you were. Maybe even more clever, because he is not trying to dispose of the jewels here in France. I have made inquiries in Marseilles, in Toulon, in Paris, in Lyons, in Lille, everywhere. They have not been offered, not a stone, unless they have gone to Belgium or Holland. Without someone to betray him, as you were betrayed"—Bellini shook his head—"he might operate for months, years. We cannot wait that long. We must uncover him before he ruins us. Before Jean-Pierre and Coco and Le Borgne are back in prison and I am left alone with no one to help me."

He beamed, his head cocked sideways.

John said, "What are you hinting at?"

Bellini nodded, his smile unchanged.

"I should never try to be subtle with you. Your mind does not work that way. Very well. We need your help."

He sat back in his chair, lifting the hand of his crippled arm before John could speak. "Let me finish. Whoever this thief is—and he will be hard to uncover, very hard—he has borrowed your style, your technique. You must have noticed it. I have studied your thefts and his, and I tell you that he is exactly the thief you were. He thinks as you did, robs as you used to, mocks the police with his actions as you mocked them. He is another Cat. You see what an opportunity it gives you? You could put yourself into his mind, plan his thefts, think a step ahead of him—"

"I can't do it, Bellini. They're looking for me now. Not him. I have the whole sentence to serve if I go back."

"They would forget the prison sentence if you gave them this thief. He makes them ridiculous. They would forgive a dozen murders to take him."

"They would forget about him if they could take me, too. They can prove that I'm Le Chat. If they find me—"

"What real risk will you run? You said yourself that they would not be looking for a middle-aged tourist. There are hundreds, thousands of middle-aged tourists here on the Côte for the season. You would be one fish in a school. They have sent a *commissaire division-naire* down from Paris to take charge of the investigation, Lepic, a good man but young. He has never seen you. Your record was destroyed, your prison photographs, everything. You would not have to expose yourself. I can give you men to help, a hundred if you want them. You remember once you said that we would have made good partners? That is it. All you have to do is think for us."

"And risk La Maison Centrale again if I slipped."

"You need not slip. Did I ever ask you to take an unnecessary risk in the *maquis?*"

"This is not the *maquis,* Bellini. I took risks then because I had reasons to take them. I have none now."

"What of Le Borgne and Coco and Jean-Pierre?"

John opened his mouth, but thought better of what he had intended to say. Bellini said it for him.

"You are not a thief, now, or a companion of thieves and gangsters. Is that it?"

"I didn't say it."

"But you meant it." Bellini wiped sweat from his face. The smile stayed. "Very well. Then think of yourself, John. You love France. You are as much of a Frenchman as you are an American, at heart. You say you can come back again some day, after it is over, after the thief is caught. I say you will never come back."

"What will there be to stop me?"

"Nothing. But how will you be able to bring yourself to return?"

Bellini was leaning forward under the lamp again. His face gleamed in the glare of light. He still smiled.

"You could come back before without fear of prison because of what we all did in the *maquis,* John. You were only part of it. You alone did not win the amnesty. Jean-Pierre did, and Coco, and Le Borgne, and La Mule, and I, and all the others together, crooks, thieves, murderers, and good comrades in spite of it. We, not you, won you off from the years in prison you are afraid of now. You didn't pay for that when you spilled a few drops of blood for *liberté, égalité, fraternité,* and the Third Republic. And you can't escape a debt by running from it. Will you ever be able to take advantage of the amnesty again, after you have abandoned us to save your own skin?"

John turned away. He walked to the window to look at the moon track lying across the calm sea.

Strollers still wandered along the promenade. The wind still rustled in the palms. Two or three miles off-shore the lights of a passing steamer winked across the water, heading south and west for Marseilles, Gibraltar, the Atlantic, and America.

And safety, he thought.

After a long time he said to the open window, "I'm not as confident as you are. It's been twelve years since I thought like a thief."

"I am confident enough for both of us." Bellini chuckled

warmly behind his back. "I have already made preliminary plans for you. You will have to go to Marseilles for a few days, to Jean-Pierre, but all arrangements have been made for your return. I believe you will be able to work best here in Cannes, where we can keep in touch with each other. With your mind and my organization, it will be easy. Relatively easy, of course. Everything is relative."

John turned around.

"You were confident, weren't you?" he said, unsmiling.

Bellini giggled.

"I am always confident of my friends. I find that loyalty repays loyalty."

"What have you done so far?"

"Only groundwork. I have been able to decide definitely on only one probable victim of the thief. I can suggest other possibilities for you to consider for yourself, but this one seems to me almost a certainty. She is a Mrs. Stevens, an American widow staying at the Hotel Midi for the season. She carries with her jewels which have been insured by a London insurance company for seventy-two thousand five hundred dollars, value accepted. I have had the figures verified. She is accompanied by her daughter Francie. How old are you?"

The irrelevancy of the question made him look up in surprise. "Thirty-four. Why?"

"Are you susceptible to attractive women?"

"Not particularly. Why, again?"

"The daughter is unusual."

"I've known unusual women before, and robbed several."

Bellini shook his head. "Not like this one. There is nothing to steal from her. She wears no jewelry of any kind, at any time. I find it very strange that the daughter of a woman of wealth does not own even a ring."

It would be even more strange that there could be two such women in Cannes. John said, "Is she a blue-eyed brunette with a keep-your-distance look?"

"How did you know?"

"I came here on the bus with her tonight."

"She wouldn't be on the bus."

"She was, although she didn't belong there. She puzzled me."

"Then undoubtedly you have seen her." Bellini beamed. "Everything about her puzzles me. Not only the lack of jewelry, but even her reason for existence. No one can live without a reason for existence. It may change from time to time, but there is always a driving force of some kind—pleasure, duty, fame, the accumulation of wealth, good works, thievery, destruction, murder. The mother's is pleasure, as mine, generally speaking, is to persuade others to do what is best for me." He giggled. "I do not know what the daughter's is, and what I do not under-stand I do not trust. Also, as you have seen, she is attract-tive. It is a dangerous combination if you let it distract you from more important things."

"There isn't anything that can distract me from staying out of prison. What else should I be warned against?"

"Several things, although the plan I have in mind is essentially simple. Tonight you will go to Marseilles with one of my men."

He talked on, chuckling as he outlined the risks John must run, giggling over the dangers to be avoided as if he were rehearsing some practical joke they meant to play on a friend. It was his way. He would giggle on his deathbed. But he was careful to overlook no detail that might be important, and John listened attentively. The knowledge that a slip would cost twenty years of his life kept his mind from wandering.

2

A SÛRETÉ NATIONALE AGENT in plain clothes strolled along the sun-baked promenade of the Boulevard La Croisette. He was hot, his shirt stuck to his back, and he envied the seven-eighths-naked vacationers sporting on the strip of beach ten feet below the promenade, who swam or dived or played ball or sprawled on the sand, coloring the beach with brief, bright bathing suits and tanned bare arms and legs. Cannes in midsummer was no place for a man who had to wear clothes. The *agent* would have given his chances for promotion, which were not good as long as Le Chat remained at large, to be lying on the beach himself, with a cold bottle of beer in his hand and no troubles.

Passing the impressive front of the Hotel Midi, he made his usual inspection of the small patch of roped-off sand which was the hotel's private beach. Several people read books or newspapers in deck chairs under the beach umbrellas, others sunned themselves. A few were cooling off in the water. The *plage privée* was more sedate and less crowded than other parts of the beach. The Midi's guests were generally sedate and exclusive.

The *agent* saw nothing that interested him professionally. A girl who came across the boulevard from the
hotel and went down to the beach wearing a zebra-
striped bathing suit that was startling even for Cannes
made him hesitate, but the man who followed her gave
him a cold look. The *agent* walked on.

John Robie, sitting in one of the shaded deck chairs
on the *plage privée,* put down his newspaper after the
agent had passed.

He was used to the *agents* who strolled La Croisette.
They were as methodical about it as patrolling sentries,
and as much alike in their sport clothes as soldiers in
uniform, or like the young men who came down to the
beach in the afternoon with the girl in the startling
bathing suit.

He looks like an American today, John thought,
watching the girl and her companion. It had been a
Frenchman the day before, an Englishman the day
before that, but they all looked much the same. None of
them lasted very long.

He watched the girl pull on a white bathing cap over
her dark hair. When she had buttoned the strap of the
bathing cap, she and the American waded into the
water and struck out for the diving platform anchored a
hundred yards out. She was a fine swimmer. The American, a husky boy, had to stroke hard to keep up with her.

She was Francie Stevens, the girl he had seen on the
bus. Since that night he had learned a few things about
her, more about her mother, even more about the
mother's jewelry, which was insured for seventy-two

thousand five hundred dollars with a London insurance company and fitted nicely into a small red leather jewel case. He was in the process of determining how the jewelry could most easily be stolen.

He still did not know the reason for Francie Stevens's existence, although the problem did not disturb him as much as it had seemed to disturb Bellini. Since he had already fallen into the old way of thinking of himself as a thief, she interested him only because she was a factor to be considered in the theft. She never wore jewelry herself.

That puzzled him as much as it had puzzled Bellini. It was not modesty on her part. Her clothes, as well as her bathing suits, were always designed to attract attention. It was not lack of money. And it was too clearly a deliberate gesture of some kind on her part to be overlooked. The summer season on the Côte offered every woman an opportunity to make two displays—one of herself, on the beach during the day, the other of her dress and ornament in the evening. Francie was noticeable on both occasions; on the beach because of the bathing suits, at other times because she wore no personal ornament of any kind at any time, not even rings or a bracelet. This and her clear lack of interest in other things that brought most summer visitors to the Côte were puzzling. Otherwise she seemed like any other pretty girl. She had a good figure and the kind of Irish attractiveness that goes with blue eyes, a fair skin, and dark hair. He thought she might be really eye-catching if she would make an effort to be.

She seems to be eye-catching enough without an effort, he thought. He had seen the *agent* on the promenade stop to stare. The next *agent* would not come by for another hour.

He opened his paper to read the war news.

It was a week since his talk with Bellini. He had gone from Bellini's office to Marseilles in a car driven by a man who asked no questions and would not have recognized his passenger as the respectable middle-aged gentleman who returned to Cannes by train three days later. John's normally straight brown hair, now black and curly, receded sharply over the temples and was beginning to gray at the sides. His eyebrows were darker and bushier, and he was moderately convex through the middle instead of concave. Pads in his shoes increased his height and made him toe out when he walked, enough to give him a flat-footed, slightly clumsy appearance. The strolling police *agents,* each of whom had a copy of a poor twelve-year-old photograph and a physical description of Le Chat, acrobat, thief, and jailbird, never gave a second look at the balding, thick-bodied man who sat reading a newspaper in a deck chair on the beach in front of the Hotel Midi. He wore tinted glasses occasionally, but so did most of the other hotel guests while they were on the beach. The sun glare from the water was strong.

"It's a matter of camouflage, not disguise," Jean-Pierre had told him in Marseilles. "As we did in the *maquis,* one adopts the coloration of one's surroundings. One blends. In your case, we blend you into a clot of tourists, like a cook blending fish in a bouillabaisse. You no longer exist as an individual. You merely contribute to the background."

The blending process had taken three days. Jean-Pierre could not give him a permanent wave or put pads in his shoes, but he had friends who came with their equipment and went away afterward as uncurious as they had come. Jean-Pierre continued the transformation with hair dye, a razor to create the balding temples, and some of the shaved hair to make bushy eyebrows. Jean-Pierre's wife sewed the light harness John wore next to his skin to change his body contours, and Jean-Pierre's sons bought his new wardrobe and luggage piece by piece on the Marseilles flea market. When it was all done, Jean-Pierre, using a fine German camera stolen from its original owner only a week before, took the photograph that went on ahead to Bellini to replace the original in John's passport.

"The harness will bother you for a time, but you will get used to it," Jean-Pierre said. "It is a necessary evil, like the shoes. There is nothing we can do with the face. The *flics* will be on watch for a green beard, so we must leave the face out in the open, except for a touch here and there. I do not approve of mustaches. The eyebrows are better. You have average features and average coloring, luckily. We do not need to hide an eagle nose. You should wear sun glasses when the other fish wear sun glasses, but not habitually. As for the rest, I am an *impressioniste,* like Papa Picasso. I do not make you older and fatter, with grease paint and false hair and a tub of lard in the middle. I create the impression that you are older and fatter, subtly. I am an *artiste.*"

"You are an *artiste,*" John agreed, looking at himself in the mirror. The illusion of middle age and physical softness was perfect.

Jean-Pierre said, "The main thing is to disguise the body. The *boche* did you a favor when they burned your prison photographs, but the body is known. That is what they will watch for, so no disclosures on the beach. You must wear the harness at all times in public, but even without the harness you would give yourself away if you took off your shirt. You have too much meat in the arms and shoulders, too little around the middle." He added innocently, "Where did you earn the muscles, John?"

"You didn't ask me when we were in the *maquis.*"

"I withdraw the question. To return to business. Be careful on the beach, but appear there regularly. You must take the sun, all Americans do that at Cannes, but never the water. You have in your baggage modest shorts, knee-length in the British style, and loose shirts with sleeves to the elbow. Wear those during the day. Be unobtrusive, but do not slink. When you meet an *agent* on the street, do not look at his eyes or at his feet, but over his shoulder, past his ear. It gives one an honest, unconcerned air. Lock your door at night before you take off your clothes, and give plenty of time to thought about your appearance before you leave your room. Keep your shades drawn. Use the dye I have given you at the roots of your hair as necessary and shave your temples daily, without fail. Let them have sun gradually. Finally"—Jean-Pierre lowered his voice, looking over his shoulder to be sure his wife was not within earshot—"catch the *salop* of a thief for us, and quick. I have not said it to anyone but you, but I am afraid for my neck. This latest business, with the newspapers digging needles into the *flics,* will have them tearing their hair, arresting everyone in sight. I have twelve years yet to go at La Maison Centrale, John."

"I have twenty," John said. "I'll catch him, or they'll catch me first. You won't have to worry about La Maison Centrale, either way. *Au revoir*, and many thanks."

"*Au revoir*, John."

The name that went with his new identity was Jack Burns. Bellini had done a good forgery on the passport. It said that Mr. Burns was in the insurance business, that he came from New York City, that he was forty-four years old, and that he had no distinguishing physical characteristics worth being noted. He had entered France through the port of Marseilles on a three-month tourist permit, without a visa. His baggage bore the proper customs labels, and his wardrobe matched the wardrobes of several dozen other visitors of Mr. Burns's approximate age and financial status enjoying the pleasures of the summer on the Côte d'Azur. As Jean-Pierre had said, he contributed to the background.

He was not afraid of being recognized, unless by Oriol. Paul would certainly know his face, and any of the Vence *boule* players, even half-blind Germaine, might still identify him. But Paul had left France, and neither Germaine nor the *boule* players had any reason to visit the tourist resorts of the Côte. As for Oriol, John had read *Nice-Matin* and *L'Espoir* carefully—in private; Mr. Burns did not read French—without finding any mention of the disappearance of John Robie from the Villa des Bijoux near Vence, or anything to connect his name with the thefts. He hoped that Oriol was keeping quiet to protect his own position. A police *commissaire* who knew Le Chat's face not only as it had looked at the time of his trial but as it was twelve years afterward could be of great help to the Sûreté. He would first have to confess to the Sûreté that he had had Le Chat in his hands and let him go free, and he might not continue to hold his post as *commissaire* afterward. John counted on Oriol's peasant caution to keep him from the confession.

In any event, Mr. Burns was staying at the Hotel Midi, and small-town police officials did not often pass through the Midi's impressive doorway. The list of hotel guests included an Arabian demigod with his entourage of bodyguards and dancing girls, an exiled ex-dictator, an East Indian princess, several members of the British peerage, and a number of wealthy Americans, including Mrs. Maude Stevens, with Francie and the red leather jewel case.

Maude Stevens was in her early fifties, friendly, plump, nice-looking except for a tendency to be haphazard with her makeup, and a heavy gambler at roulette. She would have preferred to play cards, but there were no poker tables in the Riviera casinos, and she did not understand baccarat. She had done her own washing and housework for the first thirty years of her life, helping her husband to scrape a living on a quarter section of worthless land in northern Texas. Her husband had died, her only child had been born, and the first of several oil wells had come in on the quarter section almost simultaneously. Since then, she had been repaying herself for the first thirty years. She liked her jewelry florid, preferring diamonds to other stones because of their sparkle, and she changed the pieces she wore from evening to evening, giving the world an opportunity to admire her entire collection, of which she was enormously proud.

John had no intention of making her acquaintance. But he wanted to be certain that the jewels she wore were those covered by the insurance policy, and not copies. He spent an evening standing behind her chair at a roulette wheel in the casino at Juan-les-Pins, leaning forward to make small bets on red or black whenever she placed her own counters so he could look unobtrusively at her rings. He won consistently on the red and black. Mrs. Stevens, who had been losing until then, began to cap his hundred-franc counters with her own larger bets, first ten thousand francs and then, as the luck held with them, up to the table limit of a hundred thousand. She won nearly two million francs. They were great friends before their luck changed.

He saw enough of her jewelry that evening to satisfy himself that she wore the originals, and he meant to avoid her afterward. He found it almost impossible to do. On the evening of the day after their stroke of luck at roulette he went into the Midi's Petit Bar for the single cocktail which Mr. Burns allowed himself before dinner. She shouted at him from the table where she sat with Francie and Francie's admirer of the moment.

"Lucky! Lucky Burns! Come over here! I want to buy you a drink."

He had to join them. Introducing him, she said, "This is the man I was telling you about, Francie. Mr. Lucky Burns, my daughter Francie, this is Leon, don't bother getting up, Leon, sit down, Lucky, we're all in the family, what will you drink? Waiter, bring the man something. Look!"

She showed him a pin she was wearing. It was a small diamond dog with emerald eyes and a diamond leash ending in an emerald safety clasp. He did not have to look at it closely. Even at a snap guess, it represented an investment of five or six thousand dollars.

She said proudly, "I bought it this morning, at Cartier's. It took all my winnings. The house will never get its money back now."

"I should have let you make my bets for me. I was too timid."

"Have to bet 'em big to win big, my husband always said, poor man. He never had anything to bet with. How long are you going to be here in Cannes, Lucky?"

"A few weeks. I'm not sure, exactly. It depends on whether my business can get along without me."

"What is your business?"

"Insurance."

"Give me your card, and I'll try to send some customers your way. I owe you something for the dog."

He shook his head. "Thanks. I'm on my first vacation in ten years. I don't want any business."

Francie did not enter into the conversation. He could not tell if she was bored, or preoccupied with her thoughts, or sulky because Leon paid more attention to the diamond dog than he did to her. She was there at the table with them, nothing more.

Mrs. Stevens, happy with her new jewel, kept moving the dog to new positions on her dress, until Leon said something about thieves, Le Chat in particular. The *Herald Tribune* article was still a popular subject for discussion.

Mrs. Stevens scoffed at the suggestion that she had anything to worry about.

"I keep my beads in the hotel safe," she said. "Besides, they're insured. And I've got my lucky dog to sic on any cat that comes around *me.*"

She made a gesture of petting it, and laughed. So did John and Leon. Francie smiled.

He avoided the Petit Bar after that. He was very busy in the evenings, too busy to let himself be waylaid by Mrs. Stevens.

In the afternoons, after he had taken his daily sunning on the beach, he visited Bellini. Bellini had many callers, including summer visitors who wanted to arrange motor tours or hotel reservations. Mr. Burns was one among many. He was the only one who regularly took the key out of the door lock and carried it with him into Bellini's cubbyhole.

"Mrs. Stevens will do," he told Bellini, the day after she bought the diamond dog. "The others you had in mind won't attract a thief like this one. The stones aren't worth the risk. I'll have to find some that are."

"I agreed before that you would have to make the final choices," Bellini said. "We know this thief steals as you did. He has either read about you and copied your technique, or arrived at it on his own. Either way, you must identify yourself with him, plan the thefts he will make before he makes them, so that we can be ready and waiting for him. There can be only a certain number of possibilities profitable enough and safe enough to attract him, and we need to anticipate only one of those. It is true that he has the whole of France to range in, even the whole of Europe."

"He will move either in Nice or here in Cannes next."

Bellini raised his eyebrows.

John said flatly, "I would. I have to believe that he'll think the way I do, if the scheme is going to work at all. I never went outside the Côte, and he hasn't, so far. He's covered Menton, Cap Ferrat, and Monte Carlo and Monaco, to date. There are still other possibilities, but the wealthiest people come to Nice and Cannes, and the season will be over here in another few weeks. There'll be nothing to tempt him out of season. In the meantime, he won't pass up the two most popular resorts. He can't."

"Good. Good. I am glad to hear you say it like that. You are confident. I leave it in your hands. Call on me whenever you are ready for help."

"I will. In a few days. I'm still feeling my way."

He continued to feel his way. He was sure that Mrs. Stevens, glittering nightly at the casinos, would catch the thief's eye in time, but he continued to look for other baits. One trap was good, a dozen were better. He had decided on a second logical victim for the thief and was hunting a third when the necklace of pigeon-blood rubies which had been the cause of his arrest in 1939 was stolen a second time from the wife of the Member of the Chamber of Deputies.

~§~

She had a summer apartment on the Promenade des Anglais in Nice. The thief entered through a skylight which he reached by a dangerous climb up a drainpipe. He had cut a hole in the skylight with a glass cutter, lowered himself into the apartment on a rope, and climbed the rope again to make his escape.

Another uproar followed the theft. Newspaper editorials attacking the Sûreté's incompetence continued for days, and cartoons appeared showing a black cat with a ruby necklace around its neck making a popular French gesture at a group of dazed men in police uniform. The editorials ignored the fact that the wife of the Member occupied the apartment under a name which was not her husband's, since another man shared the apartment with her, and that the police had no knowledge of her presence in Nice. Le Chat was offered to the readers of the newspapers at once as the public menace of the century and as a public benefactor exposing the stupidity and corruption of the Sûreté Nationale.

Bellini had at least one source of information in every *commissariat* and public office on the Côte. John heard of the theft almost as soon as the police did. It was a bad blow when Bellini told him the news.

"I could have had him," he said. "He was bound to go after the rubies. They're irresistible. If I had known she was in Nice"—he shook his head angrily—"I could have had him. It would all be over."

"Never mind, John." Bellini was as cheerful as ever. "In a way, it is a good thing. You said he would move in Nice or Cannes, and he has moved in Nice. Very well. Cannes is next. Will we be ready for him when he comes here?"

"I'm nearly ready now. Another few days."

"You don't think it would be worth while to go to Nice yourself? If he robs there again—"

"I wouldn't have time to plan the thefts. He's already planned them. The acrobatics are nothing, Bellini. It's the groundwork, the preparation, that takes time. That's why he needs two or three weeks each time before you hear of him in a new place. He plans all the thefts he is going to make in a neighborhood, then moves fast. I worked the same way myself."

"You know best." Bellini peered owlishly through his spectacles. "You seem certain enough of his thinking processes. Do you have any mental picture, any idea of him as an individual, his appearance, his nationality? I could send several of my people to Nice, if they knew what to watch for. Give me an idea, even a hint."

"I haven't any idea. When I try to picture him, I can only see myself. I've thought so much about what to steal and how to steal it that sometimes I forget there is another thief. He's Le Chat, myself, as if I were looking in a mirror. All I can tell you is that he's an athlete, a gymnast, possibly an acrobat, strong and agile, with plenty of nerve and a good head. A good thief."

"In other words, Le Chat," Bellini said, chuckling. "Very well. We will wait for him here and leave Nice to the Sûreté. I hope they will have better luck than they have had so far."

~§~

Lepic, the *commissaire divisionnaire* who had been sent down from Paris to take charge of the hunt for Le Chat after the publication of the *Herald Tribune* article, was not as philosophical as Bellini. Lepic was a young man for his position, and he had arrived there by working hard at his job. He had no use for incompetence or sloppy police work, and he did not believe in luck, or very strongly in anything else except his own ability.

He called a conference of his chief assistants the day after the rubies were stolen.

"Quoting *L'Espoir,* we are all as dumb as camels," he told them. "I know it, and I would not expect any of you individually to be as well informed as the thief, who could not only identify the wife of the Member by sight but has had previous experience with her jewels and could logically be expected to renew his interest in them, so that a routine police check of summer visitors in Nice might—I don't say would, but might—have disclosed the lady's identity and given us an opportunity to guard her property properly." He paused for breath. "But how many men do we have looking for Le Chat in Nice? Thirty? Forty? Fifty? All with copies of his picture, all with a physical description, all presumably alert to question anyone resembling him. And he laughs in our faces. If we have no brains, where are our eyes?"

He scowled at the only man who was not looking at the floor.

The man said, "It's been twelve years since the picture was taken. It was no good even then. It is only a reporter's snap, not a police photograph. Most of us never saw him in the flesh."

"I never saw him in the flesh myself. And I agree that the photo is a poor one. But I have his description here." Lepic slapped a piece of paper. "You all have it. This man's appearance has not changed so much in twelve years that he would be unrecognizable. I say it because Le Chat climbs drainpipes like Le Chat, and to do that he must be in the same physical condition that he was twelve years ago, or nearly so. I do not ask you to rely on a poor photograph, because it is not necessary. We have a description of him. How many men do you see outside of a circus who answer this description physically?"

He rattled the paper at them.

The man who had spoken before said, "None, or we would question them. He wears clothes to cover the body, as he probably wears whiskers and tinted glasses to hide his face."

There was a mumble of assent from the other men.

Lepic bared his teeth. He said softly, "So at a summer resort like Nice, where the whole world comes to take the sun and water, you cannot find a man with whiskers and tinted glasses who never takes a dip in the sea, never sunbathes, never appears in a bathing suit, always wears clothes covering him to the wrist and ankles, like an undertaker? In this weather."

There was no answer. One man shuffled his feet.

Lepic said, "That is all for the present. Le Chat was here in Nice yesterday. I predict that, in accordance with his usual practice, he will soon make other thefts in Nice before moving to a new locale. We have no brains. We have eyes. Let us try to use the eyes to the best of our ability. *Bonsoir, messieurs.*"

Lepic was wrong. The thief committed only one robbery in Nice. John, like Lepic, expected others, but it did not matter to him that they did not occur. He continued with his plans. Lepic, when his men had failed to discover the overdressed undertaker with a beard and tinted spectacles, made further plans of his own which did not oblige him to rely on his assistants. He was ambitious for personal glory.

John spent several hours of every evening in the casinos nearest to Cannes, at Juan-les-Pins or Antibes or the ultra-fashionable Palm Beach. The Côte was having a good season. The casinos were crowded with women who glittered as Mrs. Stevens glittered and gambled as heavily. Heavy gamblers were always so intent on the fall of the cards or the spin of the ball in its circular track that they paid no attention to the player sitting next to them, if he did not win or lose too much or stare too obviously. The appraisals he made at roulette and baccarat tables were the easiest part of his work. The drudgery came later.

Bellini helped him with names and addresses, occasionally even with floor plans or blueprints of particular villas. But John spent long hours of the night in the shadows outside one or the other of the villas, studying the house and grounds, noting at what hour the occupants came in, the order in which lights went off, and when the servants first began to stir in the morning, listening for dogs to bark, other sounds. Later he drew from memory careful sketches showing the height of a wall, and how a tree shadowed a corner of the house, and whether window shutters were regularly closed or left open as a matter of household routine, night after night. Most of the Hotel Midi's guests patronized the casinos, so there was nothing out of the ordinary about a man who frequently stayed out until dawn and came in looking tired.

He remained awake long enough to make his sketches while the details were still in his mind. He abandoned several of the sketches before they were finished; an unpredictable yard dog made one useless, another lost its purpose when the villa he had been watching closed for the summer. He was accustomed to those disappointments. He returned to the casinos and started again from the beginning.

But he was working against time, always, and Mrs. Stevens handicapped him. She gambled regularly, always alone. Francie did not enjoy gambling, and he rarely saw her in the evenings. But whenever his work took him near a roulette wheel where Mrs. Stevens was playing, she would welcome him with cries of "Lucky! Lucky Burns! Come over here! I need you! This wheel is *ruining* me!" He could never escape her after that. She would insist on following him to another table if he walked away, and since she was so talkative and friendly, taking everyone around into her conversation and attracting so much notice with her jewels, her lopsided lipstick, her enormous bets, and her loud laugh that he could not remain inconspicuous, he wasted several evenings. He finally had to go to Bellini for help.

Bellini said, "You want *what?*"

"A girl."

Bellini pushed his spectacles down to the top of his nose and looked over them. He began to giggle, the loose fat shaking under his shirt. He said, "I have many business interests, John. But I assure you that one of them is not—"

"Stop joking," John said. "I'm having trouble with Mrs. Stevens. She won't leave me alone, and she attracts too much attention. I need someone to go around with me in the evenings to keep her off."

"I see." Bellini pushed his glasses back where they belonged, still beaming. "Someone young and pretty?"

"It doesn't matter. Anybody who won't be too inquisitive. She'll have to speak English, of course."

Bellini nodded. "But she must be someone young and pretty as well. A gentleman like Mr. Burns would not be interested in an intellectual type. I have just the girl for you."

He took one of his business cards out of a drawer and wrote with a scratchy pen. When he had finished, he blew the ink dry.

"La Plage Nautique, near your hotel. Ask for Danielle. She works there. Tell her what you want with her, and how much you will pay. She has had experience with American gentlemen before."

He found the signboard of La Plage Nautique not far from the Hotel Midi's *plage privée*. It was one of half a dozen similar signboards along the promenade which advertised small sections of sand open to the public. Each *plage* had its own chairs and umbrellas for rent, its own paddle boards for hire, its own small row of dressing rooms for the use of its customers, its own *professeur de natation*. He saw from the sign that the *professeur's* name at La Plage Nautique was Claude. There was no mention of Danielle.

A small flight of wooden steps went down from the promenade to the sand. He stopped at the bottom step to look over the beach. It was crowded and active. He snapped Bellini's card against his thumb, wondering what to do with it. He could see at least a hundred girls on the *plage* who were young and pretty and might answer to the name of Danielle. He wished that Bellini had been more specific.

But Bellini had sent other Americans to La Plage Nautique with his card. Almost immediately a girl in a Bikini came up to the steps where he stood. She smiled at him.

"I am Danielle, *m'sieu*. Do you want to see me, or Claude?"

He gave her the card. She read what was on it and said politely, "How do you do, Mr. Burns?"

"How do you do, Danielle?"

He thought, Damn Bellini. I can't use this child.

She was nineteen or twenty, as pretty as a flower. She had the straight nose and heart-shaped face common to many French girls, widest at the level of the eyes and tapering to a delicate mouth and chin. Her hair was a short mop of blond curls, and her figure was still the figure of a young girl, slim and small-breasted. Her skin was golden brown from the sun. She could have been Mr. Burns's daughter, the youngest of three or four.

He told her what he wanted, feeling more ridiculous each minute. He explained that he was alone in Cannes, liked to visit the casinos in the evening but felt out of place without a companion, did not speak French—Mr. Bellini had recommended her highly—he would pay well for her time—she could be sure it would remain a business arrangement—nothing personal—

He stumbled through it. It was natural for an embarrassed stranger to stumble in the circumstances, and he did not have to pretend a poise he did not feel. He was conscious that she was studying him while he talked, measuring the balding, middle-aged man with the flat feet, wondering how he would behave after the second drink and what he meant by a "business arrangement." He knew what was going on behind her gravely polite expression. But when he finished at last, half hoping she would think of an excuse to refuse him, she said without hesitation, "I'll be happy to go with you in the evenings, Mr. Burns. I work here during the day. If that is all right?"

"That's fine."

"When do you want me to start?"

"Tonight, if you have no other plans."

"Shall I come to your hotel?"

"I'll be glad to call for you."

"It will be better for me to come to your hotel, I think. Where are you staying?"

He told her. They set the hour and arranged a price. It was very businesslike after the uncomfortable preliminaries. He felt less like a fool.

While they were still talking, Claude, the *professeur de natation,* came up and said, *"Qu'est-ce que c'est?"* to Danielle, smiling professionally at John.

She introduced him. He said, *"Enchanté."*

John said, "Tell him I don't speak French but I'm pleased to meet him."

Claude smiled again when Danielle translated. He had a good smile, even though it involved only his mouth. He was a little man with a sleek cap of black hair, hardly taller than Danielle but broad-shouldered, slim-hipped, and muscled like a weight lifter. He wore only bathing trunks, and ropes of muscle crawled under his tanned skin when he moved. John, looking at Claude's shoulders, thought idly, A good climber, if he isn't muscle-bound. And immediately, automatically: Thief?

The thought stirred him. But he knew it was senseless to suspect anyone simply because of over-developed arm and shoulder muscles, and after he had listened to the conversation between Claude and Danielle, the suspicion left him.

Claude was not clever enough to be a successful thief. He was small-minded, and as pompous as a man of his size could be. When Danielle had explained what Mr. Burns wanted of her, he said, "I do not like the looks of the *type*. He will massage your legs under the table."

"They are my legs, not yours."

"They are not the *type's,* either. Tell him to go break his head against a wall."

"I will not. It's easy money."

"And what about me and the beach?"

"I'll still be here. He only wants me in the evenings."

"Naturally. Certain hours are best for certain things. I know these *types.*"

"If he wasn't looking I'd slap your face, you imbecile. Can't you see he's harmless? Bellini wouldn't send me anyone who was one of those."

"He'll massage your legs at the very least," Claude said stubbornly. "How do you expect me to feel about that? A man has his pride."

"Oh, spread your pride on a piece of bread and eat it!" Danielle was trying to keep the anger from her voice. "You don't own me."

"I'll spread the *type* on a piece of bread and eat him if he massages your legs. Tell him that, and don't stay out so late that you can't be here on time in the mornings. And get him to patronize the beach while you're about it. I have no objections to taking his money." He turned the professional smile in John's direction. *"Au revoir, m'sieu. Enchanté de vous connaître.*

He walked away swelling his chest. The muscles rippled in his back.

"Doesn't he approve?" John asked.

"Oh, yes. I'll see you this evening, Mr. Burns. Please excuse me now."

She hurried after Claude. John did not wait to see if the argument developed further.

~§~

Danielle met him in the lobby of the Midi that night, and regularly afterward. Usually they had dinner together before going on to the casinos. Her wardrobe was not extensive, and because he thought she would feel out of place among the expensively gowned women in the Midi's huge dining-salon, he took her to smaller, less public restaurants. At the gambling-tables he always bought her a handful of hundred-franc counters when he bought his own. She liked to play, but she

insisted on turning everything back to him whenever
she won. Actually she cost him very little. She was
pretty, *chic,* well-mannered, and demanded no more
attention from him than he wanted to give her. As he
had hoped, Mrs. Stevens let him alone when she saw
that he had a companion, except for an occasional
friendly shout across the table. He continued to look for
his baits.

He saw Francie Stevens eyeing Danielle speculatively one night. Francie never paid any great attention
to him, beyond a casual greeting when they passed in
the hotel or on the beach. But on an evening when he
took Danielle to dinner at a *boîte* on the Quai St. Pierre,
Francie was at the adjoining table with a party of
friends. She paid less attention to the friends than she
did to John and Danielle, and she did not attempt to
hide her interest. The next afternoon, while he was
reading his paper in the beach chair, she stopped to
talk.

It surprised him, not only because she stopped but
because she was alone. She wore a polka-dot bathing-
suit this time. She sat down beside his chair, funneled
sand through her hands, and said something about the
heat. When they had discussed the weather, they had
nothing in common to talk about except Francie's
mother and her gambling.

"She wins and loses," Francie said. "She's lost, lately,
but the money doesn't mean anything to her. It's the
thrill." After a moment she added, "I wish I could get a
thrill out of gambling."

"You don't get much of a thrill out of anything, do you?"

"No." She stared at the sand pouring through her fingers.

"How long are you going to stay here in Cannes?"

"Until the season is over, I suppose. Mother always wants to wait until the last *gala,* so she can make a big splash."

"Then what?"

"I don't know. New York, or Florida. Or Switzerland. Or somewhere to make another splash. It depends on Mother."

"Do you always go where she goes?"

"Usually. She's too friendly to travel by herself. She's always picking up imitation dukes who borrow money from her and forget to pay it back, or try to steal her jewels. I have to look out for her jewels."

"You sound more like the mother than the daughter."

"Sometimes I feel that way."

She began to drift sand over her painted toenails.

He was trying to think of another conversational lead when she said abruptly, "I'll be glad to get out of here."

"Don't you like Cannes?"

"Do you?" She looked up at him curiously.

"Very much."

"Why? What do you like about it?"

"Why, everything."

"The casinos? The beach? Rubbing elbows with famous people? Hitting the high spots? Drinking champagne? Playing roulette all night? Being waited on, and made to think you're somebody important? Is that what you mean?"

"I suppose so."

"You know it's all put on for you, don't you? You're not really as important as they try to make you feel."

"I still like it."

She made an impatient gesture, then went on funneling sand over her toenails.

After a while she said, "You're not married, are you?"

"I never could seem to find the time."

"You seem to have the time now." She looked sideways at him, tilting her head, unsmiling. "She's awfully pretty."

"Who?"

"The girl you were with last night, at the restaurant. I've seen you with her several times."

He laughed. "You'll probably see her with me several times again. That's as far as it goes. She isn't half my age."

"What do life expectancies have to do with it?"

He was still wondering what Mr. Burns should say to an irrelevant remark about life expectancies when Francie stood up, walked down to the sea, plunged in, and swam away.

She was a strange girl. He felt vaguely sorry for her, without knowing why. But he was not unhappy when she passed his deck chair the next afternoon with her usual indifferent greeting. She had a new man following her.

Danielle, unlike Francie, was delightful company. Although she had the same keep-your-distance air about her it that he had first noticed in Francie, and did not like him even to take her arm when they crossed the street or touch her hand when they said good night—he supposed that good-night attempts by other employers had made her cautious—she talked freely of herself whenever he showed an interest. Something about her reminded him of someone he had known before. In an attempt to pin the resemblance down, he asked questions.

She had learned English in the French schools and improved it in England, where she had spent nearly a year as lady's maid. The job had ended when the lady walked in on Danielle and the lady's husband as Danielle was slapping the husband's face. She was hoping to find another permanent position that did not have complicating factors. In the meantime, Bellini placed her temporarily with summer visitors to the Côte as lady's maid, governess, or, she put it frankly, as companion of the evening for American gentlemen who did not expect a companion for the night as well. Between times she worked for Claude at La Plage Nautique, collecting rentals for the beach chairs and umbrellas, or simply standing around ornamentally in a Bikini so gentlemen could admire her figure and possibly decide to patronize the *plage*.

She was equally frank about the reason for her value to Claude. John said, "Doesn't it bother you to show yourself off that way?"

"Why should it? I know I have a pretty figure. And all women like to be admired. French women are more honest about it than others, that's all."

"What about Claude? Doesn't he care?"

"It's what he pays me for. All the other *professeurs* do the same thing."

"Doesn't he ever get jealous, or resent having people stare at you?"

"All he cares about is the money it brings in. Besides, he has nothing to be jealous about. I only work for him."

"He swelled his muscles at me the first day I talked to you."

She laughed. "Those muscles. You needn't be afraid, though. They're all he has. Nothing upstairs. It's too bad."

"Why is it too bad?"

She said seriously, "He wants me to marry him. I'd like to get married, raise half a dozen children, darn their socks, and cook soup for them. I like babies, and cooking soup. But Claude—" She shook her head doubt- fully. "I don't know. With no money, and no brains ei- ther, he isn't much of a catch."

"A husband ought to have one or another."

"He ought to have money, anyway. A man like Claude doesn't really need brains. That's what a wife is for. But if he can't afford to support a wife, where is he?"

"I don't know. Are you in love with him?"

"No. But I could be, if he had money. Or brains. We French women are adaptable."

John lifted his wine glass. "It's an honest answer. Here's to you, Danielle."

"Here's to you, Mr. Burns."

They drank the toast at Les Ambassadeurs, one of the few restaurants in Cannes which still clung to tradition. Even during the hottest evenings of the summer, only guests in dinner clothes were permitted to dine on the main floor. Others, like John and Danielle, sat at small tables on a low mezzanine, ate the same good food, paid the same high prices, and listened to the music of the same string orchestra. There were never very many people who went to the trouble of dressing formally for the privilege of walking down the six stairs from the mezzanine to the main floor of Les Ambassadeurs, but always a few. That night, while he was waiting for the waiter to bring his change, he looked down at the floor below and saw Paul.

The white dinner jacket caught his eye first. Paul was alone, and sat facing him directly. The subdued light was too dim for John to see his face clearly, but there was something, a kind of rigidity in the way he sat, which warned John that Paul's attention had been attracted. He turned his head, not too quickly, and then, as the waiter came back with his change, stood up to draw Danielle's chair away from the table.

She said something to him. He did not hear the words, but he smiled and followed her away from the table, letting his shoulders sag and his stomach push forward, trying to shrink into his clothes. He did not dare turn around to see if Paul had moved. He did not look back until they were outside in the street. Paul had not followed.

But the narrow escape disturbed him. Moments later,

while they were walking, Danielle said, "What's the matter, Mr. Burns? Did I say something?"

"Why do you ask that?"

"Just a feeling. You don't seem—I don't know—quite the same. I thought I might have said something wrong, when I was talking about Claude and getting married."

"You didn't say anything wrong."

They walked another dozen steps. Danielle was silent. He said, "I don't think I'll go to the casino tonight."

"All right. Tomorrow night?"

"Not tomorrow night, either." He disliked what he was doing, but she had given him an opportunity he needed. "Nor the night after that. I don't know when I'll go again."

She stopped and turned to face him. They were under a street light. She said steadily, "I did say something wrong. I'm sorry, Mr. Burns. Whatever it was, I didn't mean to offend you."

"You didn't offend me, Danielle." He did not try to meet her eyes. "I'm just suddenly tired of gambling, I guess. I've really enjoyed your company. If you would like a recommendation—"

"No, thank you. Good night, Mr. Burns. Thanks for everything."

She turned away. He said lamely, "Wait a minute. I owe you some money. And I don't want you to think—"

"Give the money to Mr. Bellini for me, please. Good night."

It was an unpleasant way to end a pleasant relationship, but he had to get rid of her one way or another and with a reasonable excuse. He knew he could not return to the casinos again. Paul's presence in Cannes, particularly in evening clothes, meant that he ran the risk of meeting Paul face to face somewhere under the bright lights of the gambling tables. He could not take the chance. He would have to go ahead with what he had, and trust that he had enough to bait at least one effective trap.

~§~

He had three prospects for the thief. Le Chat would have robbed, or attempted to rob, all of them.

Mrs. Stevens was the first and most obvious. His second choice was an American couple, the Sanfords. George Sanford, who made his money in California real estate, had retired at an early age with Mrs. Sanford to the Château Combe d'Or on a hilltop in a suburb of Cannes named, appropriately, Californie. They were regular visitors to the Palm Beach casino, lost enough money there to indicate they could afford more, and were as well known on the Côte for their huge parties as they were for Mrs. Sanford's emeralds. She frequently drank too much champagne to be cautious about her jewelry, and the house guests she invited to her famous *galas* were generally people who brought jewelry of their own to put on display. Mimi Sanford always announced the most elaborate *gala* of the year at the end of the summer season, when her social rivals had exhausted themselves. John had hopes for the *gala* if everything else failed.

His other choice was the wife of a Brazilian coffee planter named Souza. Souza was a dark-skinned man in his forties, a serious gambler and a system player. His wife, ten years younger than he, was a handsome, full-bodied woman who liked to flirt. She played baccarat or sat at the roulette table without any real interest in the game, her beautiful dark eyes roving beyond the cards or the spinning ball until she caught the attention of some man facing her. Once it had been John. Her flirtations were innocent enough, a look, lowered eyelids, another look, a half-smile, a little turn of the shoulder, another half-smile. It was all quite harmless, and it infuriated her husband, who grew paler and more tight-lipped as it went on, glaring first at his wife and then at the uncomfortable man across the table until he could bear it no longer. Bursting with suppressed rage, he would take his wife away from the game. They had a summer cottage in an isolated part of Le Cannet, on the outskirts of Cannes, and John spent hours in the shrubbery beneath their bedroom windows listening to them scream at each other in Portuguese. He could not understand their words, but the arguments always followed the same pattern. They would shout at each other until they were exhausted, then go to bed in separate rooms and sleep peacefully. The next evening the husband would be contrite, the wife cold and well behaved. The day following that she would be less cold and would have added a new diamond and topaz bracelet to her collection of diamond and topaz bracelets. An evening or two later, her eyes would rove again.

The diamond and topaz bracelets came from Cartier's or Van Cleef & Arpels, on the Boulevard La Croisette. He had seen the husband go into both shops. Because he had always to be on watch for watchers, he discovered that another man was equally interested in the Brazilians.

The watcher spent his afternoons on a bench in the little park across the boulevard from Van Cleef & Arpels's window, usually with a copy of the *Continental Daily Mail* for company. He was a thin, elderly man with white hair and a fierce white guardsman's mustache which looked out of place on his mild face. He did not remember to turn the pages of his newspaper as often as he should, and his clothes were more appropriate for London weather than for the Côte.

John had no opportunity to put Bellini onto him until the day after he saw Paul at Les Ambassadeurs. When he went to Bellini to report, he found the *Continental Daily Mail* reader twisting his mustache points in Bellini's office.

He said, "I didn't mean to interrupt. I'll come back later, Bellini."

Bellini said, "Mr. Paige was just leaving. Have you gentlemen met? Mr. Paige, Mr. Burns. Mr. Burns, Mr. Paige."

Mr. Paige said, "How do you do? How do you do?" jerking his head twice quickly at John. "Just about to go. You'll do what you can for us, Bellini?"

"Certainly, sir. Although as I have told you—"

"Quite. Quite. I understand. Discuss it another time. Do your best. Good day. Good day to you, sir."

He jerked his head at John again and left the room.

Bellini giggled helplessly afterward, shaking all over. Between wheezes he said, "He wants to get in touch with Le Chat."

"Who is he?"

"A special agent from the London insurance company. They've been badly hurt by claims, and he wants to make an offer for the jewelry before it is broken up. He's trying to find a contact with *le milieu*."

"Why did he come to you?"

Bellini gave his lopsided shrug. "I represent the company myself, in a small way. He hoped I would have heard if the jewels had been offered on the market."

"What did you tell him?"

"The truth. That I had not heard of a single stone being offered. This is a very clever and cautious thief, John. The police are increasing pressure on *le milieu* every day, trying to pop him to the surface like a seed from a grape. They do not believe that no one can help them. Jean-Pierre says he has received a definite promise that if they do not take Le Chat soon, they will take him. And others."

"Jean-Pierre and the others who know Le Chat might be tempted to talk, in the circumstances."

"Undoubtedly. But there still such a thing as loyalty."

"It's too much to expect that it will go as far as prison."

"It went even farther in the *maquis*. Remember La

Mule?"

"La Mule is dead and buried," John said. "Tell Jean-Pierre he'll have to hold out a few days longer. I'm ready for the thief now, or as ready as I'll ever be."

He told Bellini about Paul, and Danielle, and what he had decided.

Bellini said, "You are right. You cannot go into the casinos again. As for Danielle, it doesn't matter what she thinks. I have another job ready and waiting for her. Now you will want another kind of help. How many?"

"Half a dozen good men."

"What is good?"

"Strong, active, and handy with a *casse-tête*. Some of our old bunch, if you can get them. Like Coco."

"You can have Coco, himself, for one. He will be happy to help. I will see about the others."

"How about Le Borgne? He isn't as agile as he might be, but he has a good head."

"Le Borgne is almost respectable, as I told you. But he still has a turn to go at La Maison Centrale, and he always admired you. I think I can get him for you. And four others of the best. When do you want them?"

"As soon as possible. This evening, if you can arrange it. Seven o'clock."

"Where shall I send them?"

"Some place where I can talk to them all together without attracting attention."

"There is a small house for rent on the Rue Georges Clemenceau. It is not too far to walk." Bellini took a key from his desk. "Go first to look at it now, in the daylight, so the neighbors will not become curious later." He put his hand firmly on John's arm. "And do not think too much about prison sentences, John, either your own or Jean-Pierre's or the others. You will beat this thief. I know it."

"I'll beat him if I last long enough. *A bientôt.*"

"I see that you are learning French, Mr. Burns." Bellini chuckled, "Very good. *A bientôt.*"

He went to look at the house on the Rue Georges Clemenceau. He made himself conspicuous there; opened shutters, banged doors, walked around the garden until he was sure he had been noticed by the neighbors. Afterward he had lunch, and went down to the beach for his regular afternoon appearance in the sun.

For the first time, he went to La Plage Nautique rather than to the *plage privée* of the Midi. He wanted to see Danielle, if only to say hello. He still felt vaguely guilty about Danielle.

She was not at the beach. He remembered that Bellini had spoken of other work for her. Claude strutted up with his professional welcoming smile, his fine muscles rippling. He and John talked mostly in pantomime. John said *"chaise"* and *"umbrella"* with gestures, and "Danielle?" raising his eyebrows. Claude gave him the chair and the umbrella, but no news of Danielle. He didn't know, or didn't want to say. He set up John's chair, cocked the umbrella over it, and went away.

John was beginning to realize that he made one mistake in creating Jack Burns. That was to deprive him of the advantage of a French vocabulary.

It had not been necessary. Many of the Americans he met at the Midi spoke the language adequately, and several were fluent. Mr. Burns could have been reasonably fluent and still remain in character. It made him see how far he had grown away from his own countrymen, that he had not been able to picture a successful, well-educated businessman like Mr. Burns speaking any language except his own.

But it was a small error and a minor handicap at the most. He had made no major mistakes. Mr. Burns was a well-rounded creation, artistically as well as physically.

He looked out from under his umbrella across the sparkling blue Mediterranean water to the diving platform, where half a dozen swimmers lay sunning themselves. The diving platform always tempted him. He imagined how it would feel to be out on the board, feel it bounce and spring under him as he went off, deep down into the cool water and up again, thrashing his arms and legs to kick the cramp out of them, get rid of the stiff, tight feeling that came from his awkward walk and the bind of his harness.

He badly wanted a swim. But he knew that even if he could find some little isolated cove down the coast where no one would notice that Mr. Burns in bathing trunks was oddly muscular through the chest and shoulders, he would still have to worry about his dyed hair and artificial eyebrows. He could not take any unnecessary risk, now that he had gone so far. His luck had been good. If it held for a few days, another week or two at the most, he could have the swim like a free man

and go back to the Villa des Bijoux, to Germaine's cooking and the garden, the good dog and the hunting trips,
the scent of flowers in the evening, the *boule* games in
the village, the sweating pleasure of a difficult climb
across a cliff face, the long, lazy talks with Paul, all of it.
If his luck held. If not—

He refused to think of the alternative. He made up
his mind not to think at all until it was time for him to
talk to Coco and Le Borgne. Seven o'clock would come
soon enough.

He closed his eyes.

He was half asleep when he became aware that
someone stood in front of his chair, and was looking at
him. He came fully awake at once, still with his eyes
closed. His first thought was, *Paul?* and then, *Oriol?* No
other thought occurred to him, only the names of the
two men who could recognize him.

He breathed twice, keeping his muscles slack, and
opened his eyes.

It was Francie Stevens. Her brief bathing suit was
wet from the sea. She wore the white bathing cap. Drops
of water sparkled on her arms and shoulders and in her
eyelashes. She stood there, dripping sea water, watching him. He held to the blank, empty expression of a
man just awakened.

Francie nodded and smiled, suddenly.

"Good afternoon, Mr. Burns," she said.

He had never seen her smile like that. He had wondered more than once what an expression of animation
would do for her. Now he knew. She was alive, vital,

sparkling. The change in her was so tangible that he found it hard to recognize her. She was Francie, but another Francie, a girl he had not seen before.

He did not wholly like the change. There was something about her, something in her expression, her very animation, that made him uneasy. He said, "Hello. Where did you spring from?"

"The diving raft. I saw you come down to the beach. I wanted to ask you a question."

"You have good eyes, if you could see me from the raft."

"I have very good eyes."

"What did you want to ask me?"

"It's rather personal."

"That didn't bother you the last time we talked."

"This is different." She laughed, breathlessly. "I'm kind of excited, I guess. You needn't be, though, because I haven't talked about it to anyone else yet. You're Le Chat, aren't you?"

3

GOOD MUSCULAR CONTROL had always been his most valuable asset. He kept his face blank and his muscles loose. He felt a strong urge to swallow, and fought it down. For one short, bad moment he could think of nothing but the need to keep her from seeing the involuntary movement of his throat muscles.

She watched him, the bright, expectant smile lighting her face.

He said, "I'm what?"

"You don't want me to shout it out loud, do you?" She nodded to indicate the sunbathers lying on the beach near them. "Somebody might understand English."

"I don't think I heard you right. I thought you said—"

"I did. You are." The bright smile faded slowly. "You don't have to try to bluff me, Mr. Burns. I know. Do you me want me to tell you how I know?"

"I don't see that it matters." He put his hands behind his head, stretching. It gave him a chance to swallow, ease his tight throat. "If I'm the man you say I am, you'd better call the police. I might be dangerous."

"I don't think you're so dangerous. And I'm not going to call the police. For awhile, anyway. I want you to hear how clever I was, first. Come on, stand up." She held out her hand to him impatiently. "We can't talk here."

"Where do you want to talk?"

"We'll walk down the beach."

He was still marking time when he got up from the chair, going through Mr. Burns's movements. He had no ideas, only a realization of pressing danger. An idea did not come to him until later, while they were walking. But it was instinctive with him to turn in the direction of the Hotel Napoleon and Bellini.

Francie was occupied for a moment with the strap of her bathing cap. It gave him a chance to make the first move, take his first steps in the right direction, and wait for her to follow when she had removed the cap and shaken out her hair.

They walked on the hard, wet sand at the edge of the sea. She swung the bathing cap by its strap.

"My, it's a lovely day," she said, breathing deeply. "Did you ever see any place in the world more beautiful than this? Look at the colors of the island off there, and the sky, and the water, and the pink and blue and green buildings on the hill. I wish I could paint."

"I thought you didn't like Cannes." Mr. Burns still functioned, although only automatically.

"That was when it was dull. I don't think it's dull any more, since I found out about you. I never knew a jewel thief before. It's stimulating."

"You were going to tell me how you found out about me."

He managed a chuckle. She said sharply, "Stop acting

like Mr. Burns."

"What shall I act like?"

"Yourself. John. That's your real name, isn't it?"

"I prefer Jack."

"I prefer John. You can call me Francie."

"All right, Francie."

They were a third of the way to the Hotel Napoleon. He thought, I'm out of my depth. I'll have to get her to Bellini, somehow. He'll know what to do with her.

She said conversationally, "I wouldn't have suspected you except that I always have to look out for Mother. People have tried to steal her jewelry before. When I read about the—you—in the papers, I was sure that Mother would catch your eye. She makes such a show wherever she goes that she couldn't help it. Naturally I was expecting you to arrive in the neighborhood."

"Naturally."

"At first I was looking for somebody tall and athletic and muscular, the young man on the flying trapeze, or one of those over there, for example." She pointed at a pair of beach tumblers doing flip-overs on the sand. "That was because of your newspaper publicity. But then I realized that nobody could really do all those tricks you were supposed to do, climbing up drainpipes and flying out of windows and the rest of it. Nobody who was really a human fly and an acrobat would leave so many signs around to *prove* he was a human fly and an acrobat. The answer had to be that you wanted everybody to be on watch for a kind of superman. So, of course, you wouldn't really be a superman at all. Just someone ordinary, like Mr. Burns. And there was Mr. Burns, right under my nose."

"Very logical. I wish you would tell me how I managed all those thefts, if I'm really not a superman. According to the papers—"

"I don't think you're really as stodgy as you try to look, but that's aside from the point. You aren't a superman, you're a gang."

"I am?"

"Certainly. One man couldn't do all you are supposed to be able to do. I'm surprised the police don't see that right away. You're just the front man. And the brains, of course."

"Thank you. Have you identified my helpers?"

"Only one, so far. The cute French girl. I don't think you were very clever to let yourself be seen in public with her."

"I suppose it was careless of me."

He made deliberate footprints in the wet sand, toes out, heels deeply impressed, one after the other. He did not want to walk too fast. They were halfway to the Hotel Napoleon.

Francie's footprints beside his own were small, neat, and high-arched. She said, "I suspected you first when you scraped up an acquaintance with Mother. I always suspect anyone who cultivates Mother. She's a dear, but she's kind of a rough diamond. The only reason anybody would deliberately cultivate her would be to borrow money or steal her jewelry. You didn't try to borrow money, so you were after her jewelry." Francie turned her head to ask him in a friendly way, "Am I impressing you with my cleverness?"

"Not yet."

"I'll come to it. You were pretty good, everything considered, and it's hard to put a finger on what I mean, but you're not quite convincing, John. You're like an American character in an English novel, if you ever read English novels. You don't talk quite the way an American businessman ought to talk, nor act like one. Particularly an insurance man. I was engaged to an insurance man once. For a week." She laughed. "All he ever talked about was insurance. And baseball. You never even mention your business, or baseball, or television, or Hopalong Cassidy, or politics, or wage freezes, or high prices, or anything that you ought to talk about. You're just not American enough to carry it off."

"What am I? Russian?"

"I don't mean you aren't an American. I said you weren't American *enough*. You need a refresher course. I don't think you have been in America for a long time. How long was it, John?"

"According to my passport—"

"Oh, passports!" She made a face. "I know all about passports. I'll bet you haven't seen the United States in five years. Ten years. How long was it?"

The beach had been narrowing while they walked. Now there were rocks ahead. They could go no farther without wading.

But they were not far from the Hotel Napoleon. He

could see a curtain blowing idly in Bellini's open window. It was the least popular end of the beach, and only a few bathers were near them. Still, traffic was heavy on the boulevard they had to cross to reach the hotel. She would have to be made to go voluntarily.

He said, "Six weeks."

She shook her head. "Try again."

He said tolerantly, "Francie, you're a nice girl but you have too much imagination. You're going to cause me unnecessary trouble if you go around telling people about the famous jewel thief you've discovered. I'm on a vacation. I want to relax, not explain my way out of a French jail. If I can prove to you that I left New York six weeks ago, will you forget this nonsense?"

"No."

"What more do you want?"

"More than you can give me." He knew from her triumphant tone that she was about to play her top card. "I cabled my ex-boyfriend in New York and had him check up on all the Burnses in the insurance business. They're all present and accounted for. You don't exist. So how could you have been in New York six weeks ago?"

"Your ex-boyfriend made a mistake." He took her arm. "I'll prove it, if you'll walk a hundred feet with me. I've got a friend at the Hotel Napoleon—"

"I don't doubt it. Let go of my wrist. You're leaving fingerprints."

There was a new note in her voice, not of pain. He realized that he had given something away by the unconscious force of his grip. He had to make a conscious effort to relax his fingers slightly. But he did not release her.

She said curiously, "Maybe there is something in the superman angle, after all. You're strong, aren't you?"

"Francie, please listen. Give me five minutes."

"You're still leaving fingerprints. Let go of me."

It was flat, imperative. He released her.

She smiled again immediately. She said, "I don't know exactly why you want to get me into the Hotel Napoleon, but I can make a pretty good guess. Please don't be reckless. If I were to scream for help and accuse you of trying to drag me into a hotel room, you'd have a hard time enjoying your vacation afterward. Wouldn't you?"

"Yes."

"I'm glad you realize it."

They turned back from the rocks.

Their footprints had already disappeared in the wet sand. It was so hot in the open sun that most of the sunbathers had gone under cover of the umbrellas or were in the water. He was sweating under the harness next to his skin, but he felt cold inside. He had no more ideas. He could only mark time, take a step, leave a footprint, take another step, stop when she did, go where she led. He was on a leash.

She said, "Are you going to rob Mother first, or Lady Kerry?"

"Lady Kerry, in the circumstances. Who is she?"

"Don't be backward. I am not going to give you away,

John. I told you I liked excitement, and you're it, for the time being. Lady Kerry is the high-nosed English character your cute girl friend went to work for this afternoon."

"Danielle?"

"If that's her name. I've been expecting you to do something with her."

"I don't suppose I could convince you that I never saw Danielle in my life until a few days ago, or that I didn't know she had gone to work for Lady Kerry until you told me."

"Certainly not. I'm only surprised that you hope to get away with such an obvious plant. The Kerry jewels are famous."

He laughed, and the laugh was not wholly an effort to keep Mr. Burns alive as long as possible. The Kerry jewels were as famous as she said, but every thief in Europe knew they were copies of the once valuable originals, which had long since gone to bolster the sagging Kerry fortunes. It was too bad he could not explain the joke.

Francie said, "If I were you, I'd leave Lady Kerry alone and rob Mother."

"You would?"

"Even the French police are going to be smart enough to arrest your girlfriend after Lady Kerry's jewelry disappears, and you wouldn't want that to happen. Is Danielle your mistress?"

"No."

"It wouldn't be gentlemanly to say yes, would it? I'm

sure you're a gentleman. It's one of the things I like about you. Gentleman thief has such a nice sound." She patted his arm. "Aside from that, you can make a good thing out of Mother's jewels. They're insured for seventy-two thousand five hundred dollars, not counting the diamond and emerald dog you helped her win at roulette. But I suppose you already know what they are worth."

"Yes. No. Whichever you prefer."

"Now you sound beaten down. I'm only trying to help you, John. I think it would be a fine thing for everybody concerned if you would steal her jewels. You'd make a nice profit, she'd have the fun of spending the insurance money all over again, and the French national economy would be benefited to the extent of seventy-two thousand five hundred dollars."

"How would you suggest that I go about it?"

She frowned. "It's a problem, of course. She's never had a personal maid, so it would be impossible to plant anyone on her, and she leaves the jewel case in the hotel safe all the time except when she's asleep in the same room with it. She's careful about bolting her door, too. Are you light on your feet?"

"When I don't stumble over young women with silly ideas."

"I could arrange to leave my door unlocked some night. You could get in that way. Or why couldn't I steal them myself and smuggle them to you?"

They walked back to his deck chair. Francie Stopped there. Her eyes were bright. She said, "It would be foolproof. All you would have to do is send one of your men to get into her room sometime when she's not there and leave marks at the window to show that The Cat had come down from the roof by rope ladder. You couldn't have the diamond and emerald dog, of course, because it isn't insured, but the rest of it is plenty. Another scoop for Le Chat, more publicity in the newspapers, and the police absolutely baffled. As the French say, *voilà!* What could be prettier?"

"Don't talk so loud. Pretending for the moment that I'm really an honest insurance man, I wouldn't want anybody to hear us planning to beat a London insurance company out of seventy-two thousand five hundred dollars." His confidence was returning slowly. Even if Mr. Burns were to survive only on a leash, it was still survival. He said, "Besides, they wouldn't pay the claim."

"They'd have to."

"Not if the diamond and emerald dog were left behind."

"It has nothing to do with them. It's not insured."

"That's why they'd fight the claim. They're not stupid. A professional thief wouldn't pass up the only piece of jewelry not covered by the policy, simply by accident."

"I hadn't thought of that." She bit thoughtfully at her fingernail. "I could hide it, and give it back to her afterward."

"You'd have a lot of explaining to do."

"I'll send it to her anonymously through the mail, then."

"Your mother would have a lot more explaining to

do, in that case. I'm sorry to be so discouraging just when you are launching your career as a thief, but the only way you could collect the insurance without answering awkward questions is to make a clean sweep."

"I'm not going to let you have the dog. I'll just have to think more about it, that's all."

She put on her bathing cap. While she was tucking her hair in and fastening the strap, she said, "I'd like you to join Mother and me for a drink this evening. We haven't seen you at Le Petit Bar lately, and I may have some new ideas by then. Eight o'clock."

"I'll be glad to, some other time. I don't think I can make it, tonight."

"You'd better, if you know what's good for you. Eight o'clock sharp, John."

She smiled sweetly, turned her back, took a few running steps, and made a clean dive into the shallows. She came up on her back five yards farther out, lifted her hand to wave, then turned over and swam away, slim brown arms and white cap bobbing in the blue water.

~§~

The key was not in the lock of Bellini's door when John got there. He went down to the promenade to wait on a bench across the boulevard from the hotel entrance.

It gave him time to think. The leash was still around his neck, but it was a long one, and it allowed him considerable freedom. When he saw Mr. Paige, the

London insurance company's agent, come out of the hotel and walk away, twisting at his fierce mustache, he went back up to Bellini's office and found the key again in the door.

Bellini said, "I was hoping you would call, Mr. Burns." He took off his glasses, mopping his wet face. "This heat is savage. I am losing weight through my pores." He chuckled, patting his belly. "I have a bit of news for you."

"Paige?"

"You saw him leave, of course. Yes. He has been talking to Lepic, the *commissaire divisionnaire*. He wants to put *récompense proportionelle* advertisements in the newspapers. You know the police do not like them because they increase the market value of stolen goods. He knows it, too, and was surprised when he asked Lepic for authority and Lepic told him to go ahead, without growling about it. He gained the impression that Lepic did not think newspaper advertisements would make a difference one way or the other, as far as recovery of the jewelry is concerned, which is generally true enough. But Lepic sounds much too amiable. He has something up his sleeve. Expect something unusual from him."

"Something unusual just happened."

He told Bellini about the bombshell Francie Stevens had exploded in his face.

Bellini, characteristically, began to wheeze with laughter. Between giggles, he said, "Forgive me, John. The curse of my life is a sense of humor," then giggled again.

When he had caught his breath he said cheerfully, "So all of our work, all the planning, the careful disguise, were not enough even to deceive an idle girl with an imagination. But I warned you against her, didn't I? We were only lucky that it was she and not the police who discovered you first. At least you are not in prison yet, and with luck I can still get you away. I will send you down to Marseilles tonight, after dark."

"I have an appointment to meet her at eight o'clock. I'm going to keep it."

Bellini blinked owlishly. John said, "She complicates things, but she isn't fatal to what we're doing. She wants to help me steal her mother's jewels."

"Not seriously?"

"Seriously. If she didn't have a reason for existence before, she has one now. She wants to be a thief."

Bellini giggled again. John said, "She's after excitement, a thrill. I'm giving her a thrill. As long as I can continue I'm convinced she won't give me away. If I try to run now, she can have me picked up before I get out of the country. There's nothing for me to do but stay and hope that we accomplish something before I begin to bore her."

"But the police, John. If she could see through your camouflage so easily—"

"I've considered that, too. I don't think I have to worry any more about the police than I did yesterday. They're logical. She isn't. The whole line of reasoning she followed to decide that I was Le Chat was false.

Actually she had only one real point to work from, the fact that I'm not up to date. I don't talk about the right things for a man who has been living in the United States. But no French police *agent* will realize that, and for the rest of it, she invented things, or made facts out of nonsense. She doesn't know that I'm wearing a camouflage, or that I've changed the color of my hair. She hasn't read anything that came out during my trial. She thinks I deliberately cultivated her mother's acquaintance. She thinks Le Chat is a fake, a misdirection, and that the thefts are done by a gang. She believes I planted Danielle on Lady Kerry."

"To steal the Kerry jewels?" Bellini wheezed again. "Poor Danielle. The whole world must know about the Kerry jewels."

"The *flics* do. That's my point, Bellini. They can't follow her line of reasoning. It's a series of mistakes, all the way."

"Have you tried to point out the errors?"

"I can't, without telling her the truth. Besides, she cabled New York and had me checked there."

"No Mr. Burns in the insurance business?"

"Several. All on hand."

"So you confessed and threw yourself on her mercy."

"No. I'm humoring her. Playing games. Cloak and dagger business."

Bellini shook his head, looking as nearly serious as it was possible for him to look.

"I don't like it. She sounds unpredictable. You can't rely on her."

"I can't do anything else. I have no choice."

"We could have her"—Bellini hesitated, choosing the right word—"quarantined, briefly. If you would take her for a walk along the beach after dark—"

"I thought of that, too. I tried to bring her here, but she's too alert. And you know what would happen if a rich American girl was kidnapped in Cannes. The *mobiles* would be patrolling the streets, checking identification papers at every corner."

"You are probably right. But I am afraid for you, John."

"I'm afraid for myself," John said flatly. "I've been afraid for myself ever since I started this thing. She hasn't changed that." He made a gesture of dismissal. "I'm in it, and I can't get out. I've just got to keep going. Have Le Borgne and Coco and the others on hand at seven o'clock sharp. I've got to see the girl at eight."

"What does she want with you at eight o'clock?"

"We're going to plan the theft of her mother's jewels, I suppose. Or maybe she'll have a hoop for me to jump through. I don't really know."

Bellini chuckled automatically, although he did not think the joke was funny.

~§~

John tried to sleep during the heat of the afternoon. He put the *Do Not Disturb* sign on his door, drew the window blinds, stripped, took a cool shower, made all the preparations to rest, and lay awake, sleepless.

He could not get over the feeling that Francie held him on a leash. It was almost a physical thing, as if there were a collar on his neck and he had only to turn his head or lift a hand to feel it. She hadn't tugged hard at the collar yet, but it was there. He had to go where she led him.

If he knew what was good for him, she had said. Mr. Burns would be on hand for cocktails at eight o'clock, if he knew what was good for him. Mr. Burns would provide excitement to order. Mr. Burns would steal her mother's jewels when she told him to, but would be careful not to take the diamond and emerald dog. It was on a leash, too, and it was worth five thousand dollars. Mr. Burns was only good for twenty years at La Maison Centrale.

He could not sleep. He got up, pulled the mattress from the bed to the floor, and used it as a tumbling mat for half an hour. He was streaming sweat before he finished, but he felt better for the exercise. After he had bathed, he reconstructed Mr. Burns with particular care; the harness, the padded shoes, a touch of dye at the hair roots, a razor for the balding temples, one of his new American neckties. On the leash or off, Mr. Burns had to survive.

~§~

The daylight was fading when he reached the house on the Rue Georges Clemenceau. It was seven o'clock exactly. He saw no one in the street, a good sign that

Bellini had sent him good men. He used his key, turned on several lights, found a radio, and tuned in a Paris musical program. Someone pulled the cord of the old-fashioned doorbell almost immediately.

The six men came in singly, a few minutes apart. Coco and Le Borgne were among the last.

He did not recognize any of the other men. Le Borgne was heavier and grayer than he had been in the *maquis,* and had a respectable glass eye instead of a patch over the empty eye socket. Coco had not changed at all. He was a small man with a wide, lipless mouth, tight and mistrusting. His eyes were suspicious. All the men were suspicious, except Le Borgne. They looked at the corners of the room, and at the windows, and at each other, and at John, saying nothing. They did not know why they were there, and they did not like being there.

He passed cigarettes. He held a match, first for Le Borgne, then for Coco, while the other men lit their own. Neither Le Borgne nor Coco gave any sign of recognition, nor thanked him for the light.

He said, "Not even *merci* for an old friend, Coco?"

Coco's cigarette jutted from the corner of his tight mouth. Without removing it, he said belligerently, "Who are you to call me Coco?"

John looked to Le Borgne. "How about you, One Eye?"

Le Borgne nodded.

"Bellini told me," he said. "I would not have come otherwise. Still, it is a good get-up. The face is much the same, but in a different frame it is a different picture. I wouldn't see you on the street."

"What are you talking about?" Coco said, still truculent.

"Le Chat, nut-head. Look at the face, not the belly."

John saw recognition come into Coco's eyes. Coco said, "No," doubtfully, and then "Yes!" He took John by both arms. "Le Chat! John the Neck-Breaker! But what a barrel you've put on, man. Give me your hand so I can make sure, and not too much with the fingers. I am no *boche* sentry, remember."

They shook hands. Someone else said, "Le Chat!" in a different tone, and he heard it repeated. It was a bad name in *le milieu*. Even Coco took his hand back quickly. His eyes grew hard again, after his first enthusiasm.

John said, "The Cat you knew, Coco. Not the one the police are hunting."

"There is only one Cat," Coco said. "I read the papers."

"There are two."

A throaty female voice on the radio sang several bars of a *chanson*. No one moved. Coco's suspicious expression did not change.

Le Borgne broke the silence. He said, "Talk some more, John."

Another man, young and dark, with an evil gypsy face, threw his cigarette on the floor.

"*Merde* for talk!" he said violently. "One Cat or two, it is too many for me. The *flics* had me in the tank for two weeks because the Cat came into my neighborhood. I say—"

Coco whirled on him.

"Who are you to say *merde* to a man who fought in the *maquis?*"

The gypsy was not expecting an attack from his own side. He flared back.

"I am a citizen of the Republic, as good as the next one. I fought in the *maquis* myself. It is my right."

Coco sneered. "A citizen of the Republic! Pah! Dirty gypsy. Dirty Arab. I spit in your face, citizen."

The gypsy's dark face paled. He stood frozen, motionless. Coco stared at him for a moment, inviting trouble, then turned his back, deliberately and contemptuously.

The gypsy's hand flashed inside his coat the moment Coco's eyes left him. John, expecting the movement, was quicker. He had the gypsy by both elbows, his arms pinned to his sides, before the hidden hand could come into sight again. He held the man that way, helpless, and tightened his grip on the gypsy's thin arms until the knife dropped free of the coat and fell to the floor.

By then Coco had the *casse-tête* in his hand, and was moving in with his arm cocked to strike at the gypsy's head with the limber, shot-loaded leather. John released the gypsy, pushing him out of the way and stepping between the two men before the blow could fall.

"You asked for it, Coco," he said, picking up the knife. "Put the skull-cracker away. Next time you want to pick a fight, do it on your own time."

Coco hesitated, then shook his head and put the black-jack in his pocket.

"The citizen had more under his shirt than I expected

of him," he said, without animosity. "I retract the spit, citizen. Although it was in the face and not between the shoulder blades."

The gypsy scowled, rubbing his elbows.

Le Borgne said, "You should learn to think first and spit afterward, Coco. Tell us why we are here, John."

"Sit down. It will take time."

They sat down. The scuffle had cleared the air.

He talked for half an hour. He used Bellini's name more often than was necessary, for the value it had with these men, while he explained the scheme, what he had done, and what he hoped to accomplish. He passed around his sketches of the two houses they were to watch, and pointed out probable points of entry into them. He showed on the sketches where shrubbery would give cover for them to watch the points of entry, and where they could make a safe rendezvous. He explained the household routines, the habits of the householders, where they slept and at what hours. He said, "Both women generally wear most of their jewels when they go out in the evening, so if the thief makes an attempt he will do it when they are at home and the jewels are in the house. I don't expect anything to happen at the Combe d'Or before the *gala* next weekend, but you'll have to be ready just the same. Be most alert during the two or three hours after the lights go off, when they are in their first sleep. The thief will pick a night when they have been out late and are tired. If he comes, don't try to take him as he goes in, unless he steps on you. You won't see him in time, and you can't be certain you have the man we want unless you take him with the jewelry. Get him on the way out. He'll come back the same way he went in."

The gypsy said skeptically, "You say he will do this and that and the other thing. How do you know? How do you know he will come back the same way he went in? How do you know we will not sit on our hands while he flies out another window, eh?"

Coco said, "You are listening to Le Chat, citizen of—"

"Be quiet, Coco. I know he will come out the same way he goes in because it's the only safe route for a thief working in the dark. He maps his way as he goes. Unless he is surprised and has to jump for it, he follows the map back. Three of you can cover the whole house to watch where he goes in, but afterward you must all be waiting for him together. He's strong and agile, too much for one man to be certain of handling alone. Take no chances with him. Quiet him down as quickly as possible, and get him to Bellini. He will take care of the rest of it. Do you all have *casse-têtes?*"

They all nodded except the gypsy, who smirked unpleasantly. John said, "No knives. He is no good to us dead."

"Remember that, citizen of the Republic," Coco said from a corner of his tight mouth. "No knives. Get yourself a skull-buster or I will see to you myself."

The gypsy stopped smirking.

Another man said, "All right. We know what you want from us. What do we get out of it?"

"You get the thief. The Sûreté will take the pressure

off when they have him. You can go on about your business again."

"It's not enough. The *flics* have not interfered with my business. If I am going to sit out on my tail all night every night under a bush, someone will have to pay for it."

Another man said, "That goes for me."

John had not considered the possibility that others would have a lesser personal interest than his own in the capture. While he hesitated, Le Borgne said, "He's right, John. You and I and Coco have our necks to save. It's different with the rest of them."

"What did Bellini promise you?"

The spokesman for the bargainers said, "Something if we catch him, nothing if we fail. It's fair enough. But we want to know what the something will be."

"He has stolen jewelry worth a hundred million francs, and none of it has been shopped off yet. Bellini won't hand him over to the Sûreté without squeezing him first."

"How can Bellini hold it back?" the spokesman asked, practically. "Naturally the thief will talk."

"Let him talk. A large London insurance company has insured most or all of it. Their man is offering *récompense proportionelle* for the recovery, no questions asked, and Bellini should be able to get twenty per cent out of him. Twenty per cent of a hundred million to divide around will pay for several nights of sitting under a bush."

He let them work out the arithmetic for themselves.

They seemed satisfied. No one asked for a more concrete guarantee. The practical man said, "Good enough. When do we start?"

"Tonight."

He divided them into two groups—the gypsy, the practical man, and Coco to watch the Brazilian couple, Le Borgne and the others for the Combe d'Or. Coco would keep the gypsy in check, and the practical man, whose name was Michel, would balance Coco's impulsiveness. Le Borgne's level head was enough for the other crew. John gave them the sketches, told them how best to approach the houses without being observed, not later than midnight, and warned them to stay under cover from then until dawn, and to leave carefully.

"It will be like the *maquis* again," he told them. "Patience, caution. He may not come for days, he may not come at all, but we have to be ready from now on. If he's had time to explore he'll be ready to rob, and if he isn't ready to rob he'll be looking over the ground. Keep under cover, and don't move around. You won't need blankets, the nights are too warm, but take something to sit on. Don't doze. Sleep during the day. Don't smoke. If you feel the need for a cigarette, think of twenty per cent of a hundred million francs instead."

"Don't worry about us," Coco said. "Next time you hear from us, we'll have this imitation Cat in a basket. Eh, there, citizen of the Republic?"

He dug the gypsy in the ribs. The gypsy said something that was obscene even for a gypsy.

John said, "I have to hear from you every day. One

Eye, you and Coco report to Bellini once each morning, and leave a message if anything unusual happens. But report every day, even if there is nothing to report, because if something slips, if the *flics* pick you up, if anything keeps you off the job, I have to know about it and find somebody else to put on. Our only chance of staying out of prison is to catch this thief before we're rounded up. Jean-Pierre says he has already been warned. It is only another kind of pressure, but they might take him as an example."

"I have been warned myself," Le Borgne said.

"So have I," Coco said. "I spit in their faces. Come along, citizen of the Republic. We have work ahead of us."

The gypsy said, "Wait a minute. What about you?" He was talking to John. "What will you be doing while we squat all night under a bush without cigarettes, eh?"

"I have a trap of my own to watch. I think he will come to me first, if he comes."

"Do we share alike, regardless?"

"You share in everything. Bellini gave you his word. I give you mine."

"And I'll give you a piece of my stretch at La Maison Centrale any time you like," Coco said impatiently to the gypsy. "Or the whole thing. What are nine years in the jug to a young fellow like you? Move along, citizen."

After they had gone, John closed the house and walked back down the Rue Georges Clemenceau to the yacht harbor and La Croisette. The illuminated face of the clock in the old stone tower on the hill overlooking the harbor said five minutes to eight.

~§~

He entered Le Petit Bar at eight sharp, obedient to the leash.

Francie was there with her mother and a man who sat with his back to the door. When the man turned his head to speak to Mrs. Stevens, John saw the tip of the fierce guardsman's mustache. Mr. Paige's path was crossing his with increasing regularity.

Francie waved to attract his attention. For the second time that day, he was introduced to the London insurance company's agent. He said, "We've already met," shaking hands, and Mr. Paige said, "Oh, yes. Quite. Quite," as if he were not certain about it. He was clearly preoccupied with Mrs. Stevens's display of jewelry.

She glittered even more brightly than usual. The diamond and emerald dog was pinned to the shoulder of her dress, she had diamonds in her ears, diamonds on her fingers, and diamonds on her wrists. Her lipstick was, as always, lopsided, and she drank champagne from a glass with red smears on the rim. She was dressed for a good time, and seemed to be having one.

She said, "Hi, Lucky. Come over here and sit by me."

She patted the chair next to her invitingly.

Francie said, "We can't stay. Mr. Burns is taking me to Monte Carlo."

"Good." Her mother tossed off the last of her champagne. "We'll all go to Monte Carlo."

"You can't come."

"Why can't I?"

"You've had your share. If he's as lucky as you say he is, I want him for myself."

"Since when have you taken up gambling?" Mrs. Stevens winked at John. "You've done something to my daughter, Lucky. I don't know what it is, but she's almost human lately. Look at her, gambling and everything. She's even wearing my beads. I don't know what's come over her."

They all looked at the beads, which were hard to ignore. John had marked them from the doorway, a magnificent necklace of diamonds and sapphires. He had already appraised the necklace on Mrs. Stevens's throat at the casino. It looked different on Francie.

She wore a black, strapless evening gown, very plain in the way that only Dior or Schiaparelli could make plain black dresses. She had done her hair so as to expose her ears, with sapphire earrings at the ear lobes. The blue of the stones at her throat and ears, matching and emphasizing the blue of her eyes, produced an effect that could not have been accidental. It was as if she had chosen deliberately to display the necklace and earrings, not as ornament but as they might be displayed on a model, for themselves.

Mrs. Stevens said cheerfully, "Well, if I can't go with you, I'll have to go somewhere else. I have a hunch I'm going to ruin the house tonight, Lucky. Saturday night has always been my best night. Do you gamble, Mr. Paige?"

Mr. Paige did not take the hint. He said absently that he did not enjoy gambling. Mrs. Stevens's diamonds still had him hypnotized.

"Have to go by myself, then." Mrs. Stevens jingled her bracelets. "Take good care of my child, Lucky. And the beads, of course." She winked slyly, indicating Mr. Paige with a movement of her head. "They cost a lot of money."

Mr. Paige looked unhappily at Francie's necklace. John said, "I'll bring them both back early."

"I don't care when you bring them back, just so long as you bring them. I'm going to stay up until breakfast myself. I've got a new roulette system to work out." She snapped her fingers at a waiter. "Sure you won't have one little drink for the road, Lucky?"

Francie said firmly, "Good night, Mother. Good night, Mr. Paige," and took John's arm.

He stopped her when they were in the foyer of the hotel. "What's going on?" he said.

"What do you mean?" She was wide-eyed, innocent.

"You invited me for a drink. Now you want to go to Monte Carlo. Why?"

"I want to gamble."

"You never gambled before. And you don't have to go as far as Monte Carlo to start."

"I *want* to go to Monte Carlo."

"I don't."

The jewels at her throat winked blue and white with her breathing. She said softly, "But you'll go, won't you? You wouldn't like me to go wandering around by myself wearing Mother's nice beads, with all these thieves you read about in the newspapers waiting to steal them?"

"What are you up to?"

"I told you. I want to go to Monte Carlo. You're taking me."

"No."

"Yes you are." She had stopped smiling. "Otherwise we'll go back to Mother and Mr. Paige and talk about Le Chat. You know who Mr. Paige is, don't you?"

"No."

"You ought to. He's the agent of the London insurance company. He'd like very much to meet Le Chat. Shall I introduce you to him again?"

"Francie, you're crazy! Even for a joke—"

"I'm not joking, Mr. Burns. Are you taking me to Monte Carlo, or back to Le Petit Bar?"

A hotel *chasseur* came through the foyer, holding over his head a piece of blackboard on both sides of which a name had been chalked. Somebody was wanted on the telephone. John wished that it had been his own name on the blackboard, anything to take him away from her. He felt the leash tight on his neck.

When the *chasseur* had passed, he said, "I'll have to change my clothes."

"I'll wait for you here. Don't be too long."

Francie sat down in the nearest chair, spread her skirt, crossed her slim ankles, folded her hands, and smiled. Her eyes were very blue, the color of the sapphires.

~§~

He went to change his clothes. He did not know what Francie was planning, whether Monte Carlo was only a whim or something else, why she had put on her mother's jewels, or what scheme she had in her head, if it was a scheme. He could do nothing about Francie except go where she led him. And only the accident of her mother's decision to stay out all night to try a new roulette system saved him from having to leave his best bait for the thief waiting and unguarded.

He had been watching the bait for four nights. Mrs. Stevens ordinarily came in at one or two in the morning, Francie about the same time. According to his timing, they were both sound asleep by three. It left an hour or an hour and a half before the light of early summer dawn for a thief to get at the red leather jewel case that remained in Mrs. Stevens's room only while she slept. Even while he was still spending night hours in Le Cannet and Californie to complete his sketches of the two houses that were to be his other traps, he managed to get back to his room for the vital hour and a half before dawn. He passed that time waiting patiently in the dark by the small window of his bathroom. If the thief came at all, John knew how he would come.

There was only one way. From the first, he had discarded the possibility of an approach through the front windows of the Stevens suite, which were not inaccessible to a good climber scaling the huge neon sign on

the front of the building but were too well illuminated
by the same sign to offer a safe means of entry. All of
the hotel doors fastened with a spring lock and a strong
inner bolt, and the thief was too cautious to attempt a
break-in from a brightly lit hotel corridor in any event.
He needed darkness in which to operate, like Le Chat.
When John discovered the tiny lightwell that offered a
safe, hidden passage up through the interior of the
building, he made complaints to the hotel *directeur*
about street noises and leaky plumbing fixtures until he
at last got a room that would serve his purpose.

The room was on the third floor back, while the
Stevens suite was fourth floor front, but the windows of
both bathrooms opened into the lightwell. It was a
narrow, rectangular shaft rising from the basement
level to a skylight in the roof, and it served better as a
receptacle for used razor blades and bits of wastepaper
than as a source of light. Two small windows, paned
with frosted glass for the sake of the guests' privacy,
faced each other in opposite walls at each floor. The
other two walls were blank. There was a hatch at the
basement level by which the janitor could enter to clean
out debris occasionally, although the hatch had not
been opened in some time. During John's first night in
his new room, he waited until very late, then stripped to
a pair of shorts and went up the lightwell as a mountain
climber goes up a cleft in the rock, back and feet braced
against the blank wall. He was careful not to disturb the
dust on the window ledges, and he did not have to repeat
the laborious climb. One exploration was enough to

satisfy him that the thief could enter the shaft either from the skylight above or the hatch below.

He would have preferred the skylight himself, since there were means to fasten a rope, and it was possible for an agile man to move faster up and down a rope than by inching carefully along wedged between walls. But he was ready for an approach from either direction, and he was sure of his own ability to bottle the thief once he heard sounds of movement in the shaft. All of his preparations had gone toward that moment.

Now, for one night at least, the watch was unnecessary. He could forget Mrs. Stevens temporarily. The invisible leash kept him from forgetting Francie.

She was waiting where he had left her. She said, "Mother just left for Palm Beach. She tried to invite herself along with us again, but I discouraged her."

"Why didn't you want her to come with us?"

Francie hooked her arm through his, smiling up at him. "I hate chaperones, Mr. Burns. And I'm sure I'm safe in your hands."

The magnificent necklace sparkled at her throat like an invitation.

He hired a car at the taxi stand across the boulevard from the hotel, a huge, old, heavy Hispano-Suiza, open in back behind a glass wind screen that separated passengers from driver. The hiring process, a sign-language discussion of hours and distance and price, was only a routine to be gone through, part of Mr. Burns's camouflage. The car belonged to Bellini, and the driver was Bellini's man, the same one who had taken John to

Marseilles.

He drove them to Monte Carlo by way of the Middle Corniche. The road, high up on a cliff after they had left Nice behind, followed the curves of the coast, in and out and around above the sparkling lights of Beaulieu-sur-Mer and Villefranche and Cap d'Ail below. The stars were bright, the night air pleasantly warm, the view magnificent. Francie thought it was all lovely beyond words.

He said, "You've changed your mind about a lot of things, haven't you? Two days ago you wouldn't have seen the stars."

"I told you why. Things aren't the same when your escort for the evening is a famous jewel thief."

"Tell me why you wore the necklace tonight. Do you expect me to steal it?"

"Not right away. I thought you might like to examine it first. It's worth eleven thousand dollars. Shall I take it off?"

Her hands went to the clasp at the back of her neck.

He said, "I can't see it in this light. I'll take your word for it. I meant why did you wear it tonight, when you never wear even a ring, ordinarily?"

"I don't like jewelry, ordinarily."

"Why?"

She shrugged. "Just one of those things. Some people don't like parsnips."

"That's not a reason."

She did not speak again for some time. The car hummed along quietly, roared for a minute as they passed through a tunnel bored into the rocky cliff, then hummed again in the open. Starlight dappled the sea below the cliff.

"Mother owns seventeen oil wells," Francie said abruptly. "I'll inherit them."

"Are we still talking about the reason you don't like jewelry?"

"Yes." She spoke without looking at him. "I told you once that I had to travel with her because she's so trusting. Every thief and confidence man who sees her makes some kind of an effort. She's an invitation to them. They'd steal her blind, if it weren't for me. I've got so I don't trust anyone, not even an inoffensive, friendly man like Mr. Burns of New York. It's an unpleasant state of mind, when the slightest friendly gesture from a stranger only makes you suspicious."

"So with that necklace around your throat, you're eleven thousand dollars worth of diamonds and sapphires to any man who smiles at you, and not just a pretty girl at all. Is that it?"

She nodded. "Eleven thousand dollars worth of diamonds and sapphires and seventeen oil wells."

"It must make it difficult for you to listen to any man who might really be more interested in the color of your eyes."

"It does. Especially if he compares them with sapphires." She laughed humorlessly. "It happened two weeks ago. I left him and rode home alone on the bus. I'm sure the poor man had only been trying to pay me a compliment, and wasn't really interested in the oil wells at all. I felt horrible about it afterward. And of course it's nothing you can explain."

"Why did you put on the necklace tonight?"

"Because I don't have to worry about ulterior motives in your case. You're an honest thief. We both know what you're after. I can enjoy your company without nasty, suspicious thoughts in my mind. I don't like feeling nasty and suspicious."

"I see."

She was silent again. In time, she said more brightly, "You'll be able to go ahead with the theft in a few days. I told Mother she ought to have the diamond dog insured as soon as possible, to be safe, and since Mr. Paige was there at the hotel, we called him over for a drink. He's having a something-or-other put on the policy. As soon as it's confirmed by London, I'll let you know."

"You're very thoughtful."

"I'm not very thoughtful about Mr. Paige. He's being awfully British and tactful with Mother, trying to get up the nerve to tell her she oughtn't to go around sparkling like a Christmas tree. She knows it, and she teases him by slathering on more diamonds. He's going to feel terrible when you rob her practically under his nose. Have you decided how you're going to manage it?"

"I haven't worked out the details."

"Are you going to need any help from me?"

"I don't think so. If you don't mind Francie, could we pretend for tonight that I'm not really a burglar at all? Just Mr. Burns, on a vacation? I'd like to forget about business for a while, if I could."

"All right. No business."

They did not talk again. The car came at last off the Corniche, down the wide, winding road from the cliffs to the neat houses and pleasant gardened streets of the little principality of Monaco, to draw up at last before the ornate summer casino on its hill overlooking the bay of Monte Carlo.

He had not been in Monte Carlo since 1939. Twelve years and a war had passed it by without changing anything. The uniformed attendant who came to open the door of the car made the same bow and offered the same words of welcome as before. The quiet, sharp-eyed men in the foyer stood in the same positions opposite the door, watching the people who entered the gambling salons. Inside, everything was as he remembered it—the flowered wallpaper, the faded gilt, the ornate crystal chandeliers, all the atmosphere of decayed Victorian splendor, were unchanged. The expressionless croupiers looked the same, and he thought he even recognized the dead, burned-out faces of some of the ancient system players at the roulette wheels, hunched over their charts marking down endless chains of figures, *rouge* and *noir, pair* and *impair, manque* and *passe,* until the proper moment came for the inevitable hundred-franc bet, the satisfied nod when it won and the blank stare when it lost, but always another mark on the system chart. Nothing that he remembered had changed by as much as a single prism on the chandeliers. The American dice tables were new, but they were set unobtrusively back in an alcove, out of the way.

Even American dice tables could not affect Monte Carlo. It was timeless.

Francie said, "What are you staring at?"

"The casino at Monte Carlo." He added the explanation, "In my character of Jack Burns, of course. He's never seen it before. He's read about it—the gambling place of kings, fortunes won and lost on the turn of the wheel, broken hearts, lost hopes, a pistol on the terrace to end it all. Now he's here in the flesh. He's impressed."

"He doesn't want to overdo it, though," Francie said critically. "I'm not as impressed as all that. It looks like any other casino, only more moth-eaten. What do we do first?"

"Buy counters, I suppose. If you really want to gamble."

"I want to gamble."

They bought counters at the nearest wheel. Francie put fifty thousand francs on the red, and drew a quick, impersonal glance from the lookout on his high chair at the end of the table. Black won. While Francie was reaching to place another bet, John looked around the salon. His only immediate worry was that Paul might be there, but he did not see Paul. He had only to mark time, obey the leash. It was ten o'clock.

~§~

They left at four in the morning. Francie had won six hundred thousand francs at roulette, lost nearly as much at baccarat, experimented without much result either

way at the dice tables, and was still genuinely puzzled
how anyone could get a thrill out of gambling.

"I just don't understand it," she said. They were
driving back along the Corniche. Dawn was beginning
to pale the dark sky in the east, and the morning breeze
was cool. "Every time I try it, I think it might be different,
but it's always the same. You win, you lose, and it makes
no difference one way or the other."

"Some people get excitement out of winning or
losing."

"I know. Mother does. That's what I don't understand. The money doesn't mean anything to her. I could
understand someone who needs a hundred thousand
francs badly being excited if he won it, and could put it
in his pocket and run away with it. But people like
Mother don't care. If they really needed a hundred
thousand francs they wouldn't be gambling. It's only the
people who don't care about the money who can afford
to gamble that way. That couple I introduced you to
tonight, the Americans, were both betting two and three
and four hundred thousand francs at a time, all over the
table. It didn't mean a thing to them whether they won
or lost." Minutes later she added, "Did you notice her emeralds, or are we still not discussing business?"

She was talking about Mr. and Mrs. Sanford, of the
Château Combe d'Or. Le Borgne and his men would
waste the night at their watch. The Sanfords were
wound up for an evening. They were both mildly drunk,
very gay, and happy to see Francie. Mrs. Sanford had
embraced her so heartily that the emeralds on her neck

bruised them both. Francie's own necklace had looked pale beside the emeralds.

He said, "Even an honest man would notice stones like those. Who are they?"

"Their name is Sanford. I don't really know anything about them except that they're very rich, they have a lovely home above Cannes, a showplace, and she gives big parties. Mother and I went to one last year, an enormous thing, all the famous people in France were there. You could have stolen a million dollars' worth of jewels from the guests alone. If she gives another party this year, would you like to go? I can get you invited."

"You're not very loyal to your friends."

"Because I suggest that you rob them? That's silly. Jewels don't mean any more to them than the money they gamble with. They're all part of the show. What's the difference—the real difference, in terms of good or bad—if they lose ten or twenty million francs at roulette or to a thief?"

"Like me?"

"Like you."

"Some people could make a moral distinction."

"Moral distinctions aren't genuine. You say something is bad, I say it isn't. Where are we?"

They discussed moral distinctions all during the drive back to Cannes. Francie, who had puzzled Bellini because he did not understand her reason for existence, used the exact phrase herself when she argued that a thief's only function was to steal, as the Monte Carlo roulette wheels' only reason for existence was to win money for the Prince of Monaco, so that in the event John were to lose money at roulette and regain it by robbing the prince, no one could fairly say "good" or "bad" of either one, although in practice the Monegasque police would jail John and he could not jail the prince. She made a good case for her point of view, and although it was a peculiar conversation, he found it entertaining to listen to her serious analysis of the criminal's place in society. He had never concerned himself with the moral aspects of thievery before.

He realized, with great surprise, that he had forgotten the leash he wore and the danger Francie represented to him. He was genuinely enjoying her company.

It was bright morning when the car drew up in front of the Hotel Midi. The air was already warm, promising another hot day, and the sky was clear and cloudless. The Esterel hills in the west, beyond the pink bulk of the municipal casino and the slim, pointing masts of the boats in the yacht harbor stood out sharply against the sky. It was the beginning of a beautiful day, and it had been, for him, a much more enjoyable night than he had had reason to expect. He tried to tell Francie something of the way he felt when he left her at the door of her room.

She said, "I had a good time myself. I'm not such awfully bad company, am I?"

"Very good company, Francie."

"We'll do something again, soon." She smiled wickedly. "If your business doesn't interfere, of course."

"I'll try to arrange things so it won't. Take good care of the necklace."

"I will." She touched it lightly, almost affectionately, with her fingertips. "This is the first time I've ever been able to wear it without hating it. I'm glad you're a thief, John."

"I'm glad you enjoyed yourself."

"Good night."

He went to his own room, feeling tired and relaxed and contented at the same time. He could not remember ever having enjoyed a conversation so much, not even with Paul at the Villa des Bijoux.

It must be because she's an American, he thought, taking off his clothes. I'd forgotten what Americans are like. I've been too long away. Maybe after this is over—if I get out of it—

The thought faded. He was too tired to think. He yawned again, and lay down on top of the bed, still with the odd feeling of contentment in his mind.

He was nearly asleep when he heard the thin, frightened screaming begin on the floor above. It was Mrs. Stevens's voice, recognizable in spite of the high, hysterical note. Over and over and over again, endlessly, she screamed, "My jewels! My jewels! My jewels!"

4

HE DRESSED QUICKLY, putting on the clothes he had just taken off. He was tying the laces of his shoes when Mrs. Stevens stopped screaming, abruptly, as if she had been gagged.

Now he could hear other sounds on the floor above, voices, running feet, calls for the floor porter. He heard the elevator go up, then down, then quickly up again. A door banged. Outside in the street, the doorman began to blow his whistle, long, shrill blasts for the police.

He thought, I've blundered.

He did not stop to wonder how he had blundered, what had gone wrong. The police would be on hand soon. Questions would be asked. Mr. Burns had to be ready to put in an appearance. He took the immediate steps for his safety automatically, as a man swims when he finds himself in deep water.

He checked Mr. Burns quickly in the mirror—hair, eyebrows, shoes, body profile. A light bristle had grown on his temples since he shaved them last, but it was not noticeable to the eye, and he had no time to use a razor.

He thought again, I've blundered. I've got to do it right, now. Another blunder will finish me.

He left his room, checking Mr. Burns's actions in his mind as he had checked Mr. Burns's appearance. It would be unnatural for him not to respond at once to screams from the Stevens suite, since he had left Francie at her door only a few minutes earlier. He would not wait for the elevator. He would run up the stairs, not too quickly for a man of his age, not too excited. Mr. Burns was level-headed.

He went up the stairs, not too quickly.

A number of hotel guests had already gathered in the hallway, most of them half dressed. They crowded the door of Mrs. Stevens's room, buzzing questions at each other and at the hotel *directeur,* who was trying to push the door closed against the pressure from outside. Although he managed to hold the doorway against intrusion, he could not force the door shut. He kept repeating ineffectually, "Please! Please! Ladies and gentlemen, *messieurs et dames, s'il vous plaît!"*

John said, "What is it?" to a man in a brightly colored bathrobe.

The man said, "Damned if I know. The cat burglar has been around again, I guess. Somebody was yelling about her jewels."

Other voices began to repeat excitedly, "Le Chat! Le Chat!" No one knew anything more.

The elevator came up again. Two uniformed *agents de police* left the cage and pushed their way through the crowd. The *directeur* stepped aside to let them by, and John saw Mrs. Stevens lying on a crumpled bed, her hands pressing her eyes. Francie was bending over her.

The crowd closed in again behind the policemen, vainly. The *directeur* had managed to close the door at last.

Mr. Paige arrived a moment later, twisting at his mustache points more vigorously than usual. With nothing but a closed door to look at, the tight knot of people near the doorway had broken up into smaller groups, still questioning each other for details no one could supply. Mr. Paige went to the door and knocked.

Francie opened it. Mr. Paige went in. Francie, seeing John there, hesitated for a moment, then beckoned to him with a quick, demanding gesture. He followed the insurance agent into the room.

One of the policemen had his notebook out and was attempting to question Mrs. Stevens, who still lay on the bed with her hands over her eyes. She made small, tragic, moaning noises. Her face, as much as John could see of it, was splotchy with grief. The robe she wore over her nightgown was disarranged, and Francie went to the bed to rearrange it. Mrs. Stevens paid no attention.

The *agent* with the notebook said patiently, "If you please, madame—"

"My jewels," Mrs. Stevens whispered. "My jewels."

The hotel *directeur* cleared his throat. "She does not speak French, monsieur. I will have to translate. If you would return later, when she is more coherent, it would be easier."

"One makes a report of the crime at the moment," the *agent* said. "Perhaps mademoiselle could tell us what has happened."

He held his pencil poised, looking expectantly at Francie.

The second *agent* had been looking at her for some time. He had a Frenchman's unconcealed admiration for a pretty girl, and he liked Francie's appearance in the strapless black gown. It could have been his frank stare that had heightened her color. Something had.

She said to the *directeur,* "Tell him that Mr. Burns—this gentleman—and I went to Monte Carlo for the evening. We returned fifteen or twenty minutes ago. He left me at my door, the next room, through there. I had been wearing one of Mother's necklaces, a valuable piece of jewelry, and I wanted to put it back in the jewel case. She woke when I came in, and we talked for a few minutes. I asked her for the key to her jewel case. She said it was in her purse. I took it out, and when I went to open the case"—she pointed to it, standing open on a commode—"I saw that the strap of the lock had been cut through. I told Mother that she had been robbed. She jumped out of bed and began to scream when she saw that the jewel case was empty. I thought she was going to be hysterical, so I slapped her to keep her quiet and called the hotel desk. Then I called Mr. Paige, who represents the insurance company, since I thought he would want to hear about the theft immediately. That's all I know."

The *directeur* translated. The *agent* wrote in his notebook. Mrs. Stevens whispered, "My jewels."

"Very good," the *agent* said. "Names?"

The *directeur* supplied names and the room number. The *agent* said, "Value of the stolen jewels?"

The *directeur* asked Francie. She said, "Sixty-one thou-

sand dollars, not counting the necklace I was wearing or"
—her pause was hardly noticeable—"or a pair of sapphire
earrings."

The *directeur* made a mental calculation, and told
the *agent,* "Twenty million francs, more or less."

The second *agent* whistled soundlessly. The *agent*
with the notebook made a final note, put a period after
it with a stab of his pencil, and closed the book.

"Voilà," he said amiably. "Another nice haul for Le
Chat. Commissaire Divisionnaire Lepic will be notified
immediately. You may expect him within the hour.
Touch nothing in the meantime. *Bonjour, messieurs et
dames."*

The two *agents* saluted together and left the room.
The *directeur* excused himself to follow them.

Mrs. Stevens, her hands still over her eyes, lay quietly on the bed, no longer moaning. Mr. Paige pulled his
mustache, examined the jewel case without touching it,
then went to look out the window. When his back was
turned, Francie motioned to John in the same abrupt
way she had called him in from the hall.

They went through the connecting bathroom into her
room. She shut the door and put her back to it.

"Very neatly done, Mr. Burns," she said coolly. "You
really didn't need my help after all, did you?"

"I had nothing to do with it, Francie."

"Of course not. Your alibi is unbreakable. I'll support
it myself—after you return the diamond dog."

"I haven't got it."

"I'll give you until this evening to find it. That should

be long enough for you to get in touch with your confederates."

"Francie—"

She interrupted him. "You're in no position to bargain."

"I'm not bargaining. I'm trying to convince you that I had nothing to do with the theft."

She said brightly, "And how could you, since you were engaged in a stimulating discussion of the theoretical aspects of robbery with the daughter of the victim, miles from the scene of the crime?" Her tone changed. "Don't make me any more resentful than I am, Mr. Burns."

"If you'll stop to think for a minute, you'll realize I couldn't have planned it. We both heard your mother say she was going to be out all night. I don't know why she changed her mind."

"She lost all her money. The system didn't work."

"All right. She lost her money and came home before she intended, so the jewels were available to a thief. I didn't know that. I couldn't possibly have arranged it."

"I don't know what you arranged or who arranged what or who stole the jewels. I know you were behind it. I told you that you could have everything if you would wait until Mother had insured the dog. You couldn't wait, or you didn't want to wait, or your gang went ahead on their own when they saw a chance. I don't know. I don't care. I want the dog."

He said, " Not so loud." Someone was moving around in the bathroom behind the door to which she held her back.

"I can talk louder if it's necessary. Make up your mind."

There were other sounds from behind the door. Mr. Paige's voice said, "Miss Stevens! I say, Miss Stevens!" He rapped. "May I see you for a minute? I've found something."

"Better answer him," John said.

Francie shook her head. Her color was still high.

"The dog, first. Yes or no."

"What if I say no?"

Her eyes flashed. "Don't be a fool! I'm giving you a chance. If you don't want to take it—"

Mr. Paige rapped again. "I say, Miss Stevens. Are you there?"

"Just a minute." She put her hand on the doorknob. "Well?"

"You'll get the dog."

She opened the door.

Mr. Paige was too pleased with his discovery to be curious about them. He had the small window over the tub wide open, and dust from the window ledge was on his hands. He said excitedly, "The blighter came down the light well. There's a hole in the skylight. I'm going to have a look around up on top. When Lepic gets here, tell him—"

He was gone before they heard the rest of it.

Mrs. Stevens's weak, unhappy voice called from the next room. "Francie, honey. Bring me some aspirin. My head is splitting. Have all those people gone?"

"In a minute, Mother." Francie pushed John back through the door into her room. "Go out this way. I'll be down on the beach from after lunch until five or six. It will be safer for you to bring it to me there."

"What are you going to tell Lepic?"

"Don't worry about him. He'll have no reason to question you if I don't give him one. I won't give him one before six o'clock."

"I might not be able to get it for you that soon."

She said angrily, "Don't press me too far. It wasn't clever of you to play your game with me last night. It will be less clever of you to be late this afternoon."

She let him out into the hall. He heard the lock of the door click behind him.

In his room again, he changed to shorts and a shirt with half-sleeves, then shaved first his temples, while the razor was sharpest, next his cheeks and chin. He thought he might not have to worry about the temples again.

There was very little he could do about Francie. She was angry, not because of the theft but because she thought the evening she had found so enjoyable was only his way of keeping her occupied while his imaginary confederates robbed her mother. As long as her anger lasted, it was hopeless to try to point out that Monte Carlo had been her own idea, not his. It was as hopeless as his chance of producing a five-thousand-dollar diamond and emerald dog before six o'clock.

But his hand was steady and sure with the razor. He had nearly eleven hours in which to think of an alternative.

He heard Mr. Paige calling down the lightwell from the skylight in the roof. Another voice answered from below. He heard "Le Chat" and *"corde"* and *"agilité."*

He heard "Le Chat" again when he passed through the hotel lobby, where a reporter was questioning the harassed *directeur.* Outside, the doorman was discussing the theft with two men, one of whom had a camera which he was aiming up at the front of the building and the big HOTEL MIDI sign. The other man was Paul.

John did not break his stride. Paul was watching the cameraman. John went down the steps, averted his face, and was safely by and nearly to the promenade when the doorman called his name.

"Mr. Burns!"

He kept walking. The doorman called again, and he heard the man coming after him. He stopped.

The doorman was heavy, red-faced, a big man who held his job because he spoke the necessary languages and was impressive to look at in a blue and gold uniform. He was not a sprinter. He was breathing hard before he caught up with John.

"Excuse me, sir. There's a gentleman here—he's been asking for you—bad business about the theft, wasn't it, sir?"

John looked back. Paul was already coming toward them. The doorman touched his cap, took the tip that Paul put in his white glove, and went back to his post and the cameraman.

Paul said politely, "Mr. Jack Burns?" He gave no sign

of recognition.

"Yes."

"My name is Paul du Pré. A friend asked me to call on you."

He was a well-mannered stranger introducing himself. John said, "How do you do, Mr. du Pré?" and was conscious of his own calm. One more danger on top of the others hardly seemed to matter.

"Which way are you walking?"

"Down the promenade."

"I'll walk with you, if I may."

"Certainly."

They fell into step.

The promenade was almost deserted. It was still too early in the morning for strollers. A few cars went by on the boulevard, and a workman on a bicycle pedaled along carrying half a dozen loaves of bread balanced across his handlebars like sticks of wood. One of the loaves fell to the ground when he had to swerve suddenly to avoid a dusty Citroën that turned out of a side street without sounding its horn. The bicyclist stopped to recover the bread, mechanically cursing the Citroën.

John, who saw the buggy-whip aerial mounted on the rear fender of the car, did not look to see where it was going. Paul did. It turned in under the portico of the Hotel Midi. Several men got out and went quickly into the hotel.

Paul said, "That was the Sûreté."

"I know it."

"They're looking for you, I suppose."

"Yes."

"The doorman told me about the theft."

"He's enjoying the excitement."

There were benches at intervals along the promenade, just at the edge of the walk above the beach. Paul said, "Let's sit down and talk for a minute."

They sat down. Paul said, "Is that a false stomach you're wearing?"

"False stomach, padded shoes, hair dye, false eyebrows, forged passport. What do you want with me, Paul?"

"Not a great deal. Who was the girl with you at Les Ambassadeurs?"

The question was so unexpected, so completely apart from everything in his mind, that it had no meaning at first He had to think back: Les Ambassadeurs, Paul's white dinner jacket, a girl.

He said, "Her name is Danielle."

"Who is she? Where did she come from? What does she do?"

"Why?"

"I want to meet her."

He felt a slow boil of anger rising in him. He said, "Did you hunt me out behind my false stomach and dyed hair so I could introduce you to a girl?"

"No. No." Paul made a quick, apologetic gesture. "I'm sorry. I shouldn't have asked it that way. But I've been thinking about her so much, seeing her face—I can't get her out of my mind. Didn't you notice how much she looked like Lisa?"

His anger went away. Even in his own trouble, he knew how deep Paul's hurt was. He said, "A little. I hadn't realized it until now."

"They could be twins. Not as Lisa was when you knew her, when she was dying, but when we were married. I must meet her, John."

There was an edge of strain in his voice. John said, "You know there can't be two Lisas in the world, Paul."

"I know. I only want to get her out of my mind. It was a shock to me, that night at Les Ambassadeurs. In the dim light I thought for a moment she *was* Lisa, and I've only been able to think of her as Lisa ever since. I thought that if I could meet her, talk to her, see her as she really is, I might get over it." He went on miserably. "I have to do something. I keep tormenting myself, thinking about her. Does she—is she anything to you?"

"Nothing at all. I don't even know her last name. She works for a swimming instructor on the beach most of the time. La Plage Nautique. It's the second sign from here. Lady Kerry, at the hotel, has hired her for a few days as a personal maid. It shouldn't be hard for you to arrange a meeting if you really want to."

"I do. I must."

A man and a girl in bathing suits went by on their way to the beach, laughing at some joke. When they had passed, John said, "Is that all you want with me?"

Paul sat up, straightening his shoulders. He made an effort to smile.

"I'm not really as thoughtless as you think I am, John. I didn't come here just to bring you my own troubles. What can I do to help you?"

"Nothing, except tell me how you recognized me."

"I saw your profile at Les Ambassadeurs, before I saw the rest of you. When you stood up I thought I was wrong. I didn't see how you could make yourself look so different, so clumsy, but I was interested in the girl as well, and I asked questions until I learned your name and where you were staying. I wasn't certain until I spoke to you back there, and heard your voice. It's a good disguise. No one could picture you climbing over roofs."

"How long have you known that I climb over roofs?"

"Since Germaine told me about the police raid, and how you got away. Oriol wouldn't talk, but I read the article in the *Herald Tribune*. I'd seen you many times without your clothes, so it wasn't hard for me to guess a connection between John Robie, who climbed mountains so well, and Le Chat. To be certain, I went to Nice and looked up the report of your trial. Did you know that Oriol was the police reporter who took the testimony?"

"Yes. What is he doing now?"

"He's still *commissaire,* if that's what you mean. I don't know what there was between you two, and I'm not going to ask questions you don't want to answer, but he's bitter about your escape. It's more than just his feeling as *commissaire.* Something personal. He won't say a word, and he's hushed the whole thing over, but I can sense it in him. You made a bad enemy in Oriol."

"I seem to have made a lot of enemies."

"You needn't make any more. I want to help you, John."

"There's nothing you can do. I'd tell you if there were."

"Money?"

"No."

"It's what you steal for, isn't it?"

"I don't want to talk about it."

"You can listen, then. I'm not going to lecture. Your morals are your own business. But you'll go to prison for a long time when you're caught." Paul nodded toward the hotel, where the photographer was still taking pictures. "You seem to have brought this one off as successfully as your others. You can't keep it up forever. I have to assume that you went back to your old trade because you needed money. I have—"

"You're wasting your time."

"Let me waste it, then. I have more money than I know how to spend. We've been good friends, and I'd like it to continue. I won't enjoy visiting you in prison. How much do you need to quit now, while you still have a chance?"

"I told you I'd tell you if there was anything you could do. I don't need money."

"Why do you steal, then? Do you get a thrill out of mocking the police? Do you like to see your name in the papers? Do you enjoy being Le Chat?"

"You're still wasting your time."

"I'm trying to help you!" Paul was angry. "You're not infallible! You made a slip once before. It will happen again, sooner or later. Nobody is clever enough to go on outwitting the whole world forever. Your time will come

When it does—"

He stopped. John had stood up.

"You can do only one thing for me, Paul," he said. "Leave me alone. Forget you know me. Don't come near me again. Good-bye."

He walked away before he had to look again at Paul's face. It was not easy deliberately to kill a friendship that had been as good as his and Paul's.

~§~

Mr. Paige was telling Commissaire Divisionnaire Lepic of his discovery in the lightwell.

"The Nice theft all over again. He cut a hole in the skylight, fixed his rope, swarmed down it to the bathroom window, got in, got out, swarmed back up again with the jewels. Amazing man."

Lepic motioned to one of his assistants, pointing upward. The assistant went away.

Mr. Paige said, "He won't find anything but the hole in the skylight. The roof is loose gravel, no footprints, an easy jump to the next building, fire escape in back, four or five ways to go. Waste of time."

"The Sûreté Nationale wastes a great deal of time," Lepic said agreeably. "Sometimes we accomplish things just the same."

He set a second assistant to work looking for fingerprints on the glass top of the commode where the empty jewel case stood and put a third man at a methodical, painstaking search of the suite. It was part of the routine.

Lepic had no great faith in routine as a weapon against a man like Le Chat. But there were always gestures to be made.

His English was excellent. It let him carry on the questioning without help from the hotel *directeur,* who stood by worrying for the reputation of the hotel. Mrs. Stevens had dressed, smeared on her lipstick, and was cheerful again since Mr. Paige had assured her that the insurance money would be paid within a few days. The shock of finding her jewel case empty had made her forget things like insurance. Now, with her most valuable necklace and matching earrings still safe and a concrete promise of sixty-one thousand dollars to spend on new beads, she was almost happy. Only the diamond and emerald dog represented a real loss. Her resentment against the thief was primarily because of the dog.

Lepic said, "We draw a picture, then. The thief comes down his rope from the rooftop. He finds the small window unlocked, so he has no need for his invaluable glass cutter. He enters the window. He balances for a moment on the bathtub, leaps soundlessly to the floor, and bends his ear to the two doors, first one, then the other. He hears nothing from mademoiselle's room, investigates cautiously, and finds it empty. Good. From madame's room comes the reassuring sound of heavy breathing. Excellent. He—"

"I don't breathe heavily," Mrs. Stevens said.

"Everyone breathes heavily when he or she sleeps, madame," Lepic said. "An experienced thief would not think of entering a room in which someone slept if he could not hear the breathing. So. He enters. He slashes the strap of the jewel case—"

Lepic went to the commode and held up the cut strap. "Why does your jewel case have such a strong lock attached to such a ridiculously fragile strap, madame?"

Mrs. Stevens did not like Lepic's critical attitude. She said, "I don't know. Maybe because it was made in Paris instead of New York."

"Stop it, Mother," Francie said. "He's only doing his job."

Lepic said, "Thank you, mademoiselle. When did you take the jewel case from the hotel safe, madame?"

"When I came in.

"What time was that?"

"About three."

"Then what?"

"I put my jewels away, locked the case, put the key in my purse, undressed, brushed my teeth, put skin cream on my face, opened the window, took all the blankets off the bed because it was too hot to sleep under anything but a sheet—"

"I am interested only in the essentials. When did you first discover the theft?"

"I didn't."

"Who did?"

"My daughter."

"At what time?"

"I don't know. Ask her."

Lepic had made a bad start when he accused Mrs. Stevens of breathing heavily. But he was patient. In time he learned what there was to learn. It was not a great deal.

Mrs. Stevens, as always, had left the jewel case in the hotel safe during the day. She had taken it out before dinner, selected the pieces she intended to wear for the evening, and returned the case to the safe, to reclaim it again when she came in at three o'clock, penniless, defeated by the roulette wheel. She had locked her jewels away, bolted her door, and gone to sleep immediately. She had not wakened until Francie came in and asked for the key to the jewel case. She knew nothing else.

Francie said she had come in about six, and repeated what she had told the police *agent*. Lepic was not curious about her actions or the actions of Mr. Burns. It was enough for him that they had left the Monte Carlo casino after dawn. He said to Mrs. Stevens, "Your procedure with the jewel case was always the same, madame?"

"It was."

"So that a thief would have an excellent opportunity to learn your habits simply by observation."

"I suppose so. If he was sitting in the lobby downstairs whenever I went near the safe."

The *directeur* was horrified at the suggestion, but relieved when Lepic asked him only a few questions. By then the fingerprint man had matched all the prints on the commode with Francie's or Mrs. Stevens's, and the searcher had found nothing unusual in the suite to report except a stray ten-franc piece under a corner of the carpet. The gestures were finished.

Mr. Paige followed Lepic from the room when he left and stopped him in the hallway.

"I don't like to question your procedure, Commissioner," he said diffidently. He was ill at ease, and took his embarrassment out on his mustache points. "But I have to report to my principals. Wasn't that rather a—ah—cursory investigation of a theft involving twenty million francs?"

"In the case of a theft by Le Chat, it was more than adequate. I know what you are thinking, monsieur. But have investigated half a dozen of Le Chat's thefts, and waste less and less time, to use your own words, with each. Once the jewels are gone, they are gone. I have learned that he leaves no clues. Fingerprint powder and carpet crawling are as useless against Le Chat as your own hopeful newspaper advertisements. He will not be caught that way."

"How do you expect to catch him?"

"In my own way. By being cleverer than he is. This latest theft supplies me with an extremely important piece of information about him."

"What is that?"

"He is here in Cannes." Lepic smiled and bowed. *"Bonjour, monsieur.* Reassure your principals that their interests are being protected."

Mr. Paige frowned at Lepic's back as the *commissaire divisionnaire* got into the elevator with his men. A reassurance would not weigh with his principals against a further loss of sixty-one thousand dollars. They were inclined to demand more tangible forms of protection.

Mrs. Stevens did not think much of Lepic's investigation, either, or of Lepic himself. When they were alone she said to Francie, "I could have done better myself. He didn't even ask the manager if there were any suspicious characters in the lobby when I came in last night. Why, any American cop—"

"I don't want to talk about it now, Mother," Francie said. "I'm terribly tired. I'm going to bed."

"All right, honey. You do look worn out. How was your party with Mr. Burns?"

"So-so."

"Win any money?"

"No."

"I wish I'd given you my lucky dog to wear instead of the beads. I hate losing that dog. I'll have to borrow Mr. Burns from you and see if he can win me another one. You know, it's funny about him. He likes to gamble, but I've never seen him bet more than a hundred francs on anything. With his luck—"

She stopped, hurt. Francie had gone into her own room and closed the door.

~§~

Bellini's source of information at the Hotel Midi was a switchboard operator, from whom he got the quickest kind of service. He listened to the operator's report, then put the telephone back in its cradle and wiped moisture from his face and hands. The cubbyhole of an office was like an oven, in spite of open windows. The door, which might have provided a cross draft, was closed, and the key lay on Bellini's desk. All four men in the room, Le Borgne, Coco, and John as well as Bellini, were sweating.

"Lepic just left the hotel looking pleased with himself," he said. "He was there less than thirty minutes. He must have found something."

"There's never anything to find," John said.

"Maybe the girl has already talked," Le Borgne said.

"I don't think so. She promised me until six o'clock."

Bellini said, "Are you sure she will really talk then?"

"Unless I produce the dog."

"Then we will have to produce it, or a duplicate."

"There isn't a duplicate. Cartier's doesn't turn them out that way. It would have to be made to order."

"The money itself, then. With a story of some kind."

"The money wouldn't satisfy her. It's become a kind of an issue between us. She said I couldn't have it, and she thinks I tricked her. I have to give it up to put her back on top again. It's hard to explain."

Coco said, "I still say let me conk her. That will save explanations."

"Keep quiet," Le Borgne said.

He and Coco had been there when John arrived, reporting to Bellini as they had been told to do. Nothing exceptional had happened during the night. The Souzas had had another screaming match, and the Sanfords had not come in before Le Borgne left his post at dawn. John alone had failed to cover his end. He had an excuse, but it was still a failure.

Le Borgne said, "It was only bad luck. We haven't finished with him yet. You had better run while you can, John. Leave the rest of it to us."

"It's been too late to run since she found out who I was. I can't get away."

Bellini said cheerfully, "The air of pessimism is not natural to you, John. Have you thought of telling her the truth?"

"It's the only idea I've had. I'm trying to think of a better one."

"It should be enough. She was on your side before. If you can convince her that you don't have the dog, and that her best chance of recovering it is to cooperate, she should keep quiet."

"I think she might."

"What is the objection, then?"

"I just don't like it. The more she knows, the more hold she has. She'll have you all on the same leash she has me, if I tell her the truth."

"So?"

"In the *maquis* there was a name for a man who identified his friends to save his skin."

Le Borgne said, "This is not the *maquis*, and if it were I would still say tell her. It's your only chance."

Coco said, "I say hit her on the head, but the next best thing is clearly to talk. If she sells us, we're all sold sooner or later anyway, unless we catch this pig of a burglar."

Bellini nodded. "I agree."

"Just as long as you know," John said. "I'll try it if I can't think of anything else. Whatever happens, keep the traps covered somehow. They may save all our necks."

"On that subject, I don't like the gypsy," Coco said. "He will have to be taken off."

"Another fight?"

"Not yet, although I almost conked him last night. He smokes on the job, for one thing. He denies it, but I smelled the tobacco. For another thing, he moves around like a cow with two calves. Michel is good enough. The gypsy will never do."

John said, "Better take him off today, Bellini."

"What about a replacement?"

"I'll replace him myself, if I'm still loose tonight. If not, get somebody else tomorrow."

"If the girl sells you, I'll conk her for my own satisfaction." Coco stretched, yawned, and stood up. "Tell her that for me, and that I am expecting you under the bushes at midnight."

Le Borgne said, "We are not done yet, John. 'Voir.'"

The two men left the room.

Bellini's telephone rang as the door closed behind them. The switchboard operator at the Midi had another report to make.

When Bellini hung up, he said, "The exodus has commenced. The Arabian demigod is leaving, likewise several others including Lady Kerry, unluckily for Danielle. The thief has them worried."

"Lady Kerry hasn't anything to worry about," John said.

"Unless—"

He didn't finish it. Bellini said curiously, "Unless what?"

"I haven't looked closely at her jewelry for twelve years. She might have acquired something worth stealing in that time."

"Possibly."

John felt suddenly hopeful again, less discouraged by his own failure. A vague idea that had been in the back of his mind was beginning to take shape. It was one that had been suggested to him by Francie, and it was no better than some of her other ideas. Still, it was something.

He said, "How much do you know about Claude?"

"The muscular swimming teacher?"

"Yes."

"In what respect?"

"The possibility that he may be our thief."

Bellini chuckled. He said chidingly, "John!"

"I know. He's not clever enough to manage it on his own. But he has the physical equipment for it, and Francie gave me an idea when she told me how she reasoned that the thief had to be one of a gang. Suppose she's right. Suppose the imitation of Le Chat is deliberate, to put the *flics* on watch for Le Chat and no one else. But instead of working alone, as I did, this thief has a clever confederate. Danielle, the brains. She works during the season for people like Lady Kerry. She can't steal anything herself and hope to get away with it, but she can set up the thefts for Claude, tell him if the

stones are worth while, where they are, and when they
will be available. All he has to do is climb in the window
at a convenient moment, leave Le Chat's trademarks
where they will be found, and get out. Whether she
takes the stones or he does isn't important. Le Chat gets
the blame, they get the jewelry."

"Possible. Always possible," Bellini said. "But it is
only a bare theory. Why pick on poor Claude? Why not
any of a dozen equally agile and muscular *professeurs
de natation* here in Cannes? Or other dozens elsewhere
on the Côte? Or, for that matter, any of hundreds of
young men with Claude's biceps?"

"Because Claude has Danielle. The others don't."

Bellini nodded wisely. "You are impressed with
Danielle."

"She has a good head, she doesn't like being poor,
and in some ways she reminds me of myself at her age.
She has a state of mind. I may be misjudging her, but
I'm still curious. Have any of the people she worked for
been robbed?"

Bellini opened a drawer of his desk, searched through
a file, and pulled out a card. It had a photograph of
Danielle's neat profile on it, and several lines of typing.

He read from the card. "Lady Kerry, as of yesterday. I
placed Danielle with her myself."

"It doesn't mean anything that you placed her.
Somebody had to. Read the rest."

"Mrs. Adam Longman. She was with her in England
for nearly a year after they left France."

"I don't know the name. Read another."

"Mr. and Mrs. Roland Sauer and child, two weeks, here on the Côte."

"No theft."

"Monsieur and Madame Ferenc Boutin, also here on the Côte."

"No."

Bellini read other names. John recognized none of them. Bellini put the card back in its file.

"You see?" he said. "I am careful about these things. If Danielle, or any of my people, had even been questioned in connection with the thefts, I would have investigated."

"Just to be certain, I'd like to know if Claude can account for his time on the nights of the thefts. If he can, good. It will take him off my mind."

"That won't be difficult."

Bellini turned in his chair, reaching with his good arm to lower the window shade. It was his way of calling a messenger.

John said, "Is Claude in your pocket, too?"

"I own the concession at La Plage Nautique. In another name, of course." Bellini giggled. "Claude knows who pays him. He will answer my questions."

"Don't make them too obvious."

"Leave it to me, John. I am not entirely without subtlety."

He received several more telephone calls while they waited for an answer to the window signal. John did not understand some of the languages he spoke over the telephone, but he could tell from Bellini's mobile face, his chuckles and nods of satisfaction, that the pipelines were running. Information funneled into the little office from all over the Mediterranean coast, in French, in Arabic, in Italian, in Spanish. Bellini had a private telephone line that did not pass through the hotel switchboard, and he not only paid his sources of information well but protected them.

Besides the private telephone line, he had his own messenger service. The half-drawn blind brought a rug peddler into the office within a few minutes. He was one of a dozen or more Moroccans who hawked small, ugly rugs and leatherwork daily along La Croisette during the summer season. They were identifiable by the greasy red fezzes and Moroccan slippers they wore with their shabby European clothes, and they all looked alike. They did not sell many rugs, but they did a fair business in pornographic pictures and, occasionally, drugs. None of them was allowed inside any hotel on the promenade except the Napoleon, and then only when the window shade was drawn in Bellini's window. Bellini owned an interest in the Hotel Napoleon.

The peddler stood just inside the door, his rugs and burned-leather handbags hanging from his shoulders. Bellini spoke to him, again in a language that John did not understand. Once the peddler looked sideways at John with sly, secretive eyes. Afterward he touched his forehead with the back of his dirty fingers and went away, without having said a word.

Bellini said, "Claude will be here in a few minutes. You can wait in the other room."

John went into the next room, Bellini's bedroom, and sat in a chair against the wall behind the open door. He relaxed deliberately, loose in the chair, and closed his eyes.

It did no good. He could not stop his mind from its activity, nor control his thoughts. When he tried to visualize Claude as the thief, see him climbing down a rope into the lightwell, the picture would not come to life.

He saw only Paul, sitting alone on the bench with the hurt of rejection in his face. He thought of Oriol, whose friendship had turned to bitterness at what he believed to be a betrayal, and of Francie, coldly angry at the deception she thought he had played on her. All three had been his friends. All three would still be his friends if they knew the truth, and yet his whole instinct was against telling any of them. The feeling was as strong as his faith in Bellini. When he tried to analyze the reason for it, it came to him suddenly that he put his faith in Bellini and Coco and Le Borgne not because they were fellow *maquisards* but because they were thieves, criminals. Francie and Paul and Oriol were not.

It's because you're a thief at heart, he thought, with real surprise. You were born a thief. You're on the other side only by accident, like the gypsy.

It was the plain truth. He had stolen nothing in twelve years, had no intention ever to steal again, and yet retained a thief's distrust of those who were not thieves themselves. Like Bellini, he did not trust what he did not understand.

He was still thinking about it when he heard the door
in the next room open and close.

~§~

Claude had stopped long enough after receiving
Bellini's message to put on a dark jersey and trousers
over his swimming trunks, but he was barefooted. His
feet made no sound on the worn carpet in front of
Bellini's desk.

Bellini looked up, smiling his biggest smile of
welcome.

Claude said, *"Bonjour, m'sieu.* You sent for me?"

"I did. I have a question to ask you, Claude. Where
were you on the night of the fourteenth of July?"

John, listening behind the door, could picture Bellini
studying Claude's face, watching for a reaction. A blunt
question about Claude's whereabouts at three or four
o'clock in the morning of that same day could be something he was prepared to answer without a change of
expression. Bellini's demand would make him hesitate,
think back. The fourteenth of July was Bastille Day. A
Frenchman might reasonably forget where he had been
any other day in the year, but not Bastille Day. And the
marquee chain of the hotel in Monte Carlo had been
climbed on the night of Bastille Day, while the celebra-
tion was still going on in the street below.

Claude said, "The fourteenth of July?"

"Yes."

"Bastille Day?"

"Yes."

"It's been a long time. It's hard to remember. If I knew why you wanted to know—"

He's stalling, John thought, and felt a momentary hope.

Bellini said, "I ask for my information. Where did you pass the night?"

"I don't remember."

Bellini chuckled. "Come, come, Claude. Bastille Day, and you don't remember?"

"No."

"Think again."

Bellini took off his spectacles and beamed at Claude in a friendly way.

Claude's eyes dropped before long. He said sullenly, "Danielle put you up to this."

"Of course."

"She could have asked me herself. I can explain."

"I am asking you. Where did you pass the night?"

Claude shrugged. "With a *poule*. I was drunk."

"What *poule?*"

"Just a *poule*. Jacqueline. I don't know her last name. One of the girls who comes to the beach. I had a date with Danielle, but I got sidetracked."

"Were you with the *poule* all night?"

"Yes."

"Does she still come to the beach?"

"Yes. But I told her there was nothing doing. Danielle and I have plans."

"Tell the *poule* to come see me."

"Why?"

"I want to talk to her. If, as you say, you and Danielle have plans, somebody should tell the *poules* to leave you alone. In case you get drunk again."

"What if she won't come?"

"Convince her that she should. That will be all."

Claude stood his ground. He said stubbornly, "You don't have to tell Danielle. If you give her another story, she'll believe you. I'm already in bad with her."

"Why?"

"I don't know why. I haven't even looked at anyone else since Bastille Day. But she didn't come to the beach yesterday or this morning, and she hasn't been with the American. She told me that job was finished. I don't know where she is."

"I have given her temporary work with Lady Kerry, at the Hotel Midi. She will be back with you today or tomorrow. In the meantime, try to avoid tangling yourself with *poules,* and your conscience will stop nagging you without reason. You may go now."

"What are you going to tell her?"

"Nothing at all. You may forget that I questioned you, but only this time. That is all, Claude."

John heard the door open and close again.

He waited at the window in the other room until he saw Claude come out on the boulevard below and hurry back to his job. His fine torso in the tight jersey attracted the attention of a group of young girls who were strolling the promenade arm in arm. They stopped to look after him, giggling. One attempted a whistle. Claude paid no attention.

John went into Bellini's office. Bellini said, "Well?"

"I think he's telling the truth. But check with the girl, just the same."

"Certainly."

"And don't forget about the gypsy."

"I've already sent word."

John rubbed his eyes. It was more than twenty-four hours since he had slept last. His mind was dull with fatigue. He was sure there were other important things that Bellini should be reminded to do, but he could not think of them, or of anything else except the coming need to beg his freedom from Francie.

It was nearly noon. He had six hours before the deadline.

He said, "I've got to sleep. Can I do it here? I don't want to go back to the hotel while there's still a chance I might run into photographers."

"Of course. Close the door. I'll see that you are not disturbed."

"Don't let me oversleep. I've still got a hope, and I don't want to lose it by failing to get to the beach before six."

"I've never failed you yet, John. And you have much more than a hope with the girl. When she knows the truth about you, that you are not a thief at all, there will be even less reason for her to betray you than there was before."

"The truth about me is that I am a thief, Bellini. I just found it out. The truth about Francie is that she's on the other side, for all her talk, and if she has no other reason for existence, as you call it, it's enough that she'll probably send me back to La Maison Centrale, sooner or later, one way or another. Maybe even without trying. If I believed in premonitions, I'd say I had one."

He went into the other room and closed the door.

Bellini looked thoughtfully at the door. For once, he was not smiling. He believed strongly in premonitions.

5

JOHN'S SLEEP WAS NOT RESTFUL. The room was too hot, and he woke often with a start to look at his watch, afraid that he had overslept. The frequent shrill of Bellini's telephone in the other room and occasional voices disturbed him as well. Once he came wide awake at the sound of a voice he recognized, Danielle's.

He went soundlessly to the door and put his ear to the panel.

Danielle said, "...frightened them all, I suppose. Lady Kerry was one of the first to leave. She was nice, though. She paid me for the whole week."

Bellini's voice answered, "Does she have enough jewelry to attract a thief?"

"Mountains of it. Family heirlooms, mostly, but they must be worth a lot of money."

"Naturally she would want to take them home with her, if only for sentimental reasons." Bellini's chuckle came thinly through the door panel. "I have nothing else for you at the moment, Danielle. Go back to Claude until you hear from me."

"All right. I'd better pay your commission now."

"Of course. Business is business."

There was a silence. Danielle said, "Did Mr. Burns leave you any money for me?"

"No."

"He still owes me for two days. He said he'd give it to you."

"He must have forgotten. I'll remind him. Was he satisfied with you?"

Danielle hesitated only momentarily. "No."

"Why not?"

"I said something wrong. I don't know what it was, but he didn't like it. One minute we were good friends, talking about me and Claude, and the next minute—I don't know. Americans are hard to understand. He just said he didn't need me any more."

"What about you and Claude, Danielle?"

"You sound like Mr. Burns, *m'sieu*." Danielle was amused.

"I like to keep my files up to date. From what Claude says, I may have to change your name on my card."

"Claude says too much for his own good. I work for him as long as he pays me a salary. That's all."

"No romance, then?"

"With Claude?" She laughed. "With you, possibly. You are not pretty, but you have money and a pleasant disposition. Are you interested in romance?"

Bellini giggled at the suggestion. "My romantic years are long past, regrettably."

"Then *bonjour, M'sieu* Bellini."

"*Bonjour*, Danielle."

There was quiet afterward. John went back to bed. This

time he fell immediately and soundly asleep.

Bellini woke him about five. He held a copy of the day's edition of *L'Espoir*.

"Lepic is badly out on a limb, or else he has found something that we do not know about," he said, plainly worried. "I don't like it. He is too cautious to make promises he cannot keep. Read it."

He gave the paper to John, then went back to his office to answer the ringing telephone.

L'Espoir's front page showed a photograph of the thief's latest victim with her lipstick more lopsided than usual, another of the façade of the Hotel Midi, and a third showing the skylight, with an arrow indicating the thief's point of entry into the lightwell. The photographer had not been able to get a picture of the room where the theft had occurred, but photographs were less important to the story than Lepic's statement, directly quoted, that the Sûreté Nationale promised an arrest in the immediate future. It was the first time any such statement had been made, and *L'Espoir's* editor, frankly skeptical of Lepic's ability to live up to the promise, suggested that if nothing else were accomplished, at least the commitment would force him to eat his words publicly and confess to being the incompetent he was. From that point the editorial thundered along familiar lines of criticism.

Bellini came back.

"It is not as bad as I thought, although bad enough," he said. "They have started the roundup they promised. Jean-Pierre was first."

"They took him?"

"Not yet. He was tipped and got away. But they are looking for him in Marseilles, and if they do not find him they must find somebody. Le Borgne may be next, or Coco. I will have to get word to them quickly."

John put the newspaper down and stood up to put on his coat. He felt calm, rested. He said, "It may not be necessary. If I'm going back to prison, there's no reason why anyone else should go with me. I'll let you know how I come out as soon as I can."

Bellini said, "I'll know as soon as you do, although I am already certain that you will be able to win her help." He went to the window and drew the shade to call his messenger. "Don't be pessimistic, John. It is not like you. Something has happened to you."

He chuckled encouragingly. John said, "Nothing has happened to me yet."

~§~

In the street he saw the red-fezzed Moroccan on his way to answer the signal of Bellini's window blind. He passed one of the patrolling *agents* on the promenade, and thought, It won't take long to happen if it does happen.

His common sense told him he could convince Francie that she had no cause to betray him. But he could not escape the premonition that, whether she meant to or not, she would somehow be the cause of his downfall. If not immediately, then in time.

She was sitting under an umbrella on the *plage privée,* reading a book. The second chair under the umbrella was unoccupied.

He said, "May I sit down?"

"If you like." She added coolly, "It isn't necessary," and indicated an open beach bag on the sand at her side. "You can drop it in there."

"I haven't got it."

She leaned forward, deliberately, to look at the clock face in the old tower on the hilltop beyond the yacht harbor. He said, "It's five-thirty. In a week or two I might be able to get it for you. I can't do it in half an hour."

"You had the whole day."

"It wasn't enough. If you'll let me explain, I'll tell you why."

"I don't want an explanation. I want the dog, Mr. Burns."

It was a flat, cold demand. There was no lightness in her now, none of the friendly mockery with which she had tugged him by his invisible leash before. He knew she would not hesitate to carry out her threat if he did not win her over at once. He sat down beside her and said, "You gave me until six. I still have thirty minutes."

He began to talk, quickly, before she could deny him.

Because he had never told anyone the story before, and did not have it formulated in his mind, he began with his escape from the Villa des Bijoux. But it was not the beginning. Neither was the *maquis,* nor the prison, nor his trial, nor even his first theft. The whole story was his biography. He found that he had to go back further and further, finally as far as his memory took him.

He had been five years old when his father put him on the rings. There were only two of the Flying Robies to begin with, his father and mother, small-time acrobats in the small-time carnivals which played one- and two-day stands in the New England states. He became the third member of the troupe when he was big enough for his father to lie about his age. But he was ready long before then. He was naturally agile, and the constant grind of training his father kept him to from the first hardened his muscles and sharpened his sense of timing. Before he was twelve, he was a competent trapeze flyer. Later, when his weight and strength increased, he learned the rest.

Trapeze performers in small carnivals were jacks of all trades, never the aristocrats of the big tents in the major circuses. He learned to rig his own apparatus, do a walk on the high wire, double as a tumbling clown, substitute as readily for the equilibrist juggler as for the man who turned somersaults off the trampoline.

"I was always best at something that called for climbing," he said. He had not looked at Francie since he began to talk, but he knew he was holding her. So far. "I was strong. I had a good head for heights, and confidence in myself. Acrobats need absolute faith in their own ability more than anything else. My father lost his when he missed a catch and let my mother go over the end of the net into a bank of empty chairs. I had thrown her myself, but my throw was a good one and we both knew it was his fault. He never went on a trapeze again."

He had died soon after his wife. John was left with a few suits of tights, the muscular development necessary to climb a rope hand over hand in a way that made it look simple, and a knowledge of the rest of his trade. When he was twenty-one, able to sign a binding contract, he got what seemed to be a good offer from a French troupe touring Europe, and did not wonder, until he reached France, why a European troupe needed to take recruits from a small American carnival. The troupe was a co-operative venture that had already ceased to co-operate before he arrived. In Nice, where he heard the news, a hotel thief stole what remained of his money, his passport, and all the other means of identification he had.

"I didn't resent it, particularly," he said. He still had not looked in Francie's direction. He kept his eyes on the diving raft that floated offshore, bobbing brightly in the sunlight. "In the carnivals, a mark was always a mark, a sucker, a john, somebody to be cheated. Pickpockets and short-change men were as much a natural part of the business as the clowns. I thought of myself as another mark in a strange territory. It never occurred to me that I could go to the American consul and borrow passage money home. Even without a passport I might have managed that, but my mind didn't work that way. There were other marks around, plenty of them. I had only to find the right one."

It was the summer of 1936. The Côte had begun to glitter again, after the early dead years of the depression, and was regaining its place in Europe as an international playground for the rich and near rich. He struck up an acquaintance with a friendly British couple who drank too much. They owned a small villa on Cap Ferrat, not far from St. Jean, and they made the mistake of inviting him into their home, where he had an opportunity to look around. Shortly afterward an acrobatic thief climbed a drainpipe up the side of the villa, got in through an open bedroom window, and made off with the wife's jewels while she and her husband slept off the effects of a late evening.

He made a hundred and twenty thousand francs for the night's work, then worth about four thousand dollars, not as much as he would have got later when he had learned the language and how to value stones properly, but enough to allow him to keep up a front until his next theft. The moral aspects of thievery never concerned him. The marks were there, and climbing drainpipes was an easier and more profitable way of using his skill to make a living than any other he had known. Le Chat came into being.

To the newspapers who created him, he was a clever French thief who preyed on wealthy visitors to the Côte. John, himself one of the wealthy visitors during the summer, avoided the Côte out of season, studied French with a group of American students in Paris, read what there was available to him about the valuation of precious stones, and followed the society columns as well as lapidary trade journals which noted the manufacture or sale of outstanding gems. When he returned to the Côte the following season, he already knew whom he meant to rob, if the proper opportunities presented themselves. He was cautious, confided in no one, worked alone, and planned each theft carefully. Le Chat flourished.

"Most of the rest of it was in the old newspapers, if you had bothered to look them up," he said. "They caught me in 1939."

"Tell me the rest of it."

He did not know from Francie's voice what she felt. It was toneless.

"I tried to deal with the wrong fence," he said. "He turned me in. They gave me a fair trial and twenty years at La Maison Centrale, a prison near Saumur. The German army emptied the prison later. I went into the *maquis.*"

He told her about the *maquis,* and Bellini, and of Coco and Le Borgne and Jean-Pierre, his escape to America and his return to France under the amnesty. He said, "I was through stealing when I came back. I don't say that it was a moral regeneration. I wasn't a thief one minute, and not a thief the next. But I had enough money to live on here in France. I had learned to like the country, and I had been safe before only because no one knew who I was. It was too risky after they had my description and could recognize my style. They could send me back to do the prison sentence at any time, even on suspicion. So I retired. I bought a house near Vence and became a country gentleman."

They had been the best years of his life. He hesitated to tell her about them, but Paul and Oriol were part of the story, even Lisa, and he could not find a way to avoid the continuation. He made it as brief as he could, up until the publication of the article about Le Chat in the Paris edition of the *Herald Tribune*. From that point he told her everything, step by step, from his escape at the villa down to Jean-Pierre's escape, if it was an escape, from the police in Marseilles that same afternoon. When he had finished, he looked at his watch. It was six-fifteen. The sunlight had begun to fade.

"I can prove enough of it to satisfy you, I think," he said. "It's in your own interest to keep quiet and let me go on with what I'm trying to do. If we catch him, I'll see that your mother's jewelry is the first returned."

"A bribe to keep quiet. Is that what you are offering me?"

"If you want to put it that way."

"I wish you hadn't thought it was necessary."

He looked at her then and knew he would not need to give any proof, only an apology for having felt it necessary to offer the bribe. He said in explanation, "I've been talking my way out of twenty years in prison, Francie. I wasn't sure about you. I didn't know how you would take it."

"You can't have thought very highly of me."

"I didn't know," he repeated. "It wasn't a question of thinking highly of you. You didn't think highly of me when you believed I had tricked you. You would have given me to the police if I hadn't told you the truth."

"Why didn't you tell me before?"

"It wasn't necessary before."

"You didn't want to trust me."

"I'm not trustful by nature."

"But you trust Bellini."

"He's different. So are Jean-Pierre and the others. I had to learn to trust them to survive. Just as I'm trusting you now."

He did not want to talk further about it, or explain why there was an essential difference between his confidence in Bellini and his feeling toward her. He turned to look up at the promenade.

The rug peddler was there, holding out his gimcrack wares to the passers-by, wheedling them to buy. But he did not follow anyone far, and he kept his eye on the beach. John raised his hand, palm out, then closed his fist. The peddler walked away.

Francie said, "What was that for?"

"I was sending word to my friends that I'm still available."

They did not talk again for some time. A speedboat roared by between the beach and the diving platform, trailing a long plume of white water. A man and a girl on water skis rode the wake. When the wave of the boat's passage washed up on the beach almost to their feet, Francie said, "What are you going to do now?"

"What I have been doing. Watch my traps and hope. I would have got him last night, if my luck had been better."

"It was my fault."

"No. Just bad luck. And at least I know he's here in Cannes. I'm counting on the Brazilian woman to attract him, and the Sanford *gala* if that fails. If he doesn't try one of those, I'll have to quit."

"Can't you set other traps?"

"Not here. Not now. The season will be over. There won't be anyone around the Côte worth robbing until next year. He'll hole up until then."

"You sound positive of it."

"I'm not, but it's what I used to do. He's copied me in everything, as if he were signing my name to his thefts. The whole scheme is based on the assumption that he'll continue to copy me, do just what I have done in his place."

"And if he doesn't?"

"Then I'm wasting my time."

"You can still get away."

"Yes. I think so. But they'll get Jean-Pierre in time, probably Coco and Le Borgne as well, and give Bellini trouble. They're the only reason I stayed in the first place."

The speedboat made another pass at the beach, weaving from side to side, so that the couple at the end of the towing lines was bounced around in the wake. The girl lost her balance, fell, disappeared for a moment, and came up to swim for shore. The man hung on.

His feat of balance on the bucking water skis was wonderful to watch. John recognized the professional skill. He thought, I could be looking at the thief now. I wonder if I'll ever know.

Francie said, "You're very fond of Bellini, aren't you? I'd like to meet a man who commands that much loyalty."

"I think he'd like to meet you. You puzzle him."

"I puzzle him? How?"

"He doesn't understand your *raison d'être*. He classifies everybody according to their reasons for existing—pleasure, murder, thievery, notoriety, money-making, gambling, something. He doesn't recognize yours."

"Does everyone have to have a reason?"

"As he sees it, yes. It's logical enough."

He was saved from having to explain further by Mrs. Stevens, who called to them from the promenade, then came down the steps and trudged through the sand toward them.

"Texas was never like this," she said cheerfully. "Hello, Lucky. Don't get up. I'll just flop down here on the sand. My, it's hot, isn't it?"

She sat down on the sand under the umbrella, sighing comfortably.

"Did you hear about the excitement this morning?" she said, after she had settled herself. "I got my picture in the papers."

"I was one of the crowd. You didn't see me."

"I didn't see anyone, I guess. I was too busy yelling about my beads." Mrs. Stevens laughed at herself. "I feel better now. Mr. Paige and I just finished sending a cable off to London. I'll get my money in a few days, he says. Except for the lucky dog, of course. You'll have to help me win another dog some evening, Lucky. Whenever Francie can spare you, of course."

She gave them both an arch look.

He said, "My luck hasn't been so good lately. You'd better hope for the police to catch the thief before he has a chance to get rid of the original."

"The police!" Mrs. Stevens made a face. "That Lepic couldn't find the telephone in a telephone booth. I hate to think how close I came to letting my insurance run out before we came here. You know, if that robber had only waited another couple of days, I'd have had the dog covered with the rest of it. That's what makes me really mad. But I'm going to win another one. I've got a new roulette system. A man I met at Antibes told me that if you just play odd or even—"

She ran on about what the man at Antibes had said. John was able to excuse himself a few minutes later. When he stood up to leave, Francie said, "Don't forget that I want to meet your friend."

"I'll arrange it."

"What friend?" Mrs. Stevens asked.

"Just a friend."

"I'd like to know what's going on between you two," Mrs. Stevens said shrewdly. "You've been cooking something for a couple of days now. You aren't planning to elope, I hope."

Francie blushed. John said, "We haven't got that far yet. We're cooking up a scheme to win you a lucky dog."

~§~

He kept his rendezvous with Coco and Michel at midnight on the hillside above the cottage in Le Cannet. He was on time, but both men were ahead of him. When he came down from the hilltop to the patch of scrub that was their meeting place, Coco reached out of the darkness with both arms and embraced him so hard his ribs cracked.

"I've been sweating silver five-franc pieces wondering if you would make it," he whispered. *"Merde alors,* I would have conked the girl if she had sold you, John. What did you tell her?"

"Everything."

"She is on our side, then?"

"Yes."

"Whatever that means, in the case of a woman. Michel! *Sst!* Michel, where are you, man?"

"Here." Michel's voice came out of the dark.

"Here is our replacement for the gypsy, Le Chat himself. The thief is as good as in the bag right now."

"If he comes," Michel said, in his practical way. "But I am glad we got rid of the gypsy. Did he give any trouble?"

John said, "Bellini took him off. I don't know what he told him. Did you get word about Jean-Pierre and the *flics,* Coco?"

"Bellini sent a message for us to burrow back into the *maquis* and stay there. Le Borgne and I set up house-

keeping this afternoon in a cave back of Vallauris." Coco
snickered in the darkness. "Poor old One Eye, he is not
the man he used to be. He does not like caves any more.
He is accustomed to sleeping in a warm bed with a
nightcap pulled well over his glass peeper."

"A cave is better than a prison. You'll both have to
stay under cover until something happens to turn
Lepic's attention. He has promised in print to make
arrests, which means you and Le Borgne and Jean-
Pierre if he can't find me."

"I saw the papers. I spit in his face."

Michel said, "Do it more quietly, then. We sound like
a cabinet meeting."

Without animosity, Coco whispered, "I spit in your
face, too. Quietly."

They left Michel in the clump of scrub, which com-
manded a view of the back of the villa and its surrounding garden. Coco's point of watch was farther down the
hillside. John's was still farther below, where a small
stream entered a culvert that passed beneath the road
in front of the villa. The road came up from the town
below, winding to take advantage of the natural slope of
land, and continued on over the hilltops toward
Mougins. The villa they watched was one of half a dozen
widely separated houses at the extreme upper edge of
the town limits, beyond sidewalks and pavement except
for the single road, which was poorly illuminated at
night by lights hanging from poles at intervals of two or
three hundred meters. The roadway was mainly in
darkness except for areas of relative brilliance directly

under the lights.

One of these areas was not quite in front of the villa. It made the darkness at the back of the house more pronounced by contrast. The garden, a jungle of shrubs and vines, was marked off from the surrounding scrub mimosa of the hillside only by a low stone wall, and offered good cover to anyone approaching the house from any side but the front itself. John did not entirely discard the possibility of an approach even from the front, because he had himself robbed a house near Menton which was similarly placed with respect to a street light. But he had attended to the light first, and he knew that as long as this one continued to burn, the front was safe.

It left three sides to watch. His own preference would have been an approach from the side he was on, and he had switched Coco from there to the gypsy's former post for that reason. The villa was a three-story building, originally built to house more people than a couple and a single servant. The top floor was unoccupied, and offered an ideal entry. He had always gone in from above whenever possible, rather than from below; dogs and servants were less of a hazard on the top floors, windows were less often locked, there were many advantages to finding a way down, rather than up, in the dark, including the fact that in an emergency a man could leap farther from a high point than from a low point. The outside climb on his side was more difficult than at the back or the far side of the house, but the bedrooms were at the back, and the street light illuminated part of the far side, leaving his side in relative shadow. Not complete shadow. Even without a moon, there was enough light to make out the pale rectangular bulk of the house, the stuccoed wall that would reveal the outline of a climber.

In the mouth the culvert he took off his clothes and the body harness and exchanged his shoes for light glove-leather gymnast's slippers he had brought in his pocket. Besides the slippers, he wore only shorts. The warm night air felt good on his bare skin. The grass on which he lay at full length, with only his head above the lip of the little stream bed, had a rich, cushiony texture, and some aromatic shrub near by gave off an acrid odor, like tar. It was a familiar smell. It made him think of the *maquis,* and other nights when he had waited in other stream beds. There had been other odors as well then—blood, frequently, and the reek of gunpowder or dynamite.

He flexed his fingers. There would be no blood this time. He had learned to hate the men he had killed during the Occupation. He felt no hatred for the thief he hunted, only curiosity about his identity and the need to finish with him. He thought he felt as a professional fighter must feel, going into the ring. He meant to win, and he would do whatever damage to his opponent necessary to win. It did not require hatred.

A car came up the road. He lowered his head as the lights swept above his hiding place. The car went on over the hill and disappeared.

He found himself thinking of Francie. His premonition

about her, if it had been a premonition, had left him. He knew he would never have confided in her if it had not been absolutely necessary, any more than he would confide in Paul or Oriol unless he was forced to. But he did not see how she could harm him involuntarily, and there was no question in his mind about her willingness to help him, any more than there was a question of Paul's willingness to help him. Paul would not even demand an explanation from him. He knew it, and still he could not contemplate going voluntarily to Paul for help. He had believed at the time that his deliberate rejection of Paul's friendship had been made for Paul's own sake, to keep him from becoming involved. It was not so.

It's because you're a thief and he isn't, he thought, and remembered Francie's words: "I'm glad you're a thief, John." She had confided in him because he was a thief. He could not confide in Paul because Paul was an honest man.

He changed his position in the stream bed, partly to keep from leaving the imprint of his body in the grass where it could be seen later, partly to interrupt a trend of thought that made his head ache.

The Brazilians came home at two-thirty. They were not fighting tonight. Souza seemed to be in good humor, from the tone of his voice when he let his wife out of the car. He drove a big American sedan, too large for the garage of the villa, which had been built to shelter smaller French automobiles. He had to park it under the portico at the front of the house. John heard him slam the car doors, then try them to make sure they were locked. There was a good black market for big American cars, which were easier to dispose of even than diamond and topaz bracelets.

The lights went off in the villa at three. From then on John hardly moved a muscle in his hiding place. His eyes were alert, watching, as he knew Coco and Michel would be watching from their posts. The *maquis* had taught them all patience.

The night wore on. At dawn a milk cart came over the hill and down the road, jingling, the cart wheels grinding on the gravel of the road. The driver stopped in front of the villa and ran up the path with his can to fill a pail that had been left on the front porch. After the cart had gone on down the road, the three men reassembled in the clump of shrub up the hill.

"My bones ache," Coco grumbled. "The ground is harder than cement."

"It was just as hard during the Occupation," Michel said.

"At least we had action once in a while, and could move around. I spit in this thief's face. When is he coming, John?"

"Tomorrow. Next week. Maybe never. All we can do is wait and hope. Be here tomorrow night at the same time. Bring the news from Le Borgne when you come, and both of you be careful to keep out of sight during the day. Lepic will have your descriptions out."

"Be careful yourself. And butter the girl good, John. Make love to her, if necessary. Admire her eyes and the

swell of her bosom. I'm still more afraid of what she can
do to you than I am of being caught by the *flics.*"

"I'll worry about the girl. You look out for the *flics.*"

"I spit in the *flics'* faces, collectively."

They separated, leaving the hillside one at a time.

~§~

He did not see Francie all day. He slept in the morn-
ing, made a visit to Bellini afterward, and learned that
Jean-Pierre had still avoided capture. Jacqueline, the
girl with whom Claude said he had spent the night of
Bastille Day, had come to confirm Claude's story,
pushed along by Claude himself and too frightened of
him to be trusted as a source of reliable information.
Bellini had sent Claude away and questioned her alone.
He believed what she had to say, which eliminated
Claude as a suspect. John agreed.

There was no other news. The day's edition of *Nice-
Matin* asked baldly, *What Arrest, and How Soon, M.
Lepic?* The plain-clothes *agents* patrolled La Croisette
as usual. Everything was the same as it had been for
days, except the weather.

The sun still shone hotly in a clear sky, but a *mistral*
had begun to blow from the southwest, and the force of
the wind across the open sea piled waves up on the
beach. The Hotel Midi's tiny patch of sand was covered
with water nearly to the promenade, and the other
beaches farther along, although more sheltered from
the direct force of the wind, were not much better. The

sunbathers had no place to go except the promenade, which was over-crowded with chairs, mats, and cushions. John was making his way through the crowd when he saw Paul.

Paul stood at the edge of the promenade above La Plage Nautique, looking down at the beach. John hesitated for a moment, but what he had learned about himself since seeing his friend last made him walk over to Paul's side.

Paul was watching Danielle and Claude on the sand below, hurrying to move umbrellas and beach chairs back from the encroaching waves. John said, "She does look like Lisa. I hadn't noticed it before."

"Am I to recognize you?" Paul did not turn his head.

"We've been introduced."

"I'm glad to see you still looking well, Mr. Burns. In spite of what you said the last time we talked."

"I was expecting trouble the last time, Paul. I didn't want to have you involved. It's the only reason I said what I did."

"Does that mean you no longer expect trouble?"

"Not the same kind."

"Lepic is going to get you sooner or later. He's promised your arrest soon. My offer still holds. I wish—"

"I still don't want to talk about it. If there was anything you could do to help me, I'd ask for it."

Paul shook his head, puzzled. "I don't understand you. You're taking a terrible risk. For what? It can't be just money."

"You don't have to understand. I'd rather you didn't, at

the moment. Some day I'll explain."

"Some day it will be too late to explain."

All the time they talked, Paul had been watching Danielle. She was too occupied with her work to be conscious of the two men looking down from the promenade above. The waves were coming in fast. Claude's fine muscles bulged as he caught a heavy paddle board which was about to float off and pulled it to safety. Danielle, wading knee-deep for the paddle, was as quick and graceful as a sea nymph.

John said, "Do you want me to introduce you?"

"Will you?" Paul accepted the offer hungrily. "I've been standing here looking at her, feeling like a lout, all hands and feet and knuckles, trying to think of a way to meet her."

"You still feel the same?"

"Worse. Or better. Or more so, at least, since I've seen her again. Even the way she moves reminds me of Lisa."

"The best way to get over it is to meet her, then. Come along."

They went down the steps to the sand.

He had an excuse in the money he still owed Danielle and had forgotten to leave with Bellini. The introduction of Paul as a friend was natural and casual. Danielle was businesslike, polite, glad to meet Mr. Burns's friend, and cool to John when she thanked him for the money. Claude was too busy to pay attention to any of it. When Paul helped Danielle catch a chair that was about to drift away, John took the opportunity to walk off and leave them together. The rest was out of his hands.

The *mistral* blew all day. Either because of the effect of the dry, electrically charged wind or the suspense of waiting for nightfall, he felt a tenseness he did not like. It was an unfamiliar, unpleasant feeling. He went for a walk out along the beach toward La Napoule, but he could not walk far with comfort in his padded shoes and had to return before he had worked off his restlessness. He intended to go to his room, pull the mattress to the floor, and tumble for half an hour, the most effective way he knew to relax his muscles. But when he got back to the hotel, Danielle was waiting for him in the lobby.

She looked extraordinarily young and pretty in slacks and a slipover that emphasized the trim neatness of her figure almost as well as the Bikini. She said, "Claude had to close up for the afternoon. The beach was too flooded for business."

He waited for her to go on. It was not a reason for her call on Mr. Burns, and he thought she was hesitating to explain further.

But she was as direct as ever. She said, "Why did your friend want to meet me?"

"Any young man would want to meet you, Danielle."

"Please. I have a right to know."

"He was there, you were there, I introduced him. That's all."

"That's not all. He stayed for half an hour after you left, and it wasn't because he enjoyed standing in water up to his ankles. Was it?"

He sat down beside her. While he was trying to decide how much to tell her about Paul, she said, "I don't know what it was I said the other night that offended you. It must have been when I was talking about Claude and getting married, those things. I suppose I was too clear about what I wanted for myself. But French women don't look at such things as American women do, Mr. Burns. We're more practical than romantic. Whatever it was—"

"I wish I could convince you that you said nothing wrong at all, Danielle."

"Whatever I said, it was honest. Please be honest with me. Why did your friend want so much to be introduced?"

"You wouldn't accept an explanation that he just happened to be there, and that an introduction was polite?"

"Not in his case. There's something about me that particularly interests le Comte du Pré de la Tour. I want to know what it is."

"You're very acute."

"It wasn't hard to tell. He didn't try to hide it. Even Claude noticed something."

"What did he tell you about himself?"

"Nothing. He asked questions, who I was, and where I came from, where I was born. He wasn't impertinent, but he kept looking at me in a strange way, as if—I don't know, exactly. It wasn't just because of the Bikini. I'm used to that look. His was different. And when he went away, he asked me if he could come to the beach again.

That's a stupid question, and I know he isn't stupid." As an afterthought, she added, "Neither am I."

"No. You're not. And I suppose you are entitled to an explanation, although I hadn't expected to make one."

He told her about Paul and Lisa. His own acquaintance with Paul he did not explain, implying only that it had been in the United States rather than in France, and that he had known Lisa before she died. He told her of Paul's feeling for Lisa, and how he had reacted to her death. He said, "He saw us together one night and was struck by your resemblance to her. He couldn't get you out of his mind. He asked me to introduce him. I did. That's all."

She was silent, thoughtful. He said, "I think he only wants to talk to you, try to disassociate you from his wife, get you out of his head. It needn't end that way, though. He's very wealthy."

"Wealthy enough to afford a *petite amie?*"

"That's what I meant if *petite amie* means what I think it does. But it could go farther than that. You might even end up as the countess, if you handle him right."

"There's a difference between being practical and being cold-blooded, Mr. Burns."

"I'm not being cold-blooded. You asked me to be honest, so I'm telling you what I think. You want a husband with money or brains, or both. He has both, plus a title, good manners, good looks, and good blood. Any woman would be lucky to get him. He was emotionally dependent on Lisa and he needs someone to take her place. You're already there, in his mind. I think you would make him a better wife than a *petite amie,* but one could lead to the other. You might even fall in love with him, in time. If I were you, I'd make every effort not to let him get me out of his mind."

"Thank you, Mr. Burns. It's what I wanted to know."

She stood up to leave. He stopped her.

"Let's be friends again, Danielle."

She smiled, and put out her hand to him. He took it for a moment, felt the firm clasp of her fingers, then watched her walk away, and thought he had never seen anyone who could lend so much *chic* to beach slacks and a sweater. He was not ordinarily impressed by *chic,* since all French girls were born with it, rich and poor alike. Danielle was exceptional. Lady's maid or countess, she would never be otherwise.

~§~

The *mistral* had stopped blowing when he made the rendezvous on the hillside at midnight. The Brazilians came in at one o'clock, early for them. He expected to hear a quarrel, but it did not come. The lights went off before two. At dawn the milk cart came clattering over the hill. Nothing else had happened.

Before they separated, Coco told him that Le Borgne was complaining of rheumatism after sleeping on the ground of their cave. Le Borgne had nothing else to report except that preparations were going forward at the Combe d'Or for the coming *gala.* Lights were being strung over the *terrasse* and through the château gardens.

"One Eye says if they keep stringing lights, there won't be any way for a thief to approach the house except by burrowing," Coco said.

"He'll burrow, then," John said. "There'll be two or three hundred million francs there for the taking. I wouldn't pass it up."

"You wouldn't pass up this Brazilian *poule,* either, and what good has it done us?" Coco did not enjoy life in the cave any more than Le Borgne. It soured him on everything. "I think this dung-heap of a thief has retired for good."

Michel said, "It's only two days since the last theft. Patience."

"I spit in the face of patience! You can talk. You sleep in a warm bed when you sleep. I sleep on a layer of pebbles."

"They'll give you a warm bed at the nearest jail if you want one," John said. "Stop grumbling."

Coco growled apologetically. "Eh, don't mind me. I have to grumble for the exercise. Tomorrow night at the same time. And if he does come, I want first clout at him, to pay for the pebbles."

He slapped his palm with the limber, shot-loaded leather of his skull-cracker.

John was back at the Midi by sunrise. He stopped to chat for a moment with the doorman about roulette and his luck for the evening. Afterward he slept, woke at noon, and read the newspapers.

Nice-Matin repeated its leader of the previous day, word for word. *What Arrest, and How Soon, M. Lepic?* There was no other news. The Sûreté *agents* patrolled La Croisette as usual, the sun was hot, the beach crowded, the sea green and inviting in the shallows, deep blue farther out.

He did not call on Bellini. There was nothing for him to report, and Bellini would get word to him if there was anything he should know. When he made his regular afternoon appearance on the beach, he found Francie and her mother back in their usual places.

Mrs. Stevens was asleep in the shade of the umbrella. Francie was reading. She closed her book when she saw John, and came to meet him.

"Let's go for a stroll. I've got something to tell you."

They walked down the promenade to the far end of the beach, past the Hotel Napoleon and beyond, to where there was no beach, nothing but rocks and a solitary fisherman squatting with his pole. The patrolling *agents* never came that far.

Francie said, "Mother and I spent all day yesterday cultivating the Sanfords. We've been invited to the *gala*. So have you."

"Why me?"

"I thought you might want to be there, if you expect something to happen. You don't have to go if you don't want to."

"I'll probably still be watching the other house, but I've got three men covering the Combe d'Or. They'll take care of anything that happens."

"I just thought—I wanted to help, if I could."

He had not counted on the possibility that she would take positive action on her own, and he did not want to find himself at cross purposes with her. His arrangements were too final, too carefully planned. He said, "I don't need your help, Francie. All I asked is that you keep quiet and give me a chance to work things out my own way."

"Are you so sure of yourself that you can't accept help?"

She said it in the same way Paul had said it, half angrily.

"I'm not sure of myself at all," John answered. "I don't even know that what I'm trying to do will work. If it doesn't, if I slip somewhere and get caught, it won't do you any good to be mixed up with me and a gang of ex-convicts."

"I'm not worried about it."

"There's no sense in taking unnecessary risks."

"Maybe I want to." She was defiant. "Maybe I've found what your friend Bellini would call a reason for existence."

"Excitement?"

He regretted it immediately. Her expression changed. She said, "Let's go back."

They did not speak again until they were back at the beach where Mrs. Stevens slept on the sand. Francie picked up her book.

"The *gala* begins next Friday night, and the house guests will stay through Sunday," she told him. She was again the girl he had known before she guessed his identity; withdrawn, disinterested. "If you intend to go, we'd better go together, since I had to explain to Mrs. Sanford that we were particularly close friends in order to get you the invitation. I'll try not to bother you unnecessarily until then."

There was nothing he could say. He left her as he had found her, reading.

~§~

The *mistral* began to blow again that night, springing up suddenly after he had reached his place in the stream bed and removed his padded shoes and harness. It was always an unpredictable wind. It came from the southwest when it blew, but nothing else about it was consistent. Sometimes it was cool, sometimes hot and dry, sometimes warm and moist, bringing rain. That night it was dry and warm, blowing out of a clear sky. It made a rushing noise over his head where he lay, whipped the scrub brush of the hillside, bent the trees, made the hanging light across the road from the villa dance on its pole, so that shadows fled sideways and jumped quickly back into position again. The stars overhead were bright, but the thin, fading moon would not rise until just before dawn. It was the kind of a night that Le Chat had always liked best; darkness, moving shadows to hide another moving shadow, a rush of wind and the scrape of rubbing branches to hide small noises. There was a charged, electric feeling in the air. All three of the watchers on the hill felt it.

The light on the pole made a tinny creaking noise as it swung. Occasionally an automobile came up the road from the village below, but none stopped. From where John lay, he could see lights in the windows of the nearest houses. The music of a radio or phonograph came faintly from somewhere, but it did not continue for long. House lights gradually went out at ground-floor level, came on again upstairs, and winked out one by one as the households slept.

He felt thirsty. The stream whispered in its bed a few feet behind him, but he did not trust the water. He broke a dry twig from a bush at his elbow and put it in his mouth to start the saliva running, then watched the shadows. Once or twice he changed his position to avoid crushing for too long the grass on which he lay.

His mind followed the same track it had followed for two nights. He hardly felt even curiosity about the thief any more. He had thought his way completely around the closed circle which was the mystery of the thief's identity, and was finished with it. All he could do now was wait for the moment of action, hope that it would come as he had planned it. In the meantime, his thoughts were of Paul, and Bellini, and Francie, and Oriol, and Danielle, and the discovery he had made about himself, that he was still a thief.

He had had time to reason it out. The distinction between thief and non-thief was a state of mind, not a surreptitious entry through a skylight. Just as a burglar did not cease to be a burglar between actual housebreakings, he need not necessarily change his nature after age and stiffening joints made it impossible for him to climb to second-story windows. He himself was a thief because his attitude toward stealing had never changed. He was retired, not reformed. He was still Le Chat, with Le Chat's mind.

Or I wouldn't be here doing the Sûreté's work for them, he thought. Set a thief to catch a thief. Whoever had said it first must have been a thief himself, to see so clearly the thief's mind.

He changed his position on the grass.

Souza and his wife came in at two. They were still on good terms. John heard the woman's low, lazy laugh at something her husband said while he was locking the car. He thought, No arguments tonight—early to bed. And then, checking the time in his mind, calculating how long it would take them to fall into the first sound sleep, he thought, Three-thirty to four.

He watched the shadows more carefully now, and did not change his position again or think too much. The lights came on in the house, burned for a time, and went out. Somewhere in the distance a dog barked two or three times. There was no other sound but the rush of the wind through the scrub and the tinny creak of the street light on its pole, no movement but the dancing shadows.

Souza's first shout, more than an hour later, was a wordless yell, meaningless. John thought the Brazilian must be having a nightmare. He had seen nothing, heard nothing but the normal night sounds, and neither

Coco nor Michel had come from their posts to report anything unusual. Yet in an instant Souza was screaming, *"A moi! Vite! Vite! A moi! A moi!"* and there were other noises.

A light came on in one of the bedrooms, where Souza was shouting. Almost immediately a woman screamed, and Souza gave a different kind of shout, this time of pain. Another male voice inside the house called urgently, words that John could not distinguish. The woman screamed again.

The rest followed quickly. His position at the side of the villa kept him from seeing the fugitive until a man's figure appeared suddenly on the roof of the portico, outlined by the glow of the light in the road. He hesitated there, looked back, then climbed a railing and jumped, disappearing from sight as he dropped into the garden below. Seconds later another man stood on the roof of the portico.

He did not follow the first man over the railing. Something bright gleamed in his hand. John saw, from the strained tenseness of his figure and the way he stood, his extended arm following like a pointer the track of the invisible running man in the garden, that it was a pistol he held, and that he was waiting for a clear shot.

The second man was not the right size for Souza. That much he saw as well before the pistol roared, steadied, and roared again. His mind cried silently, Don't kill him! He's no good to anyone, dead. But then he heard the scrape of running feet on gravel and knew the fugitive had safely reached the road. He was running for the sheltering scrub of brush across the road from the villa. John knew how quickly a man could disappear from sight and how safely he could hide in that protection. Only a *maquisard* could find another man in the *maquis*. If the runner ever reached it—

He slid backward into the stream bed, ducked his head and shoulders, and crawled quickly through the mud and water of the culvert. He heard the gun roar again as he went in, then only the noise of his own splashing. There was no further sound when he came out on the far side of the road, neither running feet nor gunshots, nothing but the tinny creak of the hanging light on its pole, now almost over his head. But there was a ditch along the roadside, and a screen of grass to hide him. When the man with the gun came to roll the body in the road so he could see its face, and stood for a long minute silently looking down at it, John was close enough to hear his heavy breathing.

Because he had never seen Commissaire Division-naire Lepic before, he did not recognize him. But the dead man was the dark-faced gypsy from whose knife thrust he had saved Coco, and when it was safe for him to move again he went back through the culvert and up the hillside to the rendezvous, to tell Coco and Michel that their patience had been for nothing. Another trap had failed.

6

"I KNOW HE WASN'T THE MAN we were expecting," he told Bellini, hours later. "It's out of the question."

"I don't see how you can be so certain," Bellini said. "It seems to me that you are challenging your own judgment. I agree that mine is also open to challenge, since it was my own man who betrayed us." He chuckled. "Honor among thieves is not what it used to be. Still, the gypsy was a burglar, as we know."

"A burglar," John agreed. "But not the burglar. He couldn't have robbed Mrs. Stevens, any more than he could have climbed the marquee chain in Monte Carlo. Both of those thefts were done by a professional."

"He was not entirely an amateur, John."

"I mean that he didn't have the physical ability to pull himself two stories up a hanging rope. It takes training, and more than average strength. He tried to cut Coco's throat the first time I talked to them together. I stopped him. I had my hands on him, and I know he can't be our man. It would be enough for me even without the other things, the clumsy way he jumped, and running under the light where Lepic could get a clear shot at him, and using his knife on Souza. He wasn't our man. There isn't a possibility I could be wrong."

"Lepic doesn't seem to agree with you."

Bellini indicated the newspaper he had been reading.

John said, "I'm not convinced of that. What he believes and what he says for publication needn't be the same thing. I think he must know as well as I do that his scheme missed fire. But he promised an arrest, and the gypsy can't deny anything. And it makes Lepic look good."

The story did make Lepic look good. Although it had been written hurriedly to meet a deadline, and there had not been time for photographs, the *commissaire divisionnaire* had come into his own at last. The black scarehead said, *Le Voleur Est Mort!* The article that followed went on to credit Lepic with a clever scheme to trap the jewel thief who had been terrorizing the Côte for so many weeks. He was quoted as saying that the failures of the Sûreté Nationale's most expert men to find and identify John Robie, the man once known as Le Chat, had led him to doubt that the thief they hunted was in fact Le Chat, in spite of a universal acceptance of this belief by others. At the same time that he had continued his search for John Robie, he had arranged an inviting trap for the actual thief with the co-operation of M. and Mme. Souza.

Several sentences about M. Souza's coffee plan-tations and Mme. Souza's jewels followed. The Souzas had been approached by the *commissaire division-naire* and asked for their help shortly after the robbery,

in Nice, of the wife of the Member of the Chamber of
Deputies, on Lepic's assumption, proved correct by the
later theft from Mrs. Stevens, that the thief would move
to Cannes. Lepic, working in the utmost secrecy so as
not to betray his plans, had persuaded Mme. Souza to
make a deliberate public display of her jewelry, and had
passed several nights in the Souza villa, smuggling
himself in each night from the back of Souza's car. He
was on hand when the thief at last made the expected
attempt. The robber had apparently entered the house
sometime after the servant went to bed and before the
Souzas returned from an evening at Antibes, bringing
Lepic with them. Souza, whose part it was to remain
awake and give warning to Lepic, had instead grappled
bravely with the burglar in Mme. Souza's bedroom, and
sustained a superficial but painful stab wound in the
chest. Lepic, arriving on the scene too late to seize the
thief before he could make his escape from the house,
had shot, meaning to wound him and bring him down.
The bullet, regrettably, had struck a vital spot. The
unfortunate criminal had paid for his misdeeds with his
life, *hélas!*

Hélas! was conventional in any French newspaper
report of violent death. It was the reporter's contribution. Lepic had not expressed his own feelings, neither
regret nor triumph. He was a faithful public servant
reporting the successful performance of a disagreeable
duty so that his detractors could judge for themselves
what kind of a man they had been criticizing.

"Do you think he really shot only to wound?" Bellini

said.

"I don't know. He was aiming carefully, but it's hard to tell what he was aiming at. He reminded me of the way Le Borgne looked when he used to sharpshoot at Germans through a window at night. He meant to get a hit. I don't think it mattered to him where it was"

"If he believes the story himself, he must have wanted the gypsy alive, to talk. The whole thing will collapse unless he traces the stolen jewelry."

"The reporter makes the same point. It's only a suggestion so far, but it will be made again, and somebody is bound to wonder about the difference in techniques, in time. Lepic will be in worse hot water than before."

"Still, even if he knows the truth himself, he has a breathing spell. He's escaped further criticism, for the time being at least, he leaves the thief—meaning you—believing that all is in order for another operation, and he can still remain in the field of action with the excuse that he is tracing the jewelry. I think he may be even cleverer than we expect, John."

"If it's clever to be able to make something out of a blunder," John said. "Whatever he believes or doesn't believe, he was a fool to try it alone. He must have wanted the personal glory badly. Two or three men there with him would have made it unnecessary to shoot."

Bellini chuckled slyly. "You watched Mrs. Stevens alone."

"That was a different thing."

"I know, I know. I was making a joke to express my relief that the gypsy is not alive to talk about us. Actually

his death may help us by relieving the pressure. The
Sûreté made several arrests yesterday in Toulon and
Marseilles, including more of my own men."

"Jean-Pierre?"

"Jean-Pierre is safe for a while yet, as long as he does
not come out of his hole." Bellini giggled. "Although he
says he finds the inactivity depressing, as well as bad for
his business. One thing I do not understand is how the
gypsy hoped to succeed with the robbery, John. He
knew you were watching the house."

"I gave him what amounted to a blueprint showing
how to do it. I told him just what to expect from the
thief, when we would wait for him and where we would
watch. He did it the other way. He got in before we were
there, and I suppose he meant to leave the house after
we had gone, before anyone awoke. It might have
worked, except for Lepic."

"I should have suspected the gypsy when he offered
no protest at being taken off a job promising such a
good reward." Bellini shook his head. "My judgment is
failing. What shall we do now?"

"We still have the Sanford *gala.* Do you have anyone
who can get close to Lepic?"

"Possibly. What do you want to know?"

"Whether or not he really believes the story himself.
I'd like to make sure. If he doesn't he'll certainly cover
the *gala,* and that means you'll have to take Le Borgne
and his men off before they stumble over a *flic* in the
dark."

"Who will watch the Combe d'Or in the event that Lepic

does not?"

"I will. As a guest. Francie Stevens got me an invitation, which I declined and which I'm now going to accept after excusing myself for hurting her feelings by refusing her help."

Bellini said, "It is always dangerous."

"To go to the *gala* as a guest? Not as dangerous as it would be for Le Borgne and his men outside."

"That danger is the same one you have been in since you became Mr. Burns. I was referring to the danger you risk when you hurt a woman's feelings by rejecting that which she offers voluntarily, whatever it may be." Bellini beamed wisely through his glasses, looking more like an owl than ever. "My judgment is still good about women. I think I should meet Miss Stevens and talk to her myself before you go any further."

"She's no mystery, Bellini. You've imagined her to be something she isn't."

"Nevertheless, do me the favor."

John shrugged. "I'll bring her this afternoon. After I've knocked my head on the ground for her, first."

Bellini tittered. "Pride, John?"

"I don't know. I'm having trouble understanding what it is I feel, these days. All I'm sure of is that I wish I could finish it off, one way or another."

~§~

Mr. Paige also wanted to finish off, one way or another. He had a check from the London insurance company for sixty-two thousand dollars in his pocket, payable to Mrs. Stevens, when he read the newspaper story with his lunchtime cup of tea. The size of the settlement check made him more than ordinarily careful. After he had finished his tea, he went to the local *commissariat* and asked for an interview with Lepic, who did not want to see anyone but knew better than to refuse to talk to a man who was able to go over his head.

Mr. Paige came right to the point.

"Sixty-two thousand dollars," he said. "That's twenty-two hundred pounds, nearly twenty-two million francs. I've the check in my pocket now. Speaking in confidence, of course"—he pulled at his mustache—"I'm very much disinclined to deliver it if a recovery of the stolen jewelry appears imminent. Thought I'd speak with you about it first."

Lepic said, "I haven't been able to trace her jewelry yet, or any of the jewelry. It will take time."

Mr. Paige thoughtfully teased his mustache tips to needle points. "Shooting the thief wasn't wise, if I may say so."

"No one regrets his death more than I do," Lepic said stonily. "It was an unfortunate accident."

"Quite. You're positive he was the man?"

"I have no reason to change the story I gave to the newspapers."

"That's hardly a direct answer, Commissioner," Mr. Paige said mildly.

"It's the only one I can give you."

Mr. Paige knew when he was wasting his time. He stood up to leave.

"You know your business." He spoke as mildly as before, "I won't try to interfere. But my principals are not going to be satisfied for a minute until the jewelry comes to light, and my principals have influence in Paris. Disposing of the thief may be enough for your superiors. It won't be for the insurance company. The jewels, Commissioner, the jewels. The total is now one hundred and twenty-two million francs, if you have forgotten."

When he had gone, Lepic locked the door, sat down loosely, and looked blankly at the floor.

His ambition had put him into his own trap. Ambition and the desire for the glory that would come from a single-handed capture of Le Chat had led him into the first mistake. The rest had followed because of his confidence in his own cleverness.

He had set a trap for a thief, the trap had clicked shut, a thief had been caught. He had not meant to kill the gypsy. It had been an accident, as he said; he wanted a confession and the jewelry, not the thief's life. But a dead thief was still the sign of success, and when he stood in the road looking down at the gypsy's body, already savoring the public triumph he had earned, and saw that the man he had killed was not John Robie, it was harder for him to discard the fact of success than it was to discard his belief that John Robie was the man he wanted. The first lie had been to deny that he had expected to catch John Robie. He had tried to qualify his story to the newspaper reporters, but he could not bring himself to confess failure. Now it was too late. The story had traveled faster than he expected. Already the Ministry had telephoned from Paris to congratulate him on his success.

There had been a reprimand along with the congratulations. Single-handed strategies were not orthodox procedure, and the Ministry did not approve of killings, even of criminals by officers of the law. He was reminded that *la belle France* was not Chicago. But results were what counted. The Ministry expressed its appreciation of his success, and implied that it would express its appreciation even more tangibly when he had effected a return of the stolen jewelry to its proper owners. That was important. Most important.

He could have denied the truth of the story then. He had not been able wholly to abandon the hope that he might still have his reward. But when Oriol, driven at last out of his shell by the report of the death, had come to see the body for himself and flatly told Lepic that he knew the dead man was not the thief, assuming the blame for his own mistakes so that Lepic would not give up the hunt and promising to make a disclosure, at any expense to himself, if it were not carried on, Lepic's shaky hopes crashed.

He did not waste his energy damning Oriol for not coming forward sooner. He needed Oriol's help.

"I tell you frankly that your mistakes will cost you your position, Commissaire," he had said. "As my mistakes will cost me mine, unless between us we find Robie quickly. I have gone too far to change my story now, and the recovery of the jewelry is absolutely essential. No one will ask questions if we deliver the jewels. The whole world will ask questions if we do not. You are sure you can recognize him? We must be absolutely certain we have the right man this time."

"As sure as I am that I could recognize my own brother. I played *boule* with him for three years, drank his wine, and had him in my own home." Oriol spread his thick, callused peasant's fingers, then closed them into a hard fist. "He gave me his word that he was through thieving."

"I give you mine that we will both be publicly disgraced if we do not take him before he can steal again. We still have a chance. Go home, keep your mouth shut, and stay in touch with me."

"What are you going to do?"

"Be on hand when he attempts another theft."

"When will that be?"

"I can do no more than make a guess, Commissaire. If it is wrong, we are finished."

Mr. Paige's later visit had only made it clearer.

Mr. Paige was far from satisfied when he left Lepic. He strongly doubted that Lepic believed all he said he believed, and he was not hopeful about a quick recovery of the stolen jewelry in any event. But the possibility kept him from delivering the check for sixty-two thousand dollars to Mrs. Stevens, and when she trapped him in the lobby of the Midi to ask when she could expect her money, he told her that the *commissaire divisionnaire* had said she might expect her jewels back very soon instead. He was vague about how soon was very soon.

"But I have to have *something* before Friday night," she explained impatiently. "I'm going to the Sanford *gala*; everyone who is anyone will be there dripping with diamonds, and I can't go practically stark naked, with nothing but a single necklace. Now that they've finished with this awful thief, poor man, I don't see why I can't have either the money or my jewelry."

"Quite. Quite. Unfortunately the money hasn't been forwarded, and the jewels haven't yet been recovered."

"Well, why haven't they?"

Mr. Paige was so uncomfortable because of the bare-faced lie that he twirled his mustache points the wrong way, unwinding them. "The thief wasn't able to tell anyone what he had done with the stolen goods."

"They shouldn't have shot him until he did, then."

"Quite."

"Didn't he leave a map or something?"

"I'm afraid not."

"Well, all I can say is that it was all very badly managed. I never thought much of that Lepic character anyway. Do you think he can find my jewelry before Friday night? That's two days and a few hours."

"I'm sure he'll try his best."

Mrs. Stevens sniffed. "Whatever that is."

She told Francie about it during the afternoon. She had decided that an immediate investment of her own money at Cartier's and Van Cleef & Arpels was the only sure way to insure herself against appearing barefooted and in rags at the *gala*. It kept her running from shop to shop for the rest of the day. John found Francie alone on the beach and was able to make his apology without witnesses.

She wore the zebra-striped bathing suit, and lay sunning herself on the sand with a straw beach hat over her face to shield her eyes from the glare. When he spoke to her, she removed the hat long enough to say hello, then put it back so that it hid her face again. It was not a gesture of rudeness; her greeting was pleasant enough, and the hot sun made an eye shade excusable. But she withdrew behind the hat as effectively as if it had been a door closed between them.

He said, "I shouldn't have said what I did the other day, Francie. I did it without thinking, and I apologize for it. I would have apologized even if I didn't intend to ask for the help you offered me and I refused."

The hat kept him from seeing her expression. She took so long to answer that he thought she as ignoring him. She said at last, "I was trying to bring myself to apologize to you."

"To me? Why?"

"For not minding my own business. I should have realized that you would have to manage your own affairs in your own way. I did, later. That's why I haven't pestered you since."

"You never pestered me, Francie. I tried to explain. I don't want you to get into trouble if something goes wrong. I wouldn't ask you now if there was any way to avoid it."

"Isn't it all over?"

"No. Lepic didn't get the right thief."

"He told Mr. Paige he had, according to Mother."

"I think it's a smoke screen. I think he's inviting another theft. Whether he is or not, I still expect something to happen at the *gala,* and I want to be there." A moment later he added, "You won't involve yourself. All you have to know about me is that I'm a fellow American at the hotel."

"So that in an emergency I can always claim that you deceived me as you deceived everyone else, and go my own merry way unsullied? Is that what you mean?"

"Yes."

He thought she sighed. He couldn't be certain. He couldn't tell what she was thinking by watching a straw hat, and he doubted that even if she took the hat away her face would tell him anything. His apology hadn't changed things. She was still the girl he had known first, the one who could sit at a table with him and others, smile when somebody spoke to her, and not be there at all. He had the feeling that she was neither for him nor against him now, only withdrawn.

He said, "Do you still want to meet Bellini? He asked me to bring you to see him."

"When?"

"Any time. Right now, if you like. It's not far."

He expected her to say that Bellini no longer interested her. Instead, she pushed the hat away, stood up, reached for a robe hanging on the back of a beach chair and belted it around her.

"I think meeting Mr. Bellini would be very interesting." She brushed the sand from her slim bare legs. "I hope he knows something about American girls."

"He won't be surprised to have you call in a bathing suit, if that's what you mean."

"That's what I mean. What else would I mean?"

He didn't know what she meant.

~§~

Bellini bubbled welcome like a boiling teakettle when John brought Francie into the little office.

"I am honored," he said breathlessly. "I am delighted." He put his heels together, bowing deeply. "I am overwhelmed. Do sit down, Miss Stevens. No, not that chair. That is for visitors whom I wish to drive away as quickly as possible. Wait."

He struggled to pull up another chair that was too heavy for his bad arm, chuckling at his own clumsiness.

"How is your charming mother?" he said, beaming, red-faced from the effort before John could help him. "I have not yet had the pleasure of meeting her, although I know her by sight. A lovely woman."

"Very well. The robbery upset her, but she's recovered from it."

"There is no further news of her jewelry?"

"No."

"Regrettable. Regrettable." Bellini peered amiably over

his spectacles. "I am sure it will be recovered in time, and in any event there is always the compensation of the insurance. I am a great believer in insurance of all kinds, particularly against theft. There are so many dishonest people about nowadays. One cannot be too careful."

Francie laughed. Bellini, delighted with his own wit, laughed with her.

She said, "I thought John was exaggerating when he told me about you. I see that he wasn't."

"He has been talking about me?" Bellini looked at him with mock reproach. "I don't trust him. He has probably filled you with all kinds of wild stories."

"Very wild."

"He is like that."

"He told me something that I found very interesting. Something you said about me and my reason for existence, or lack of one."

"It was tactless of him." Bellini shrugged his good shoulder. "But it is true enough. At the time, I had not been able to classify you, and it disturbed me. I had a certain professional interest in you and your mother. John has undoubtedly told you about our little plot."

"What do you mean by 'at the time,' Mr. Bellini?"

"Since then I have discovered your *raison d'être,* of course."

"What is it?"

Bellini giggled. "Don't you know, Miss Stevens?"

They looked at each other for a long moment, the fat, round little man beaming brightly, the girl calm and serious. Something that John did not understand passed between them, because Francie said at last, "I wasn't even sure myself. Is it so obvious?"

Bellini raised his hands in exaggerated horror. "It's not obvious at all. Quite the contrary. I arrived at it only by a process of elimination."

John said, "What are you talking about?"

"Miss Stevens's reason for existence, naturally."

"What is it?"

Francie tried to say something. Bellini spoke first.

"Currently, I would say it was to help us at the difficult task we have set ourselves. Always one *raison d'être* at a time. Do you agree, Miss Stevens?"

She nodded.

The secret she shared with Bellini was too subtle for John. As Bellini had once told him, his mind did not lend itself to subtleties. He said, "In that case, we had better get down to it. Did you warn Le Borgne off?"

"He will have the message by now."

"Good. The next most important thing is to try to find out what Lepic intends to do, if we can. We have two days."

"I have had no luck with him, so far. He does not talk where any of my men can overhear, if he talks at all." Bellini cocked his head to look at Francie. "Perhaps with an attractive spy in the enemy camp, one with a legitimate reason to ask leading questions because of her mother's jewelry—"

He left the suggestion dangling delicately in the air.

Francie said, "I'll call on Mr. Lepic in the morning,

unless John objects."

"Why should he object?"

"He doesn't want me to soil my morals with anything underhanded. He's a great believer in moral values. We had an argument about it once."

Bellini looked from her to John and back, then began to giggle. Francie was still serious. It irritated John, not so much that she mocked him but because she did it so gravely. He wished Bellini didn't find something to laugh at in everything she said.

~§~

The following day was Thursday. The newspapers had had time to give proper attention to the death of the thief. There were photographs, one of the villa where the robbery had been attempted, one of Lepic, his back to the camera in accordance with Sûreté procedures, pointing to the portico from which the gypsy had made his leap, an excellent studio portrait of Mme. Souza wearing a low-cut gown and most of her jewelry, a photograph of the dead man's head and shoulders. The gypsy was identified by name, and his known record reviewed—several arrests on suspicion, detentions at the *maison d'arrêt,* no convictions. There followed a tabulation of the thefts that had occurred on the Côte since the beginning of the summer season, listing names, dates, locations, and amounts stolen.

The accompanying editorial comments, although generally kind to Lepic in a cautious way, still suggested that the death of the thief would prove to be unfortunate in more respects than one, since none of the stolen jewels had been traced. One writer who had been most critical of the Sûreté was not even kind. In his opinion a job half done was not finished, and a botched job worse than one half done. Where were the stolen jewels, M. Lepic? There was an implication that the writer intended to withhold judgment, a hint that he, at least, was not entirely convinced of the truth of Lepic's story.

"It will be more than a hint in a few days," John told Francie when she came to report the results of her call at the *commissariat*. "Even if the thief doesn't break into print again, Lepic has got to deliver before somebody challenges him to prove what he says. Do you think he believes it, or is it all a bluff?"

"I don't know. I couldn't get a thing out of him. Mr. Paige told Mother that the insurance money would be held up until the police either recover her jewels or say that they haven't been able to trace them, so I had a good excuse to ask for something definite from Lepic. All he would tell me was that he expected to be able to locate the jewelry within a few days. He wouldn't budge from that."

"He must know he failed. He can't have gone as far as he has in the Sûreté without brains. He'll have to cover the *gala*."

"If you're certain of that, you needn't risk going yourself."

"It doesn't follow. If I thought he and the Sûreté could handle it, I wouldn't be here at all."

"But it will be so dangerous for you. If you're right about him, he'll be expecting you there."

"Mr. Burns has been under his nose all the time. He hasn't seen me yet."

"Mr. Burns can't hope to go on deceiving the whole Sûreté Nationale forever."

It was developing into another argument. He had got along better with Francie when she was urging him to let her help steal her mother's jewels for a thrill.

He said, "Let me worry about it. I know what I'm doing. You said the other day that you weren't going to interfere."

"I meant it when I said it. I didn't know you were going to be such a complete fool."

"Whether I am or not, it's no more true now than it was when I started. I'm not risking anything I haven't been risking all along. If you really want to help me, do what I ask you to do and let me handle the rest in my own way."

He was talking to the air before he finished. She had walked away.

She avoided him until Friday afternoon, when they were to leave for the Sanford party. On Friday morning the follow-up stories of the thief's death had moved to the middle pages of the newspapers and appeared side by side with a list of guests who were to attend the annual *fin de saison* gala week-end at the Château Combe d'Or. Mimi Sanford had arranged for proper publicity.

The hard-headed editorial writer pointed out how fortunate it was for all concerned that Commissaire Divisionnaire Lepic had disposed of the thief in good time, since otherwise the *gala* would offer an unparalleled opportunity to bring off the robbery of a lifetime. Among the expected guests was the most famous of all Parisian *couturières,* as well known for her jewelry as for her dress creations, and a one-time American cinema star, now the Princess Lila, whose late wedding to her royal Oriental bridegroom had made international headlines partly because she had been married in a bridal gown decorated with six thousand precious stones, wearing with it her husband's gift of a string of pearls said to have been originally presented to the Queen of Sheba by King Solomon. The prince, occupied with affairs of state, would not attend the *gala,* but there were others nearly as important to Mimi Sanford's social triumph—the heir to a doubtful European throne, a Turkish cabinet minister, minor celebrities of various nationalities, and, at the bottom of the list, Mme. Maude Stevens, Mlle. Francie Stevens, M. Jack Burns, and M. le Comte du Pré de la Tour.

The unexpected news that Paul would be at the *gala* was a blow. John and Francie had met in the lobby and were waiting with the luggage while Mrs. Stevens made a last minute flying trip to Cartier's to buy a diamond sunburst she could not possibly do without after hearing about Princess Lila's pearls, which were insured for a hundred thousand pounds sterling. John said, "I didn't know Paul even knew the Sanfords. I'll be handcuffed with him there. He'll keep his eye on me every minute."

"Doesn't he know the truth?"

"Only that I'm Le Chat. He's tried twice to bribe me to stop stealing."

"Why haven't you told him the rest of it?"

"The same reason I didn't want to tell you. I don't want to get him involved."

"You'll have to involve him now. If he's your friend, why do you hesitate to trust him?"

"I do trust him. I have to trust him. He could give me away any time. But trusting him and trying to explain to him are two different things."

"Why? You explained to me, when you had to."

The trend of the conversation, why did he do this, and why not that, and what was his reason for another thing, told him that she was inviting him to reveal more for her to criticize. Ever since their visit to Bellini he had been conscious that her attitude toward him had changed. He did not understand the change, except that it had made her antagonistic in a strange way, not so much of what he did, but of what he was, as a person. He gave her another opportunity to call him a fool.

He said, "If I hurt your feelings again, it's because you asked me to. Paul is honest in a way you aren't. You're not a thief, but you would have helped me steal your mother's jewels. Maybe a touch of crookedness will help you understand why I feel a debt to Bellini and Coco and Le Borgne. It's the only thing that kept me here from the beginning. I could have got away, but they were my friends, the only friends I ever had before

I knew Paul. That they're crooks doesn't make any difference. I owe them my help. Paul could never understand that. I don't know how to describe him except to say that he's so honest himself he can't even picture thieves and honest men in the same frame. You have to be one or the other, in his eyes; an honest man on the side of honest men, or a thief among thieves. He can understand me as one or the other. But for what I am, a crook who doesn't behave like a crook and still won't cross over—"

He made a helpless gesture. He could not explain further.

Francie said, "He should be able to understand loyalty."

"He'd argue that I don't owe any to thieves, if I'm not one myself. I can't make him see that being a thief is a state of mind. He'll pin me in a corner and argue me blind, whatever I tell him or don't tell him. I've got to keep him away from the *gala,* if I can."

"How?"

"I don't know. If I can't do anything else I'll have to try to explain, but I don't want to."

"Any more than you wanted to explain to me."

"No."

"You're even a bigger fool than I thought you were."

She said it just as she had said it before. It was neither an insult nor a joke, only a statement of fact.

"You'll convince me in time. Excuse me for a few minutes. I have to make a telephone call."

He left her before she could see his irritation, and wondered what had made him think he could explain to her. The growing antagonism between them was as tangible as a fence.

There was a telephone in the hotel foyer. He called the *domaine* and was told that M. le Comte would not return before Monday. Paul's housekeeper could not say if he had gone directly to the Combe d'Or. Because he knew of only one other place where he might hear news of Paul, he walked down the promenade to La Plage Nautique.

Claude and Danielle were quarreling about something. Claude said, *"Ah, flûte,"* insultingly and walked away as John came down the steps. He did not bother to turn on his professional smile for Mr. Burns's benefit.

Danielle was flushed and angry. John said, "Have you seen Paul?"

"He was here this morning. I don't think he'll ever come back. That pig Claude! I could kill him!"

"What happened?"

"He's unbearable!" There were tears in Danielle's eyes. "He—he insulted Paul. He called him an awful name."

"Why? What did Paul do?"

"Nothing, really. But he's been here every day since you brought him, and even Claude couldn't help seeing how he feels about me. This morning Paul asked me to a weekend party at a friend's house, a *gala* some Americans are giving—"

"I know about it. I'm going myself."

"You know how respectable it will be, then. But Claude—oh, he said horrible things to Paul, swore at him, wanted to fight him." She shook her head violently, so that tears flew from her eyelashes. "Paul is so clean and gentle himself. He doesn't understand how anyone can behave like an animal."

"He's made quite an impression on you."

"Of course he has. He's the finest man I ever met."

She wiped her eyes on her wrist. John said, "Are you going to the *gala* with him?"

"I can't. I'd only embarrass him."

"If you mean because someone might ask questions, wonder who you are—"

"It isn't that." She wiped her eyes again. "I'm sure he wants an opportunity to ask me what you thought he might ask. I don't know how to answer him."

"Accept him. He'll give you everything you have always wanted."

"I don't love him, Mr. Burns. I like him a lot, but that's all."

"I thought you had a practical attitude about those things, Danielle."

"Not with Paul. He's too decent. And he was too much in love with Lisa. He told me about her. I can't substitute for her. I can't give him back what he's lost. I'd only make him miserable, in the end. And myself." She sighed unhappily. "I wish you had never brought him here."

"I'm sorry, Danielle. I didn't know it was going to turn out so badly."

She could not tell him anything more, and he knew of

no other place where he might find Paul except at the Combe d'Or itself. It was too late for him to do anything about Paul, either for Danielle's sake or his own. Nothing remained for him but to go to the *gala,* and hope that he would be able to meet the problems there as they arose.

~§~

The Château Combe d'Or was one of the showplaces of the Côte. It stood alone on the top of a hill above Cannes, commanding a view of the entire sweep of sea between the Esterel hills on the west and the Maritime Alps on the east. On a clear day, George Sanford could see from his front window the blue line of Corsica visible to the southeast. The Romans who colonized the Mediterranean coast had first recognized the advantages of the hill as a lookout point, and fortified it. Only the reinforcing wall of the circling road they had built to the hilltop still remained. The crumbling watchtower left behind by the backwash of the Roman Empire had been replaced in the fifteenth century by a stronger, higher tower crowning a stone castle that was part fortress, part pavilion for the favorites of the court. The château had collapsed in places over the centuries, but it had not suffered so badly that Sanford, with plenty of money and shrewd sense of property values, had been unable to see its potentialities.

He was proud of the restoration he had made. An ancient growth of ivy climbing one side of the château to the tower top made the castle appear, from a distance, as medieval as it might have been originally. But part of the old moat that once surrounded it had been turned into an emerald-tiled swimming pool, the rest planted with shrubs and flowers, and the former barren square of the courtyard was now a clipped green lawn between the pool and a wide flagged *terrasse* where guests could dine or dance on a summer evening or drink their host's good brandy and smoke his fine cigars. The château would accommodate fifty guests, and at least once a year it was full. No longer with a running moat and drawbridge to cut it off from the rest of the world, it still had an air of isolation, weather-beaten and ivy-covered, its tower rearing alone at the peak of the hilltop. The terraced gardens on all sides extended to the foot of the hill, where the Roman road began. George Sanford meant to have no neighbors who might build other houses to spoil his view. The Combe d'Or was a retreat for him and his friends.

Most of the other guests had already arrived when the untalkative driver of Bellini's big car brought John, Francie, and Mrs. Stevens to the château late in the afternoon. The swimming pool was full of bathers. Mimi Sanford came dripping from the pool to welcome them and invite them to change for a swim before the sun went down. But she was a good hostess. She would not urge them to do anything they did not want to do, except enjoy themselves. She was delighted that Mr. Burns had been able to accept the invitation to her party, and did not make it necessary for him to explain why he could not accept an invitation to the swimming pool.

He had already studied the floor plans of the château. Mapping the gardens had taken him two successive nights, but Bellini's connections made it easy to obtain copies of the architect's blueprints for the reconstructtion. Bachelor guest quarters were in the west wing, one of two which extended from the main body of the building like arms embracing the *terrasse*. As he had expected, he was given a room in the west wing. Francie and her mother were lodged in the central building, the old castle keep. Since the kitchens, the huge dining hall, and service rooms filled the east wing, he could localize the area in which a thief might expect to find Mimi Sanford's emeralds, the *couturière's* collection, and the Princess Lila's two-hundred-and-eighty-thousand-dollar string of pearls. He had asked Francie to gather as much additional concrete information about the location of guest rooms as possible. Otherwise they had not spoken to each other since leaving the hotel.

The man who carried his bag to his room spoke only French. John thought it was safe for Mr. Burns to have learned enough of the language to ask if le Comte du Pré de la Tour had arrived at the château. The man went to inquire. While John was waiting he locked the door and took from his bag the building plans he had brought with him.

He had not had time to spread them out for further study when a knock interrupted him. He hid the blueprints before he went to the door.

It was Paul. He came in and waited until John had shut the door behind him before he said, "The valet told me you wanted to see me."

"I asked him if you were here. I didn't expect him to send you."

"My room is just across the hall. What do you want?" Paul was quite calm.

"I saw your name on the list of guests. I thought I'd better talk to you."

"If you knew I was going to be here, you shouldn't have come."

"I had to come."

"You'll have to leave, then. I'll drive down to Cannes and telephone you so you can say you've been called away unexpectedly. It will take me about half an hour. You can make up your own story for Mrs. Sanford in that time."

"I'm not going to leave, Paul."

"I say you are."

"No. You have to trust me."

Paul's calm broke. He said furiously, "Trust you? Stand by and let you rob my friends without lifting a finger to stop you? I can't believe that anyone would ask it! Even a thief ought to have a sense of decency. To come this way, as a guest—You can't do it! You can't expect me to close my eyes to it!" Paul kept his voice down with an effort. "Get out of here. Make an excuse and go, or I'll give you away. I swear it."

"You'll send me back to twenty years in prison if you do."

"I'm giving you a choice. For God's sake, John!" It was like a groan. "You don't give me any at all."

"Will you believe me if I say I didn't come here to rob anyone?"

"Don't talk nonsense!"

"I give you my word."

Paul made a contemptuous silencing gesture. "Don't say it. I have no faith in your word."

"Listen to me, Paul! I've got to convince you—"

"I've done listening to you. You have half an hour to think of your excuse. If you haven't left by the time I get back, I'll expose you. Get out of my way."

He shoved by John, who stood between him and the doorway. John said, "Wait!" and put out his foot to block the door as Paul reached for the knob. Without hesitation, Paul hit him.

All of his bitterness went into the blow, which landed solidly on John's unprotected chin. It knocked him across the room. He did not lose consciousness until he brought up against the wall, but then the strength drained suddenly out of his legs. He felt himself falling.

When his eyes focused again he was on the floor, his back to the wall. He did not know how long he had been sitting there. The door stood open. He shook his head to clear it, got up, automatically closed the door and locked it, then went to the window.

The bathers were still sporting in the swimming pool. The fading daylight had not changed perceptibly. He knew he could not have been unconscious long, but he did not realize how short the time was until he saw Paul come out on the *terrasse* below and hurry across the lawn toward the rank of cars that were parked beyond the moat. He was almost running. Without once looking back he got into a car and roared away, faster than was safe on the narrow, winding road. Another car coming up the hill, a dusty Citroën with a buggy-whip radio aerial mounted on one rear fender, had to risk the extreme edge of the road to avoid a collision.

He had seen the Citroën before. He watched it continue up the hill and pull into the parking space Paul had just left. Oriol got out.

Although the sunlight was nearly gone, he recognized Oriol's stocky figure immediately. He thought the second man who got out of the Citroën was Lepic, but he had seen Lepic only once, at night, and could not be certain.

He watched the two men come toward the château, saw George Sanford leave a group of his guests on the *terrasse* and go to meet them, saw them talk together briefly. Sanford beckoned to a servant. The man went to the car in the parking rank and came back carrying a pair of suitcases. The whole group moved together toward the west wing.

He had his door open a crack when they came by his room. It was not enough to let him see into the hall, but he heard George Sanford grumbling.

". . . don't like it," he was saying. "I appreciate your position, Commissioner, and I'm sure you know your business, but I'm still not happy about it. Now that you've disposed of this what's-his-name burglar who was causing all the rumpus, I don't see why we can't relax and forget about jewel thieves. I have to tell you that Mrs. Sanford has been against the whole thing from the start."

Another voice said smoothly, "The Sûreté can never forget jewel thieves, Mr. Sanford. Our work never stops. The elimination of one criminal does not mean there are no others. The very fact that we have finished with one thief will invite others to expect us to be lax. That is why I have asked for secrecy. I assure you. . . "

The voices faded as they moved down the hall. He could hear no more, only a mumble, then a door closing.

The servant's footsteps came back alone. He waited. A door opened again, he heard the mumble of voices, then words as they passed his room a second time.

". . . among my own guests?" George Sanford said indignantly.

"Certainly not. Still, it will be easier for you to introduce us as guests than hide us, and we will remain as much in the background as possible. Our main reason for being here is to mount a guard during the night, the same scheme that was successful at the Souza villa."

"It's a waste of time. The Combe d'Or is impregnable to a thief. And I won't have any shooting, whatever happens. Damn it, Commissioner—"

"No home is impregnable to a determined thief, Mr. Sanford." The smooth voice went on. "I hope as much as you do that nothing will happen. But even if I did not feel a responsibility to protect Mrs. Sanford's emeralds, I could not conscientiously. . . Princess Lila's pearls. . . irresistible to any thief. . . international complications if. . . "

The voices faded. John released the breath he had been holding, closed the door, and turned the key. His main feeling was one of relief that all his problems were now one, simple and elementary. Mr. Burns and Mr. Burns's troubles were finished.

He took off his clothes, the body harness, and the padded shoes and packed them away in his bag with the blueprints. The eyebrows would have to be soaked off with hot water. He did not have time for that, and they were not important. He put on a gray slipover and gray flannels, the glove-leather slippers, and buttoned his passport and his money in his hip pocket. Mr. Burns's passport was worse than useless to him now, but he kept it. If it served for nothing else, it was a tie to something he had hoped to have.

Before he had finished his preparations, all but a few minutes of Paul's promised half hour had passed. The room was growing dark, but he did not turn on a light. When someone came along the hall and rapped lightly on the door panel, he thought it was the call to take Paul's telephone message, and waited silently for the man to go away.

The rap came again. Francie's voice said, "John."

He let her in. In the semi-darkness she did not immediately notice the change in his appearance. She said, "Why don't you turn on a light? I've got the rooms located for you. Princess Lila is next to Mimi Sanford, Mother's room is next, then mine—oh!"

She had seen the profile of his body when he passed between her and the window to look out. The lights strung across the lawn and *terrasse* had come on, and the tiled pool, now illuminated by underwater flood-lights, glowed like one of Mimi Sanford's emeralds. Most of the bathers had left the pool to join other guests sitting on the *terrasse*. He looked for Oriol and Lepic among them, but saw neither man. He could not move safely until he knew where they were.

Francie said, "What have you done to yourself?"

"Tossed Mr. Burns overboard. He can't make another appearance."

"What happened?"

He told her about Paul, and of Lepic's arrival with Oriol. He said, "I have a few minutes before Paul telephones. He'll give me away if I don't leave, Oriol will identify me if I stay, and Lepic is bound to be curious about anyone who disappears without an explanation. He'll investigate when Mr. Burns can't be found to answer an urgent telephone call, so be ready for questions. Let your mother do most of the talking. She won't have to put on an act."

"What are you going to do?"

He put his hand on her arm to silence her. Footsteps were coming down the hall again. There was a knock, another, a call, *"Téléphone, m'sieu,"* another, louder knock. In a moment the footsteps went away.

"That's it," he said. "It will be a few minutes before they begin hunting for me. Better not let them find you near my room."

"What are you going to do?"

He looked down at the *terrasse* again. Lepic was there

now, standing apart with George Sanford, talking earnestly. Oriol was nearby.

He said, "Tell me the schedule for the weekend. Just the hours after dark."

Whatever else he might think about Francie, he was grateful for her quick intelligence. She said, "Tonight, only music and dancing on the terrace. Everyone is too tired from traveling to stay up late. Tomorrow night, the *gala,* costumes and a pageant, Midsummer on Mount Olympus. Mr. and Mrs. Sanford are to be Jupiter and Juno, the rest anything in character. Nothing special has been planned for Sunday night. Almost all of the guests are leaving Monday. What—"

"Tomorrow they'll be up all night, and the jewelry will be on display, so that's out." He was thinking aloud. "Tonight or Sunday. I'd do it tonight. They'll sleep better. The pearls, if nothing else." He reached for her hand. "Come over here and point out the Princess's room. Mrs. Sanford's room is the fourth pair of windows from the opposite wing, on the top floor, not counting gables. Just under the eave."

She came over to the window. Her hand felt cold, and she was shivering.

"The Princess is next on the left, toward this wing." Her voice sounded thin, strained. "What are you going to do? Please tell me."

"Go up on the tower and wait." It was wholly dark in the room now. He could not see her face. "If he gets by Oriol and Lepic, I'll be watching for him. If he doesn't come tonight, I should be able to last until Sunday, unless they tear the place down to find me. If he doesn't come Sunday, I'll try to get to Italy before I'm picked up. If I don't reach Italy, I won't have to make any further plans."

She said nothing. Her shivering increased.

"Twice you told me I was a fool," he said. "I may have been, as Mr. Burns. I'm not now. This is what I know how to do best. Will you do one more thing for me?"

He thought she nodded. He said, "Tell them I—Mr. Burns—told you I had to leave unexpectedly, and had no time to say good-bye. It will keep Paul from talking, and it ought to make them look for me somewhere else. If I get away with this, I'll owe you more thanks than I have time to give you. If not, I'm still grateful for what you've done. Good-bye."

He pressed her cold fingers before he released them. She still said nothing, nor moved, except to shiver more violently than before. He was disappointed that she did not wish him good luck, or say good-bye. It would have been only a small gesture for her to make.

He left her standing by the window, opened the door cautiously, and saw that the corridor was empty.

Paul had done him one favor in identifying the location of his own room across the hall. He took Mr. Burns's bag with him and hid it under Paul's bed, where it might escape detection for a while, then went quickly and quietly to the window.

It was high and narrow, a slit in the thick outer wall of the castle overlooking the gardened moat. He had to squeeze to get to the ledge outside. He was on the opposite side of the wing from the *terrasse*. There were no lights in the garden below him. He listened for voices, watched for the gleam of a lighted cigarette in the dark, heard nothing, saw nothing. Stretching to his full height from the ledge, he reached above his head and explored the old wall with his fingers until he found a crevice between the stones. He began to climb, a gray shadow against gray rock.

7

HE CLIMBED CAREFULLY BUT STEADILY. There were no windows above him, only blank wall and an overhanging eave. When he found a crevice big enough for his toes, he rested. Otherwise it was a test of strength and grip, harder than climbing a rope because he could not clasp with his palms, but not greatly more difficult than scaling a cliff face. His fingers found holds where the centuries-old mortar between the stones of the wall had weathered. He held his weight on the hard hook of one hand while he groped with the other for a new hold, pulling himself upward as patiently as a snail on stone. He moved like a snail, not thinking, letting his arms and legs and fingers think for him—pull, hold, reach, grip, pull again, hold, grope, find a foothold, rest.

The overhanging eave was hardest to pass. He had to sidle crabwise on the wall to find both a momentary handhold and toehold in the right positions, then stretch to his limit to reach the gutter at the eave edge. He would not voluntarily have scaled the eave in that way, given any other choice, because he could not properly test the strength of the gutter before trusting his weight to it. But it did not sag during the moment he hung suspended from it. He pulled himself up to the roof.

His fingers ached from the strain of clinging to small holds, and the climb had made him sweat. He rested.

A faint afterglow still remained in the sky. He studied the roofs he had still to cross, marking a path that would not take him in front of a dormer window. He had to pass the length of the wing and over the main, higher roof tops to the tower, which rose from the juncture of the opposite wing with the central mass of the castle. The roofs were of slate tile, smooth and steep. Slate was always dangerous to climb, not only because of its smoothness but because each tile was hung on a single nail which pulled loose easily under strain and might let the tile slide with a revealing clatter. And although there were no dormers over-looking the roof in either wing, several broke the top outline of the main building, one or two showing lighted windows.

He crossed above the dormers, making his way along the gutter to the inner end of the wing, up the angle the roof made with the joining wall, jumping from the peak of the wing to catch the gutter at the eave of the higher roof, then up the rise of the roof corner to the top. Only the tower stood higher. The central roof was a series of disconnected gables and sharply peaked turrets, so that his path along the ridges of the roof top, balanced as delicately as a wire walker to avoid a misstep on the sheer slopes of slate, took him up, down, and at angles until he reached the base of the tower.

The eaves and the bulk of the castle itself had shielded

him until then from the view of anyone who might look up from the terrace. The tower was more exposed. He knew there was a stairway inside, and a door opened at the tower base onto a shallow rampart. But he did not try the door. He made his way around the tower on the narrow rampart walk to the outside, where it was blocked by the thick growth of ivy climbing from the moat below, then up the strong ladder of vine to the crenellated tower top and at last over the parapet.

From that remote perch he overlooked the entire château: the roofs, the gardened moat, the glowing emerald pool, the lighted terrace. The terrace was a stage in the theater made by the box of the extending wings. He was too far above the foreshortened figures on the stage to hear their words, but the pantomime, the dumb show of gesture and movement, stage crosses, entrances, and exits, told him what was going on.

He watched the action of the play with the same sense of detachment that always came to him when he looked down from a high place. He did not feel that he was part of the play. It was Mr. Burns they were excited about, not himself.

~§~

The valet coughed at Mimi Sanford's elbow. She was too engrossed in listening to the *couturière* describe the changes she meant to introduce in the fall fashions to notice him at first. He coughed again.

She said, "What is it?"

"Mr. Burns, madame. He's wanted on the telephone. An urgent call."

She looked around the *terrasse*. Mr. Burns was not in sight. She had forgotten him, and it made her feel guilty. She was a conscientious hostess.

She said, "He must be in his room."

"I just came from his room, madame. He doesn't answer."

"I haven't seen him since he arrived. Ask Mr. Sanford."

The valet asked Mr. Sanford, who was standing with Lepic and Oriol on the lawn where they could see the rise of the castle walls, explaining why any suggestion of thieves breaking into the Combe d'Or was nonsense. It was his firm opinion that once the castle doors had been closed and bolted for the night, nobody alive could enter his home except by dynamiting a way, and not easily even then. He was giving reasons for his faith, in terms of wall thicknesses, when valet came to make his inquiry.

"Burns?" Sanford said blankly. "Who the devil is Mr. Burns?"

"The friend of Mrs. Stevens and her daughter, sir."

"Oh, him. I didn't even know he was here. Ask Mrs. Sanford."

"I've already asked her, sir. She told me to speak to you."

"Well, I don't know. Ask Mrs. Stevens, then."

Mrs. Stevens did not know, either. She looked around for Francie, but Francie was nowhere in sight, and the

Princess Lila's description of life with Oriental royalty was too entertaining to be interrupted. It was another ten minutes before the valet could attract attention to the fact that Mr. Burns was either dead or unconscious in his room or had vanished into thin air.

George Sanford went reluctantly to search for his guest. Lepic, with growing curiosity, accompanied him. When they found Mr. Burns's room empty and his luggage gone, Sanford was at first relieved not to discover a body, then puzzled, finally indignant. He could not satisfy Lepic's curiosity. He had met Mr. Burns only once, casually. Mrs. Sanford had invited him to the *gala* at the request of Mrs. Stevens, or possibly Miss Stevens.

It was all Sanford knew. He did not remember what Mr. Burns looked like, beyond the fact that he was middle-aged and slightly bald.

Mrs. Stevens was startled to find Lepic suddenly at her elbow, asking questions about Mr. Burns in a demanding way and with more signs of excitement than he had shown at the loss of her jewelry. She said, "He's a gentleman staying at my hotel, a friend of my daughter's. Why? What's happened to him?"

"I would like to know myself, madame. Where is your daughter?"

"I haven't the faintest idea. Probably in her room."

"Please take me to her room."

Mrs. Stevens looked down her plump nose and said, with considerable pleasure, "At the moment, the Princess Lila and I—"

Lepic cut her off.

"I demand that you take me to your daughter, madame," he said harshly. "At once!"

Mrs. Stevens decided not to argue. He did not show the same patience of manner she remembered. She took him to Francie's room.

Francie was lying in the dark. She had a splitting headache, and did not want to talk with anyone. But she told Lepic of the message Mr. Burns had left for his hosts, that he had been called away unexpectedly without time to make his apologies. She did not know when or how he had left the château. She answered Lepic's questions listlessly, describing Mr. Burns's appearance, clothes, and mannerisms, what little else she knew about him. When Lepic had rushed off, she asked her mother to turn off the light and leave her alone. She had no desire to talk further about Mr. Burns or anything else. It was a very bad headache.

Mrs. Stevens, returning to the *terrasse,* found everyone else more than eager to discuss Mr. Burns's mysterious disappearance. Who was he, and why would anyone behave in such a peculiar manner? No one had seen him go. It was certainly strange of him not even to say good-bye to his host and hostess.

Mrs. Stevens apologized to Mimi Sanford.

"Though I can't say it surprises me," she said cheerfully. "There was always something strange about him. He was the luckiest man at roulette I ever met, and he never bet more than a hundred francs on anything. I think he was a little crazy. In a nice way, of course."

Lepic did not think that Mr. Burns was crazy. He took Oriol aside and said, "I think we've got him! Paul du Pré is missing, too. So is his car. The servants say he drove off in a hurry just about the time we arrived. Didn't you tell me he and Robie were close friends?"

"They used to be. Did the servants see anyone else in the car?"

"They weren't watching for anyone else. It has to be more than a coincidence that they both disappeared at once."

"I'm not so sure. I don't think Paul would help him beat the law. Besides, the description is all wrong. John had more hair and less belly, and it isn't his technique to smuggle in as a guest."

"Hairlines and bellies are easy to change," Lepic said impatiently. "So are techniques, if you can't get in any other way. I tell you, we've got him!"

"We've got somebody," Oriol conceded. "I'm not convinced that it was John Robie."

"Who else would have a reason to run?"

"Any crook could recognize the Citroën and know we weren't making a social call. But go ahead and set your lines out for him. It won't be any worse than a waste of time. I'm going to stay here."

"Don't use that tone with me, Commissaire." Lepic's voice was sharp. "I'm still your superior. You'll do what I tell you."

Oriol laughed, bitterly, without enjoyment.

"You'll be my superior if and when we take Le Chat," he said. "Right now we're a pair of betrayed virgins trying to keep the truth from the neighbors. Go set your nets, Commissaire Divisionnaire. I'll stay here."

Lepic's face flushed. He turned on his heel and hurried away, across the lawn and through the gardens of the moat to the car park beyond. The Citroën roared off in a spray of gravel.

~§~

John saw it go, and knew what Lepic's departure meant. He could only guess why Oriol remained.

Paul returned only a few minutes later, while Lepic was still on his way to put the *brigade mobile* in action. Paul's shoulders drooped as he came across the lawn. He walked heavily, without his normal spring of step.

Oriol went to meet him. The pantomime was clear. Oriol asked his question. Paul shook his head. Oriol asked other questions. Paul continued to shake his head. He knew nothing about Mr. Burns, and had an explanation for his own absence from the château. The explanation did not satisfy Oriol, who put out his hand to stop Paul when he turned away. Paul brushed the hand off. Oriol watched him cross the terrace to speak to his hostess, who took his arm and presented him to the princess, the *couturière,* Mrs. Stevens, and several others. He showed only polite interest in Mr. Burns's puzzling disappearance, still the main subject of conversation, but it was something he said, some suggestion made in apparent innocence, which sent Mimi Sanford, the princess, and most of the other women hurrying in fright to their rooms to reassure themselves that they had not been robbed.

Oriol followed them. The women came back in time, laughing at themselves and each other, to chide Paul for a ridiculous suggestion. Oriol did not return.

John heard him exploring the roof, several hours later. Dinner was over, coffee and liqueurs had been served, and several couples were dancing to the music of a small orchestra that played on the terrace. The flurry caused by Mr. Burns's disappearance had been forgotten. Francie had still not come to join the other guests. But she had sent her excuses, and no one missed Oriol, the other absent guest, except George Sanford, who was relieved that he did not have to explain Oriol to the princess and the *couturière*.

Oriol intended to see for himself if Sanford's claims about the castle's impregnability were justified. He still did not believe that Le Chat would come to the Combe d'Or by invitation.

He worked his way up through the château from the bottom floors, peering through windows and trying doors. Most of the guest-room doors he found securely locked. He hoped the windows he could not try were locked as well, although he knew locked windows would not be a bar. Neither would the apparently unscalable walls under the windows. There were drainpipes. And when, after climbing interminable flights of narrow, winding stairs, he reached the roof tops and found the ladder of ivy ascending to the parapet of the tower, he smiled wryly to himself at Sanford's boasts. The château might be successfully defended against armed assault, as Sanford claimed. It offered no protection against the entry of a man like John Robie.

John heard him first when the door at the base of the tower squeaked open on heavy hinges. He did not risk exposing himself by looking over the parapet. He knew it would be Oriol.

A flag pole rose from the tower top, and a trap door connected with the stairs inside. He waited, listening to the man below cautiously explore the narrow rampart walk out to the block of the ivy vine, heard him go back into the tower and the bolt of the door slide home, then went over the parapet to burrow into the screen of vine ten feet below. He hung there for a quarter of an hour, breathing through his mouth so the dust in the ivy leaves would not make him sneeze. But Oriol did not try the trap at the tower top. When John was certain that it was safe to move, he went back to his high perch. He was not disturbed again.

The orchestra stopped playing early, before midnight. The guests were not enthusiastic about dancing. Most of them found that hours of travel to reach the Combe d'Or, combined with George Sanford's brandy, made them sleepy. They drifted away from the terrace by ones and twos and threes until only Paul and the orchestra remained, finally only Paul.

He sat alone, smoking one cigarette after another, not moving until George Sanford came back to the terrace and spoke to him. Sanford's gestures said that he did not like to disturb his guest's solitude, but it was time to drop the portcullis and lift the metaphorical drawbridge. Paul followed him inside. The huge double doors of the castle swung shut. Bars dropped into place. Moments afterward the lights in the emerald pool winked out, then those on the terrace. The Château Combe d'Or was sealed for the night.

There were still lights in many of the castle windows, and no need to maintain a watch until they went out. But John had a view of more than the rooftops.

For what it had been originally, a lookout point, the tower top was magnificent. Only the high irregular line of the Esterel stretching far in the southwest blocked his view of the starlit Mediterranean. There was no moon, and the brilliance of the lights marking the curving coast road was sharper in contrast with the velvet darkness of the night. Against the shadowy backdrop of the Esterel hills there were first isolated bright sparks, then strings of bright sparks together to mark the grand sweep of seashore north and east from Théoule toward La Napoule and the blaze of illumination that was Cannes. The château stood at the upper peak of a chain of hills running down into the sea at the sharp hook of Cap Croisette, and the white, floodlighted bulk of the casino shining at the tip of the point glowed like a pendant on a necklace of light which continued toward the northeast with the coastal road, bending around the crescent of Golfe Juan to Cap d'Antibes, bending again in a wider crescent to melt into a larger, brighter pool of light, Nice in the distance, continuing beyond to the clustered sparkle to Cap Ferrat, beyond that to another, dimmer necklace marking the beginning of the Corniche road which led along the cliffs to Villefranche, Beaulieu, Monte Carlo, Menton, and finally to the Italian border sixty miles away. The whole Côte d' Azur lay under his eyes.

Sixty miles of jewels, he thought, and the hope that had carried him failed utterly. With a thousand opportunities at hand, it was beyond reason to expect the thief to come to the Combe d'Or.

But he built his confidence again with the thought that he had reasoned correctly about the theft from Mrs. Stevens. The fabulous pearls were a far greater temptation. In all his career he had never brought off a theft that would pay as well as the pearls. He had known of them in his time, marked them for an attempt if the opportunity presented itself, but until the prince presented them to his American bride they had never come into his territory. He knew with certainty that he would have taken any risk to steal them, given an opportunity. And they would be beyond reach after Sunday night, gone from the Côte and from France. The thief had to come.

He held to the belief. It was the reason for his existence.

He did not doubt that he could last until Sunday night if it became necessary. He would have to remain exposed on the tower top during the following day and most of the next night, but it would not be impossible to leave the château during the height of the *gala* and return before dawn. There were farms in the hills back of the Combe d'Or where he could find food and water, and a dozen ways to scale the outside walls even without the ivy. Lepic would have his net laid by morning, but it would cover roads and borders, not the near countryside. Oriol was the man he had most to fear.

The thought of Oriol made him turn from the lights of the coast line to watch the roof tops again.

Windows were darkening, one by one. As time passed, he could mark the tide of sleep rising in the castle by the way in which darkness came first to the lower floors, then to the master bedrooms and guest rooms, last of all to the dormer windows in the roof, where the servants slept. A few lights, mostly in the dormers, still burned when a distant church bell pealed a single note. He did not know if it marked one o'clock or the half hour.

When the bell rang to mark the passage of another half hour, it was again a single chime. One dormer was still alight. He avoided looking directly at the glowing pane, to prevent his eyes from adjusting themselves to brilliance. After the window darkened at last, there was only starlight to show him the faint sheen of the gray slate roofs.

The church bell rang two o'clock. The Combe d'Or slept, dark and soundless. He watched the roof, the eaves, the gutters for a shadow. He could not see into the blackness of the dark courtyard of the moat, but there was no need for it. The château, built to withstand strong ground assaults, was vulnerable only to a climber who, like Le Chat, worked down from the high

To Catch A Thief   237

places. If he came, he would come over the roof tops.

The bell pealed two-thirty. The air had begun to cool perceptibly. A breeze rustled the ivy.

He changed his cramped position without taking his eyes from the roof. He was beginning to feel thirsty. If the parching *mistral* began to blow he would dry out quickly. Rain would be even worse. He could not hope to last a day and a night in the rain without shelter and still retain the free use of his muscles. When a breeze rustled the ivy again, he turned to look at the southwest sky, searching for a sign of clouds blotting out the stars.

There were no clouds. There was no sign of the *mistral*, not even a breeze in his face. But the ivy rustled again.

He thought, quite calmly, Careful. Don't make any mistakes now. Let him come.

The ivy whispered, and whispered again. He could not see beyond the overhang of the rampart walk without exposing the outline of his head and shoulders against the sky. He felt his pulses beat with the intermittent movements of the climber on the vine. He began to breathe deeply through his open mouth, steadying himself for the effort to come. He bent to test the ties of his slippers, scuffed the soles against the stone on which he stood, rubbed his palms on the rock of the parapet to dry them and roughen the skin, tightened his belt, flexed his fingers. The ivy whispered more loudly now—rustle, pause, rustle again, finally a pause that was not followed by another rustle. Only then he looked down from the parapet and saw the shadowy figure below make its way along the rampart walk and unhesitatingly, surely, confidently out on the sharp peak of the roof top.

He swung down the ivy to the rampart in a surge of released tension. There was no need to wait longer, nothing left to plan, no need to hope. The time had come.

The shadow was visible several yards ahead when he followed it. He had not been able to conceal the sounds of his descent from the tower top. He knew he had been seen, as much as anything could be seen in the starlit darkness. There was no identity to the shadow ahead except a dim grayness. He saw it only for a moment before it faded into blackness.

The disappearance did not worry him. He was between the shadow and the ladder of ivy. To escape, the thief would have to leave the roof and make his way to the ground by some other means. He was confident that he could descend as fast, or faster, by any path. The thief might dodge him for a while in the angles of the roof gables and turrets, but he could not begin a descent without appearing on the eaves or attempting to work back toward the tower. John stood in his way.

He moved to the end of the peak where the shadow had disappeared. The angle of a joining dormer went down, the corner of a gable went up. There was no other path, nothing but impassable slates. He went up and caught sight of the shadow at the far end of the gable before it disappeared again.

It became a three-dimensional chess game, each move

according to prescribed rules, following definite lines. Short cuts were impossible. A misstep on the slates would have sent either of them sliding helplessly, with only the gutters at the eaves to stop a fall. They could pass along the roof peaks, diagonally in the angle of joining gables, up and down the slope of roof corners, or by way of the gutter. John did not move as rapidly as the thief. He was at a disadvantage in that he had to explore each shadow, study each pocket of darkness when he came to it so that he might not overrun his quarry, opening an escape to the tower behind. He meant to force the shadow ahead of him and down to the roof of the west wing, where there were no corners to hide in, no rising gables or descending angles to dodge across, nothing but a single roof peak, a straight line ending in sheer fall to the moat and the end of the chessboard.

He almost missed the shadow lying flat and motionless at the outer end of a dormer he was about to pass. The thief's ruse, failing, trapped him in the same way John hoped to trap him on the wing, but in a smaller space. There was nothing behind him but a drop to the courtyard, nothing on either side but the slope of dormer into another steep slope of slate.

John moved out on the dormer peak, cautiously. He expected the thief to risk a swing down from the end of the dormer to the eave below and from there along the gutter or down the wall to the courtyard. He was prepared for both moves, either of which would put him at an advantage. He was not prepared for the soaring jump the thief made instead to an adjoining dormer.

It was a tremendous leap, one he would have hesitated to attempt himself. His own muscles tensed in an unconscious effort to assist the jumper. The thief failed to reach secure footing, came down heavily on the slates, slipped, and saved himself by catching at the peak of the dormer. Tiles split, slid, and went clattering off the eave into the courtyard, to shatter on the terrace.

~§~

Oriol heard them fall. He had made another round of the château since it quieted down for the night, and was considering taking his post at a window in the east wing from which he could watch the windows of the Princess Lila's bedroom and Mimi Sanford's bedroom. When the slates fell, he was instantly alert. There was no reason for slates to fall on a windless night.

The chance of his position let him see the light that came on immediately in one of the roof dormers. He marked the position of the dormer and hurried up the stairs, cursing the castle builders for having made the stairs so steep and winding, his own shortness of breath for making them more difficult.

An angry man in a nightshirt answered his knock when he found the room he wanted. He was one of the cooks, who had to be up at five o'clock and needed his rest.

"How do I know what happened?" he grumbled. *"Merde,* what a household! As many guests to cook for as there are worms in the potatoes, no sleep—"

"What woke you?"

"A thump, dirt in my face, stars peeking at me through a hole in the roof. Right over the sack full of soup bones they give me for a bed, too. What do I do when it rains, eh? It's a situation calling for thought when a student of Escoffier and a citizen of the French Republic—"

He shrugged and went back to bed, muttering. Oriol was already running down the hall.

His wind was gone when he climbed the last flight of stairs and unbarred the door at the base of the tower. He stopped to breathe on the narrow rampart, peering off across the roof tops.

The light in the cook's window had gone out. He could see nothing except the beginning of a sharp roof peak leading off into darkness, but he knew how far the fall was on either side. He did not have a head for heights. His earlier exploration of the precarious rampart walk had made him dizzy at the thought of the drop he could not see. But while he hesitated, still breathing hard, he heard slates slide and clatter again.

He had no light, no time to hunt for a light, and no stomach for roof tops in the dark, nothing to drive him but stubbornness and a mistake he meant to redeem. He set his jaw, lowered himself from the rampart until he was astride the roof peak, and began to inch forward into the darkness.

~§~

John had dislodged the second fall of slates. He was being driven to take increasing risks to keep the fleeing shadow ahead of him. The thief had seen his intention, and was making every effort to escape the trap.

He felt a reluctant admiration for the other man's sureness of foot. The chase would have been a test even in daylight. In darkness, with visibility extending only as far as the next step along a knife edge of ridge peak or up the steep climb of a gable corner, it was a feat. Except for the unavoidable fall on the dormer, the thief had made no sound to indicate a misstep. John had slipped twice, once saving himself only by the friction of his palms flat on the slates and a scramble that dislodged the tiles before he could get back to the peak he was protecting.

The thief had not yet attempted to escape by going over the eaves, but there would be nothing else left for him once they were on the roof of the wing. Nimbleness of foot would not help him then. Only sureness of grip and strength of arms and shoulders counted on a wall. Still forcing toward that end, John lost sight of the shadow again.

He stopped, searching for it along the eaves, unwilling to move farther until he saw that he was not opening another way of escape. When he heard the scrape on the roof far behind him, he thought for a black moment that the escape had already been made.

But immediately he caught sight of the shadow again, almost to the drop-off that would take it down to the wing, and knew that someone else was on the roof.

Oriol moved by hitching himself along the ridge peaks with his hands. He came like a turtle, with a turtle's steadiness of purpose. He could not keep his heels from scraping the slates, but he was not trying to be quiet. He knew Le Chat was ahead of him. He wanted Le Chat to know that he was coming.

He called into the darkness, "John!"

John recognized the voice, but even before Oriol called his name he had guessed who it was. As surely as Oriol knew that the noise on the roof top meant Le Chat was there, so John knew that only one man had the dogged determination to hunt him there in the dark on his own ground. He moved forward, driving the shadow toward the end of the roof.

Oriol called, "John Robie!"

His voice came clearly across the roof top.

"Lepic has the net out for you. If you get away from me, you'll never escape him. Give yourself up."

There was silence. Then the patient scraping noise began again.

John moved ahead of it. The shadow was now at the extreme end of the roof, on the eave. There was no way to go from there except down to the wing.

Oriol's voice came again. "I know you're here, John. I'd rather take you myself than let Lepic do it, but you're finished, either way. Give yourself up."

Because John was moving along the roof peak and

had his back turned, he did not see the flash of the shot when Oriol worked a pistol out of his pocket and fired it into the air. The bright red pencil of flame went straight up.

Oriol meant to arouse the household, not kill another thief.

All John saw with the echoing report of the shot was his own shadow outlined for an instant on the tiles. The flare that showed him to Oriol let him see that the other shadow was gone. Expecting the roar of another shot and the shock of a bullet in his back, he raced along the peak, down the slope of the last roof corner. The gun banged again while he ran, but he was over the eave before the third shot. He swung from the gutter and dropped, not hoping to land on the safe perch of the roof peak below but prepared to fall flat to either side, according to the angle of slate his feet met.

He did not fall. Hands reached out to steady him. He turned instantly to seize and hold the figure beside him, and knew in the immediate moment of contact, unmistakably, that he had caught a woman.

Tight in the grip of his arms, not struggling, she whispered, "Let me go, John Robie. We have to help each other now."

"Danielle!"

He thought she started at the sound of his voice. It might have been only his own muscular reaction to the shock. He released her. Before he could even attempt to think, bring his mind to accept the stunning fact of the discovery, she said quickly, "There's the first light now.

He'll be able to see us as soon as he reaches the eave. We have to get off the roof. I've got a rope."

She crouched on the peak where they stood. Another light came on somewhere above them. He saw that she was exploring the roof top with her hands, rapidly, although without sign of panic.

He still could not think.

An angry voice shouted from a window. More lights were coming on. He heard the scrape of Oriol's approach on the roof above.

It released him from the momentary paralysis of thought and action. He took Danielle's arm and brought her erect beside him.

"There's no time to fix a rope," he said. "We'll have to go over the eave. The wall isn't difficult."

"I can't reach from the eave. I would have tried it before if it was possible. I'll have to—"

"I'll make a bridge for you. Stay close behind me, and when I go over watch my hands for a signal. Quick!"

He went down the angle between roof and wall and along the gutter, no longer with the need to accept a reality he still could not grasp, all of his mind now on the escape. The thought did not enter his head that he might get away more easily alone, or that he should try. Afterward he could not remember any conscious change of attitude in himself, from pursuer of a thief to the thief's ally. One identity had merged into another while he was both hunter and hunted, so that it seemed wholly natural to find himself providing a path of escape for the girl he had risked his liberty to give to the police. It was not because she was someone he knew and liked, nor because of her sex. She was a thief, he was a thief. Oriol threatened them both.

He swung down from the eave at what he judged was the point he had come up. It took him a moment to find the hand hold and toe hold he knew to be there. He was firmly braced between wall and eave when he felt Danielle's light touch on his fingers clinging to the gutter. He lifted one finger against her palm as a signal.

She came down from the eave and across his body to the wall like a squirrel, found a grip, held her own weight. He swung in behind her.

The angry voice was shouting again. They heard Oriol call back, urgently, the angry voice replying, other voices.

He said, "Are you all right?"

"Yes." Danielle was flat against the wall by his side. "Shall I go first?"

"We don't have time to make it to the ground before they head us off. The first window is about twenty feet straight down, two yards to your left."

As if in response to a cue, the slit window below them lighted. Danielle said, "Someone is awake in the room."

"The whole place will be awake in a minute. It's Paul's room. He's our only hope."

A second window on the same floor with Paul's room showed a light, then another a floor below. Oriol was shouting urgently from the roof top. They began to descend.

~§~

The room was empty when they squeezed in through the narrow slit window. Paul was outside, in the corridor. They heard his voice and the voices of other guests aroused by the shots and the shouting. But no one passed the open doorway to see them before they had crossed the room, so when Paul, in pajamas and a dressing gown, came in, he found them there behind it.

He had not quite shut the door when he caught sight of them. He stood that way, motionless, his hand on the doorknob. The color drained slowly out of his face as he looked at them. Danielle was dressed, like John, in gray slacks and jersey and soft leather slippers. She wore a dark beret which hid her bright hair, and a length of strong light line was wound around her slim waist like a belt. Even without the dust of the roof staining her clothes and John's to show where they had been and the way they had come, their clothing alone would have betrayed them for what they were, two thieves.

Paul closed the door, turned the key, then switched off the light.

"You'll both feel more at home in the dark," he said emotionlessly. "It's safer for you, and I'd rather not have to see you, if you don't mind."

Danielle said, "I'm sorry, Paul."

He did not answer her. They heard him sit on the bed. When he spoke again, minutes later, it was in the same lifeless tone. He said, "It would have been less cruel to tell me the truth when I asked you to, John."

John had his ear to the door, listening for sounds in the corridor. He was too fully occupied to realize that Paul had come to a natural conclusion until Danielle said pleadingly, "Whatever else you think—"

"Quiet! It will keep."

John listened at the door. There were voices, but none nearby. They could talk in safety.

He said, "We'll get out of here as soon as we have a chance. While we're waiting, I'll tell you what I was trying to tell you yesterday when you knocked me out, Paul. I should have told you before then, and I won't try to explain now why I didn't. But I never lied to you. I didn't know anything more about Danielle than I said. I don't know any more about her now, except that she's what you thought I was."

He told the rest as briefly as possible, stopping now and then to listen at the door panel. At the end he said, "I warned you that there couldn't be two Lisas. But it should hurt less to know this one is a thief than to think something else about her."

Paul said, "Is it true, Danielle?"

"Yes." Her answer was barely audible.

They heard footsteps coming along the corridor, and two voices arguing. The argument went on past the door, down the corridor.

John said, "That's Oriol. He'll never quit."

Danielle said, "Why don't you give me to him? Why didn't you give me to him on the roof, if you had risked so much to find me?"

"I don't know. It never occurred to me. I didn't have time to think about it. I—"

He stopped. The footsteps had come back. The low-voiced argument was still going on. It continued outside the door for a moment before someone knocked.

Paul said, "Who is it?"

"Oriol. I want to talk to you, Paul."

Paul turned on the light. The color had returned to his face, but nothing in his expression told them what he meant to do. John reached for Danielle's arm to bring her against the wall, where they would be shielded by the door when it opened. It was as instinctive as everything else he had done since learning her identity.

Oriol and George Sanford were in the hall. Sanford looked angry, Oriol stubborn.

Paul said, "What is it?"

"I'm sorry, Paul." Sanford was both angry and embarrassed. "I have to apologize for this."

"I'll make my own apologies," Oriol said. "John Robie was on the roof tonight. I almost got him. He didn't have time to get away from this wing, and I think he would come to you for help if he was trapped. Do you know where he is?"

John held his breath. Danielle was tense at his side.

Paul said, "No. Do you want to search my room?"

"I won't permit it!" Sanford said furiously.

Oriol ignored him. He said, "I know you don't lie, Paul. But you held something back from me last night, when I asked you about Mr. Burns. I don't know what it was, but now I want to know I've heard the plain truth, and all of it. Give me your word."

"I give you my word that I haven't seen John Robie at any time since coming here, and that I wouldn't protect him if I knew or suspected where he was. Is that enough?"

"That's enough. I'm sorry I disturbed you."

The door closed. The footsteps went away.

Paul stared at the door panel in front of his eyes until there was no sound in the corridor. Then he shook his head quickly and turned to grin at John and Danielle.

The grin was an effort, but he managed it. He said, "That puts us all on the same side, doesn't it? Two thieves and a liar on his word of honor. What do we do next?"

John let out his breath.

Danielle began to unwind the rope that was around her waist. She avoided looking in Paul's direction, and when she spoke it was not to him but to John.

"May I go now?"

"How?"

"Out the window."

"Oriol will be watching the wing. He knows I'm here somewhere. We'll have to wait."

"I'd rather go, just the same."

"You can't."

She rewound the line obediently. He said, "Where did you learn to climb a rope?"

"In a circus."

"What's the rest of it?"

She bent her head more than was necessary to see the

end of the line she was tucking into place as her waist. He said, "Paul is entitled to know, as much as I am. We've both paid a high price to protect you, in our own ways."

She bit her lip. Afterward she gave no sign of emotion. She spoke calmly, always to John. Paul never took his eyes from her face.

Her story was so much like John's own that he knew, as she went on, what was to follow. The only difference between them was that she had been trained first for the ballet, as a child. Her parents had been dance enthusiasts, wealthy enough to provide her with the long schooling they hoped would produce a star. It had been an apprenticeship to which she submitted without enthusiasm until she was thirteen, when a side wash of the war and a flight of bombers wiped out the ballet school, her home, her family, and everything else she knew, leaving bare survival a problem for an adolescent girl in a devastated country occupied by an invading army.

"I had relatives in Switzerland," she said. "They brought me out of France, but they were poor and practical. I had to support myself. I could dance on my toes and do an *entrechat,* but I didn't know how to churn butter or milk a cow. The nearest thing they knew to the theater was a Swiss circus that came around the countryside once a year. I went with it."

It had been another kind of apprenticeship, more arduous than ballet. But her earlier schooling helped her. She had poise, trained muscles, and agility. In time

she learned acrobatics and the trapeze. From trapeze
flying she graduated to the high wire, first as part of an
act, ultimately to star billing as Monsieur Daniel, the
Aerial Clown, with a mustache and baggy clothes to
conceal her sex, since by strict Swiss law girls of sixteen
were not permitted even to attend a public cinema,
much less appear as paid performers in a circus.

"It gave me the idea for something different," she
said. Although she still did not look at Paul, some
change in her tone made both men realize she was
talking to him now, not John. "I don't know when it was
I decided to do what I did, if I ever made a decision. I
don't think I had to. I wanted things—security, and
leisure, and a nice life, not to be a performing monkey
on a string three times a day. Another girl might have
got away from it by finding different work. I didn't. I
can't tell you why the idea of stealing didn't make me
ashamed. I suppose people have different ideas of—"

Paul said, "You don't have to explain anything to me,
and John must understand. Go on with the rest of it."

"At first I thought I could use Monsieur Daniel, with
the mustache and a man's clothes, to hide behind. I did,
in Switzerland. But there was nothing big to steal there,
and I didn't intend to be a thief any longer than
necessary to get what I wanted, so I left the circus and
came here. I had a new idea when I met Claude. I
thought I could use him instead of Monsieur Daniel.
But he wasn't clever enough to trust, and I went on with
Monsieur Daniel until I heard about Le Chat."

John said, "It would have been better for both of us if

you had stayed with Monsieur Daniel."

"'I didn't even know that you were still alive. But Le Chat was exactly what I wanted, a real thief, known, photographed, and identified. I read everything I could find about you, your trial, the reports of your old thefts, and copied you in everything so they would look for you instead of me."

"When did you identify me?"

"Not until tonight, on the roof. Oriol called your name. Besides, there aren't many men who could have followed me as you did." She smiled quickly, to apologize for the small boast. "I knew from the beginning that Mr. Burns didn't go to the casinos just to gamble hundred-franc counters. I thought you were probably an insurance detective, like Mr. Paige, hoping to find the thief spotting jewelry. You made it easy for me to see Mrs. Stevens. I didn't know you and Mr. Burns were the same man until you spoke to me on the roof."

"I suspected you, for a while. But I thought Claude was your climber. I forgot that women don't develop the same kind of muscles. And you never let me touch you."

"I never let anyone touch me. It was too dangerous."

Paul said curiously, "Why?"

John took Paul's hand and put it on Danielle's shoulder, at the point where the muscle from the shoulder blade ran up into the neck. Under the softness of her flesh it was like a hard rope.

Paul said, "I see."

He left his hand on her shoulder. Danielle did not move away from the contact.

She said to John, "What else do you want to know?"

"Did you intend to rob the Souzas?'

"I was planning it when Bellini sent me to Lady Kerry. That gave me a chance at Mrs. Stevens instead. I saw her come in that night. She was alone, she'd had too much champagne, and I knew she'd sleep well. It took twenty minutes."

"I was waiting for you every night but that one. I had the Souza villa covered, too. I guessed every theft you would try in Cannes, including this one. Why did you come here when you knew I'd be here?"

"I told you I didn't know who you were. I wasn't afraid of Mr. Burns. Kind, innocent Mr. Burns, who introduced me to his—good friend Paul—"

Her steady voice wavered and broke.

Paul's hand was still on her shoulder. He made her turn to look at him.

"His good friend Paul, who had fallen in love with you and couldn't change if you had robbed the French treasury and burned it to the ground afterward," he finished. "This isn't the way I intended to ask you, but it will do. Will you marry me?"

She tried to say something, could not, and shook her head. He said, "I meant to ask you when I invited you here. All the things you wanted I can give you if you'll have me, Danielle. I offered to buy John off when I thought he was the thief. Let me buy you."

She still could not answer him, only shake her head. The eagerness that had been in his face left it. He took his hand from her shoulder.

John said, "What else do you expect her to say, Paul? Give her a chance. You can't buy her out of trouble. She has to do that herself. Do you still have the jewelry, Danielle?"

She nodded.

"All of it? Unbroken?"

"Yes." She swallowed and found it easier to talk. "I was going to take it to Holland and sell it there, after I got the pearls. I was afraid I'd make the same mistake you did, in France."

"You'll have to give it up. You can have Paul instead, if you want him, but they'll never stop hunting us until the jewelry is returned. If we turn it back—let me think for a minute. I've got an idea."

It did not come to him all at once that there was a way they could both go freely from the château. He only knew certainly that to end the search for the thief a return of the stolen jewels was essential. But he had had an idea for his own escape since Danielle said she thought Mr. Burns and Mr. Paige were working toward the same end. Mr. Paige had the influence and power of the London insurance company behind him. If it could be brought to their side, purchased with the free return of a hundred and twenty-five million francs' worth of jewelry—Paige was hard-headed—the recovery was what he wanted, not a conviction.

His mind raced over the possibilities. He could see his own way out. Francie would have to help again, with Danielle. If she was still on his side, they could both go free.

He looked at the window and saw that the sky was already light. "What time is it?"

Paul said, "Nearly five."

"We'll have to wait until seven, at least. I've thought of a way to send you and Danielle out of here together."

"How?"

"Never mind. I'll tell you when I'm sure it will work. Where is the jewelry now, Danielle?"

"In my room. In a suitcase."

"That's what you'll pay to stay out of Lepic's hands, then. As soon as you're safe, get the suitcase and take it to Bellini with a note I'll give you. After that, you and Paul are on your own. You can decide for yourselves where you want to go from there. Give me a pencil and paper, Paul."

He sat down and wrote the note to Bellini.

~§~

He wrote a second note which Paul carried to Francie's room shortly after six o'clock. The sun was up, and the heat of another blazing day had begun to make itself felt. It was a good beginning. Bad weather would have made his scheme more difficult.

Paul returned in a few minutes. John said, "Did she ask any questions?"

"She read the note and said it would take her about half an hour. That's all. She didn't seem surprised."

"Good. Where is Oriol?"

"Still arguing with Sanford. Sanford isn't so skeptical

now, since he's seen the hole in the roof, but he still doesn't believe you're inside the château. Oriol knows better. He's trying to reach Lepic by phone."

"You'll have to get away before Lepic comes. He knows Francie by sight. Do you have a pair of bathing trunks?"

"Yes."

"Put them on, and a robe."

Paul went into the bathroom. When he came back in swimming trunks and a beach robe, John said, "The minute Francie arrives, you go. Start your car, and give Oriol plenty of time to notice that you're leaving. If he comes after you to ask why, tell him the seashore is the only place you can think of where you might escape insults from the police. Be unpleasant enough to show you haven't forgotten this morning. When Danielle gets there, let him see her, but leave as quickly as you can without acting as if you were in a hurry."

"I know how to do my part. What about you?"

"I'll go a different way. I wouldn't be trying this if I weren't certain I could get out myself, so don't worry about me. There's nothing to do now but wait."

They waited. The valet came by with a *petit déjeuner* of coffee and rolls. Paul took the tray at the door, and they shared the breakfast, drinking from a single cup. Paul, touching Danielle's fingers as the cup passed between them, looked happier than John had ever seen him.

Danielle spoke hardly at all. She realized that what happened during the next few hours meant either an end or a beginning for her. Although she was accustomed to facing risks, and gave no outward sign of worry, John knew what was going on in her head. She was, as always, practical. If and when she escaped Oriol and Lepic, there would be time for Paul.

Francie arrived before they had finished the coffee. She wore the zebra-striped bathing suit he remembered, a robe over it, the white bathing cap, and sandals. There were dark circles under her eyes. Nothing in her attitude indicated either reluctance or eagerness to play the part he had given her. She looked only once at Danielle, briefly, and asked no questions.

Paul left the room immediately. Francie said, "There are a few people on the terrace, but none near the pool. I put my toe in the water, then walked away. No one paid any attention. They're still talking about burglars."

"Was your mother there?"

"She's still in her room. She hasn't dressed yet."

"That helps. What about the other bathing suit?"

"I only had this one with me. I can change clothes with her, if you want me to."

"It isn't necessary. The robe will cover her. You're taller than she is, but it won't be noticeable. Roll up your slacks and put on the sandals, Danielle."

Francie took off the sandals and gave them to Danielle, who put them on, then the beach robe, finally the bathing cap. With a towel tied like a scarf at her neck, she was effectively disguised. There was only a small difference in height to show that she was not the girl who had already appeared on the terrace to dip her toe in the swimming pool.

John said, "The rest is up to you and Paul. Go down the first stair you find on your left when you leave here, cross the terrace, go on by the swimming pool, and get into Paul's car. If anyone calls to you, wave and keep going. Let Oriol look at you if he's there. He'll lose interest as soon as he sees you're a woman. Don't try to hide your face, and don't hurry."

"I understand."

"That's all, then. Get the jewelry and the note to Bellini as quickly as possible."

"You're putting a lot of faith in me, aren't you?" Danielle said.

"If you mean because you might not deliver the jewelry, I don't think so. You can't have it and Paul, too. You'd rather have him, wouldn't you?"

"Yes."

"Make him a good wife, Danielle. He deserves it."

"I'll do my best." She put out her hand. "Good-bye, Mr. Burns. I know it isn't your name, but it's the way I think of you. No one ever did so much for me."

"Bellini would say it was loyalty among thieves." He pressed her fingers. "Good-bye. Good luck."

She turned to Francie, hesitating to hold out her hand.

"How do I thank you?" she asked.

"I'd rather you didn't try," Francie said. "I can't say you're welcome until I know what else is going to happen. I'll still give you to the police if it's—necessary. I hope it won't be."

Danielle said, "Oh," not in alarm but in under-standing.

Francie nodded. "Just so you'll know why, if it happens," she said. "Nothing personal. Good-bye."

John missed the by-play. He had gone to the window.

Neither the terrace nor the pool was visible to him, but part of the circling road that descended from the hilltop was in sight beyond the gardens of the moat. After Danielle had gone, he watched the road, counting minutes. He feared most of all the bad luck of Lepic's arrival before they got away. If the Citroën came up the hill before Paul's car went down—

Francie said, "How are you going to get away yourself?"

"Bellini will buy me out with the jewelry." He watched the road.

"You're sure?"

"I'm sure. A hundred and twenty-five million francs is worth more than I am."

"It would have been easier for you to give her to the police, as you planned."

"I had to change my plans, Francie. I didn't know she was the thief."

"It makes a difference that it was Danielle?"

There was still no sign of a car coming in either direction. He said, "It makes a difference that Paul is in love with her. But right now I'm not sure I could have turned anyone over to the police. Hunting a thief is one thing. Sending him to prison is something else. I know what prison is like."

"If Bellini can't do what you expect him to do, you'll go back. You know that too, don't you?"

"I know Bellini's capabilities."

"I'm glad you have faith in him. Is there anything more you want from me?"

"No. The rest of it is up to Bellini."

He heard the motor first, then saw the car, Paul's car, going down the road. It passed quickly out of his sight, but he watched the road for another full minute for signs of pursuit before he turned away from the window.

"They made it," he said. "Now—"

Francie had gone.

It surprised him only because he had not heard her go. Because he knew the chambermaid would come by soon to make up the room, he got his suitcase out from under Paul's bed, made sure no one was in the corridor, and took the bag across the hall to his own room, which the maid would not need to visit. There he brought Mr. Burns back to life for his final appearance, put on the padded shoes and harness, touched the roots of his hair with dye for the last time. He was careful not to pass in front of the windows, but he watched the terrace and saw Francie leave the château an hour later.

Somebody's uniformed chauffeur carried her bags and drove her away. Mrs. Stevens went to the car with her. There seemed to be some kind of an argument going on between them, but Mrs. Stevens came back from the car park alone.

Francie was showing good judgment. Her mother's innocence would be obvious to anyone who questioned her, but she herself could not safely remain to explain, if it occurred to anyone to ask, who it was that had left the château wearing her beach robe and sandals. He felt better to know that she was gone, free from possible trouble.

He waited for Bellini to bring Mr. Paige. There was never any doubt in his mind about Bellini.

Lepic arrived at the château first. He, Oriol, and George Sanford were talking on the terrace, Oriol pointing to the roof tops, then to the wing, Sanford shaking his head in disagreement at something Oriol said, when Bellini's heavy old Hispano-Suiza came purring up the hill. Bellini and Mr. Paige got out and came side by side across the lawn toward the three men on the terrace. Even from his window John could see the beaming, happy smile on Bellini's round face.

~§~

Bellini remained unobtrusively in the background, chuckling to himself now and then at some subtlety in Mr. Paige's words. He had coached Mr. Paige carefully along the general lines of what was to be said, but the phrasing was Mr. Paige's. Bellini appreciated his delivery. He liked doing business with a man who was not only hard-headed enough to see where his own interests lay but had a sense of humor as well.

Mr. Paige introduced himself to George Sanford.

"Paige," he said crisply. "I represent the London insurance company. This gentleman is Mr. Bellini. Good morning, Commissioner."

George Sanford said wearily, "This is all utter nonsense, Mr. Paige. I don't know what you may have heard, but I assure you there has been no theft of any kind. You're all making a fuss about nothing at all. If I sound rude, I'm sorry, but you're also causing me and my guests a great deal of embarrassment."

Lepic said, "If there wasn't a theft, it's only because Oriol was here to prevent it. He saw a man on the roof. And if you can see the hole where he fell, as he says, there's no argument."

"A hole on the roof?" Mr. Paige twirled his mustache tip. "I'm afraid my principals will have to assume responsibility for the repairs, then, if for nothing else. I rather fancy it was my own man who caused the damage."

Lepic said, "Your *what?*"

Bellini giggled. Mr. Paige twirled the other mustache tip.

"My operative," he said. Against his expectations, he was enjoying himself. He had not forgotten Lepic's cold treatment of him at the *commissariat*. "Mr. Burns."

Lepic's face went suddenly gray. George Sanford's chin dropped. Oriol, who could not follow the conversation in English, said to Lepic, "What is it?"

Lepic paid no attention.

"Where is he?" Mr. Paige asked pleasantly.

Sanford said, "Why, I don't know. He disappeared last

night. We thought—I'm afraid I still don't understand, Mr. Paige. You say he was your operative?"

"An operative of my company, to be exact." Mr. Paige twirled both mustache points simultaneously. "He has been working with me and Mr. Bellini"—Bellini bowed, beaming—"for some time to effect a recovery of the jewelry stolen here on the Côte during the last months. Until this morning I confess we were not wholly convinced that Commissioner Lepic had disposed of the thief, and for that reason I thought it wise to put my own man here to protect our interests and those of your guests who are our clients, particularly Mrs. Sanford and the Princess Lila." Mr. Paige coughed gently. "Had I known that Commissioner Lepic intended to take the same steps himself, my own precautions would not have been required, and the imposition on your hospitality unnecessary, Mr. Sanford. I seem to have misjudged Mr. Lepic in more ways than one."

Lepic's face was like a dead man's. Mr. Paige went on. "Your action in shooting the thief was not as unfortunate as I believed it to be at the time, Commissioner. His death permitted his friends, who held the stolen jewelry for him to take advantage of one of my *récompense proportionelle* advertisements of which you were so doubtful. The reward was claimed this morning." He paused long enough to make the effect he wanted. "The stolen jewelry has been recovered. I have already given the news to the papers."

Oriol said in Lepic's ear, "What's going on? What's he saying?"

"The jewelry came back!"

Oriol was as stunned as Lepic had been. But Lepic, with a few seconds to react, sensed that a game was being played on him. He said flatly, "I don't believe it."

"I assure you that I have inspected it myself and found everything in order, including some pieces not insured by my company. Of course I have had no way to verify those against inventory, but I have every reason to trust the good faith of the man who surrendered the jewels to me.

"Who?"

"One of the guarantees explicitly offered in the advertisements, as you will remember, Commissioner—"

"Who was it?" Lepic said fiercely.

"—is that no questions would be asked," Mr. Paige finished. "The reward has been paid, the jewels will be returned to their owners by me, and you yourself have ended the thief's potentialities for crime, Commissioner. There seems to be no need now for anything else except to offer apologies for the small deception it was necessary to play on Mr. Sanford and to ask Mr. Burns—ah, here he comes now. Good morning, Burns."

"Good morning, Mr. Paige." John came across the terrace on cue. "Good morning, Mr. Bellini."

"I'm delighted to see you again, Mr. Burns," Bellini said, chuckling. "Delighted."

~§~

John did not feel safe until he and Bellini were in the car, on their way down the curving hill road. The strain of the few minutes on the terrace had been enormous. He had not dared to meet Oriol's eyes. He knew that Oriol had recognized him at once, but Oriol's mind worked slowly. The return of the stolen jewelry destroyed the whole foundation for his belief in John's guilt, and without it he did not know what to believe. He retreated to the only safe ground he knew, silence.

Lepic was certain of only two things—that Mr. Burns was not what Mr. Paige said he was, and that he did not know enough of the truth to jeopardize his career by challenging Mr. Paige until he knew more. His uncertainty kept him baffled during the time it took John to apologize to his dazed host for his deception and leave with Bellini before it occurred to Sanford to ask about his disappearance and reappearance. Mr. Paige remained to invent explanations as required.

"I had to persuade him to act as the rear guard, but I think he's enjoying it," Bellini said. "Lepic gave him several uncomfortable moments. He's getting his own back." He wheezed and giggled. "Did you see Lepic's expression when you came across the terrace?"

"I was watching Oriol," John said. "He was the only one who really worried me. He's a bulldog."

"Bulldogs are not a breed to take action without being sure of themselves. Lepic is more dangerous to you still."

"I don't see how he can be. He's committed himself to the point where keeping his mouth shut and accepting the credit is the only alternative to exposing his own mistakes. Oriol can still send me away any time he wants to. He'll have to know the truth before I can go back to the Villa des Bijoux."

"Telling the *flics* the truth is always a mistake. However, he is also a *maquisard*. It can be arranged for him to learn a small part of it, enough to restore your position with him." Bellini wagged his head, tittering. "Not everything, of course. It is hardly believable. Who would have suspected that our lovely Danielle was so clever? I was dumbfounded when she brought your note."

"I told you once that she reminded me of myself. She has the same type of mind."

"Not entirely, luckily for all of us. She suggested a small modification of your scheme which was a great improvement."

"What was it?"

"Your idea to surrender the jewelry without reward was selfish, in view of the help given us by others. Mr. Paige was prepared to go as high as twenty per cent. I found him willing to co-operate at the level of ten per cent instead. It is not what we could have had, but it will make a nice melon to cut among our night watchers. And ourselves, of course."

"Give mine to Jean-Pierre, for the damage to his business."

"Why not a token of appreciation for Miss Stevens as

well? A small jewel of some kind would be appropriate in the circumstances—but I forgot that she never wears jewelry. Something else."

"I'll try to find out what she'd like as soon as I get rid of these clothes and the hair dye. I didn't have a chance to thank her before she left the château."

"She left? When?"

"An hour before you got there."

"Alone?"

"Yes. Her mother wouldn't miss the *gala,* naturally, but she couldn't stay herself after we had smuggled Danielle out in her clothes."

"She could have remained in her room." Bellini frowned. "I don't think you should wait to discard Mr. Burns before calling on her, John. I have a feeling that her *raison d'être* may be undergoing an adjustment."

"It's about time you told me what her *raison d'être* is."

"You still don't know?"

"At a guess, I'd say it was to criticize. She's done nothing else for three days but point out my shortcomings."

"Then it is essential that you do not give her further cause to criticize you."

Bellini picked up the old-fashioned speaking tube that hung at his elbow.

"L'Hotel Midi. *Tout de suite.*"

The driver nodded, and increased the speed of the car.

~§~

Before Bellini let him off at the hotel, he repeated something he had told John before.

"Yours is not a subtle mind, John. It functions well enough, but the line is single-tracked. You have been preoccupied for a long time by something to which you had necessarily to devote yourself. Now you have time to think of more than the survival of yourself and your friends and a return to what you were before. Consider this question: Do you really want to go back to your old life at the Villa des Bijoux?"

"I don't have to consider it. I know."

"Think about it just the same, and let me hear your final answer later. In the meantime, give my regards to Miss Stevens."

He puzzled over the question while he was crossing the lobby, in the elevator, and during the time it took him to walk down the corridor to Francie's room. He could not decide exactly what Bellini meant by it. The implication seemed to be that he might find life at the Villa des Bijoux drab after his spell of activity as Mr. Burns; that having once returned to thievery, or pseudo-thievery, he would not be able to go back again to the garden and the dog and the books. But that was nonsense. Thieving had never been more than a business to him, a means to an end, as Mr. Burns had been. The best part of his life was wrapped up in the Villa des Bijoux and what it stood for. There was nothing he wanted that he could not find at the Villa des Bijoux.

Or so he believed until he knocked at Francie's door, and for an interval afterward, when she had let him in and before he saw the evidence of her hurried packing. But he did not fully understand the significance of Bellini's question until he had asked his own.

"I'm flying back to the States this afternoon," she answered.

He knew then, all at once, not with his single-tracked mind alone but in his heart and stomach. Even then, it took time for him to realize that she was running from him and, at long last, why.

He said, "What about your mother?"

"She's staying. I've decided it's time she learned to take care of herself. If she can't it's the insurance company's worry, not mine. Not any more."

She faced him, her hands clasped in front of her, unsmiling, waiting for him to go. Her hair was disarranged, and there was a smudge of dust on her cheek. It was the first time he had seen her looking like that, the first time he had seen her at all.

He said, "I got away. It's all finished."

"I'm glad."

"Bellini sent his regards."

"That's nice."

She was still waiting for him to leave. He said bluntly, "Why are you going back to the States?"

"It's my home."

"Do I have anything to do with your going?"

"No."

"Would you stay if I asked you to?"

"No."

"Will you come back?"

"No."

"I can follow you."

"It would be a waste of time."

"I'll have to waste it, then." He pulled up a chair and sat down with his arms crossed on its back. "Go on with your packing, if your mind is made up. Bellini says I've got a one-track mind, and I know what I want, even if I'm late in finding it out."

"What do you want?"

"You."

"You can't have me."

"Why? Because I've been stupid until now?"

"Because you're still stupid."

He thought he knew why she said it, and it did not discourage him that she had put up another of her protective barriers between them because he was a good thief and knew how to surmount barriers between him and something he wanted as badly as he had found he wanted Francie Stevens. But he was clumsier than usual. The chair he had been sitting in went over with a bang before he reached her.

Afterword

In Search of the Villa Noel Fleuri

In his travel writings David Dodge always speaks affectionately of the villa that he rented in the South of France. He loved its idyllic situation in a lush garden on a hillside near the coast, with wide and glorious views of the Mediterranean. But he does not provide anything as banal as an address of the house where he and his family (wife Elva and young daughter Kendal) lived in 1950-1952.

This was where Dodge got the original idea for his best-known novel *To Catch a Thief*, basing it around a real event, a cat-burglary at the much grander villa next door. This was where he worked on the manuscript, producing it at top speed in 1950, assisted by Elva as editor and typist.

Dodge does not provide the name of his villa for over a decade. In 1962, in *The Rich Man's Guide to the Riviera*, when he was still best-known as the author of the novel behind the Oscar-winning Hitchcock film, he names it as the Villa Noel Fleuri, so called because part of the garden was in bloom at Christmas.

Now, was the Villa Noel Fleuri its real name, I wondered, or is Dodge being super-tactful and concealing it, just as he disguises the Carlton Hotel in Cannes as the Hotel Midi in *To Catch a Thief*?

Randal Brandt, who set up and maintains the wonderful website, "A David Dodge Companion" (www.david-dodge.com), had no further information. Neither did Dirk Dominick, who writes the blog "le stuff" (lestuffblog.com) and has been searching out locations used by Alfred Hitchcock in the film. A trawl of the internet produced no results. The one person who might have been able to guide us, the Dodges' daughter Kendal Dodge Butler, sadly passed on a few years ago.

There was only one way to proceed. Armed with as much evidence as we could muster, my husband and I went to spend a week in Golfe-Juan to see if we could trace the Villa Noel Fleuri.

We arrived at the small art deco station in Golfe-Juan in the early evening, after a day spent on trains. We'd left St Pancras Station in London early that morning on the Eurostar to Lille, transferred to the TGV (the French high-speed train) and then travelled almost the whole length of France to Cannes, after which it was just a five-minute journey on the regional TER train to get to Golfe-Juan.

That evening there were astonishing fireworks along the coast which flowered suddenly like sea-anemones and then disappeared. Fireworks are a particular feature of summer on the Cote d'Azur. We discovered later that this was one of the end-of-season displays (in mid-September), which reminded us that we had arrived in Golfe-Juan at just about the time that the final chapter of *To Catch a Thief* is set.

Golfe-Juan is still a charming small town with an old port (where the Dodges arrived by launch from their transatlantic liner) and a newer port which opened in 1989. Some traditional sailing-boats can be seen in the ports, and modest cruisers, but there are also palatial modern yachts bristling with GPS equipment, Cayman Island registrations and gangways labelled "private." To the west of the old port there are sandy beaches and then, west of them, 19th-century villas built just above the rocks right next to the sea, and there are more villas up on the hills within a stone's throw of the coast. In the town, there are now far more villas and apartment-buildings than there were in 1950 when the Dodges arrived. But, especially in comparison with recent vile architectural excesses elsewhere on the Cote d'Azur, Golfe-Juan remains small, unspoiled and reassuringly traditional. A road runs alongside the quay, which is now named after the yachtsman Eric Tabarly, and tables and chairs are set up on the quayside pavement, looking out over the old port, on the opposite side of the road from the old-fashioned little café-bars and restaurants to which they belong. Waiters walk back and forth across the road through the traffic with stunning nonchalance.

Within a day of our arrival we discovered from the relevant French civil service department (taxes—say no more) that French municipal archives are organised in such a way that in order to get at records of a particular property one needs to know either the name of the *owner* (and the Dodges were renting) or the official number of the *cadastre* (plot) on which the property is built. At the very least, the exact location of the property in a finger-on-the-map sort of way is required. We knew none of these, so they showed us the door, sighed heavily, and got on with attending to the queue that had built up behind us.

We moved on to the Municipal Archives in Antibes, a large department in a small street a short distance from the railway station. We asked the charming archivist (*all* the French archivists we met were charming) about the Villa Noel Fleuri and discovered that we were in the wrong place for Golfe-Juan house records. For those we needed the Municipal Archives in Vallauris (Golfe-Juan and Vallauris, the pottery town most famous for its association with Picasso, are regarded as a single entity for administrative purposes). So we asked the archivist about L'Ermitage, the guest-house (*pension*) in Juan-les-Pins-Antibes where the Dodges stayed when they first arrived in the South of France, and she found some headed letters and bills from it from the 1920s, 1930s and 1950s—happy days when "L'Ermitage, Juan-les-Pins" was an adequate address—but there was nothing which provided enough detail to pinpoint the building in an area now filled with elegant villas.

There is, however, a road called Chemin de l'Ermitage in east Antibes, so we went for a walk there, concentrating on the area closest to the beach "La Salis" alongside Boulevard James Wyllie, since Dodge mentions the guest-house's proximity to the beach (very important if you're accompanied by a nine-year-old). And we found an old archway with the words "L'Ermitage" carved into it, leading to a narrow road which connected with Chemin de l'Ermitage. We couldn't find the guest-house, but the trail to the Villa Noel Fleuri beckoned...

As soon as possible we met up with Dirk Dominick. Over lunch at a table overlooking the old port in Golfe-Juan, as the waiter strolled back and forth through the traffic, we reviewed our evidence. We drew up a list. What did we know about the Villa Noel Fleuri?

1.   It was definitely in Golfe-Juan (mentioned in travel articles and at least two travel books).

2. Dodge describes its location in *20,000 Leagues Behind the 8-Ball* (thoughtfully retitled *With a Knife and Fork Down the Amazon* for the British market):

> "I can close my eyes now and recover that first glimpse. The house stood on a hill in Golfe Juan between Juan-les-Pins and Cannes. We reached it by a side road which left the main highway skirting the gulf and wandered up the hillside between mossy old stone walls covered with climbing rose vines and sodded in the cracks with Flanders poppies. At the top of the hill a little gate with a tinkling bell attached to it

opened into a huge jungle of garden full of greenery: cork-oaks, bamboo, palms, birds-of-paradise plants, camelia shrubs, open grassy places and more Flanders poppies... The house was built on the edge of the cliff, down which the path continued to the foot of the garden fifty yards below. The *terrasse*, shaded by climbing vines of wisteria, overlooked the whole sweep of the Mediter-ranean from Cap d'Antibes to the Iles de Lerins, and the front windows of the *salon* faced, across about a mile of water, the front window of the cell in the fortress on the Ile Sainte Marguerite where The Man in the Iron Mask whiled away his time two hundred and fifty years ago."

3. It must have been fairly near the railway line. Dodge mentions, in a cautionary note in an article for *Holiday* magazine about renting a villa abroad, that the Villa Noel Fleuri was on the same spur of rock as the railway line, and the trains from Marseilles made it shake as they passed.

4. The cat-burglary which Dodge was temporarily suspected of committing, and which provided the basic idea for the plot of *To Catch a Thief*, took place in the neighbouring villa, where a "millionaire industrialist" and his wife were hosting a dinner-party for celebrity guests including the fashion designer Madame Elsa Schiaparelli. In a 1966 article for *Holiday* about famous

jewel robberies, Dodge names this much grander villa as the Villa Eden Roc (the first time he has provided a name for it).

We got out our local map of Golfe-Juan (free from the tourist office), and pored over it. We agreed that we should be looking for an area on the Cannes side of Golfe-Juan because, when she wasn't boarding, Kendal was allowed to go to school in Cannes on her bike. We looked at the railway line, which runs very close to the coast in Golfe-Juan, and at the little roads which wound up the hills in the direction of Vallauris. We drew an oblong on the map to mark the most likely area, crossed our fingers, and piled into the small violet car which Dirk was driving and which he'd borrowed from a friend ("I've been told to treat this car like a very distinguished old lady.").

We headed west towards Cannes along the main road and took almost the first of the steep little roads which meander up the hills. Dirk drove slowly, concentrating on the road, while my husband and I looked for house-names and argued about the dates of domestic architecture (pre- or post-1950?). Suddenly he said, "Villa Eden Roc!" when I was looking in the opposite direction. Had we really found the major clue to the location of the Villa Noel Fleuri?

We piled out and looked at the building. It was large, grand, pink, divided into apartments (including one for the *gardien*), and clearly much younger than the building which Dodge knew—but villas in the South of

France are constantly being refurbished and rebuilt. The big question was: was it built on the same site? [The original Villa Eden Roc was actually built on the rocks right next to the Med by the 19th-century architect Georges Massa in an astonishing conglomeration of styles. It was later, sadly, demolished, but photographs of it survive. Massa designed the villa for himself, which is just as well, as I wonder whether anyone would have loved it as he did.]

We walked around, *20,000 Leagues Behind the 8-Ball* in hand. On the downhill side of the Villa Eden Roc, there was a locked-up little gate with steps going steeply down into a lush garden bursting with overgrown plants and shrubs, where tall palm trees towered over a small square villa (at a guess 19th-century) which had bricked-up windows and appeared to be unoccupied.

We checked off the points on our list. Had we found the Villa Noel Fleuri?

There are various other leads to follow up with contacts in the South of France, especially press coverage of the burglary in *Nice-Matin*, which, with pleasing symmetry, is the local paper which John Robie buys to hide behind in the opening chapter of *To Catch a Thief*. And now that we can put a finger on the map to show exact location it might be possible to obtain details of the small square villa's history and current and previous ownership. This is surely a situation in which it would be invaluable to have the investigative assistance of Henri Bellini...

We are in the process of making a programme about the search for the Villa Noel Fleuri for BBC Radio 4, to be broadcast in the U.K. early in 2011. We have done the location recording in and around Golfe-Juan, but the follow-up research is ongoing. Please listen to the programme online if you can.

BBC Radio 4 Arts Feature: *In Search of the Villa Noel Fleuri* 6th January 2011

BBC Radio 4 Saturday Afternoon Play: *To Catch a Thief* David Dodge's novel dramatised by Jean Buchanan, 8th January 2011

Jean Buchanan
Oxford, September 2010

Now Available from Bruin Crimeworks...

James Hadley Chase

NO ORCHIDS FOR MISS BLANDISH

FLESH OF THE ORCHID

Fredric Brown

KNOCK THREE-ONE-TWO

David Dodge

DEATH AND TAXES
TO CATCH A THIEF
& coming soon: ***THE LONG ESCAPE***

Paul Bailey

DELIVER ME FROM EVA

Bruno Fischer

HOUSE OF FLESH

Elliot Chaze

BLACK WINGS HAS MY ANGEL

Visit the scene of the crime
@ *www.bruinbookstore.com*

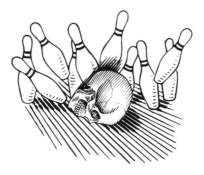

Printed in Great Britain
by Amazon